AuthorHouse™
1663 Liberty Drive
Bloomington, IN 47403
www.authorhouse.com
Phone: 1 (800) 839-8640

All Scripture quotations in this publication appear from the King James Version (KJV) of the Holy Bible.

Greek words and meanings are from Vine's Expository Dictionary of Old and New Testament Words and Vine's Complete Expository Dictionary with Topical Index unless referenced otherwise.

Published by AuthorHouse 07/02/2019

ISBN: 978-1-5462-7479-7 (sc)
ISBN: 978-1-5462-7480-3 (e)

Library of Congress Control Number: 2019900158

The Paradoxical Union

Book cover, layout, and design by the author
Melveena D. Edwards, Ph.D.

Author photos by Jehan Daugherty
Jehan, Inc. Website: https://www.jehaninc.com/

Logo graphic designs by NetMinistry Technology Corporation
Website: https://www.netministry.com/

Editors
Davonna L. Booth-Minor, B.S.B.A., M.B.A., D.R.A.
Ruben A. Minor, B.S.B.A., M.B.A., D.R.A.

Print information available on the last page.

authorHOUSE®

DEDICATION

The Paradoxical Union — is a Christian-based novel dedicated to minister's wives, elect ladies or first ladies; and those in ministry. Additionally, it is intended for those who are "experiencing or have experienced domestic violence or also called intimate partner violence—IPV," (CDC, 2018) every form of abuse, marital bondage or interrelationship strongholds, betrayal and infidelity when seemly contradictory. This novel is a fictitious invented prose narrative of a book with a complex approach of a "must tell all," story surrounding the global epidemic of domestic violence or IPV; and general abuse. This novel is a deliverance tool, healing aid, and godly instrument based on real events to catapult individuals with a distinct need to find answers or a godly "way to escape, that ye may be able to bear it" (I Corinthians 10:13). This writing typically represents a main character and action with some degree of realism in the context of ungodly marital entanglement, but whereby the reader will receive assistance with reversing emotional pain and disappointment to gain HOPE, strength, encouragement, freedom, liberty, joy, health, and wholeness through the process of survival.

Acknowledgments

"MY INEVITABLE HOPE"

I thank God, give honor, and glory to the most omnipotent God, who is the head of my life and center of my joy. I recognize God first and foremost for without whom I do nothing. God is the universal and inevitable hope and empowerment for all who will yield to His word.

I worship God today with expressed love for what He has done for me, and how God has reversed my pain and life disappointments to gain HOPE, strength, encouragement, freedom, liberty, and joy in my life.

I acknowledge my family, friends, and community who have encouraged and supported me in my research, and in authoring this short story. I honor you all for your ongoing prayers, and appreciation for my global concerns with staggering statistics relevant to "domestic violence also called intimate partner violence—IPV" (CDC, 2018) and (sometimes named domestic abuse, relationship abuse or family violence); mental health issues, reported worsening public health problem of suicidality (suicidal ideation, thoughts, attempts); and reported homicide cases.

Humbly,
—Melveena D. Edwards, Ph.D.

FOREWORD

Words cannot express the joy that I feel celebrating my mother's new life, and especially the writing of this book of inspiration and healing. There is such a special bond a mother and daughter have; we are connected like no other relationship. My mother is the bones of my spine, keeping me straight, and true. She is my blood, making sure it runs rich and strong. She is the strength in my beating heart. My mother is a REAL SURVIVOR. I celebrate the re-emergence of her smile that was deeply hidden for multiple years. I celebrate her walking in her beauty now traded for ashes; she has exchanged sackcloth for diamonds and silk! Just as God has promised He will continue to restore the years that the cankerworm and palmerworm tried to destroy. I love you mom for your essence. You are a TRUE woman, regal, and pure!

—*Davonna L. Booth-Minor,*
Your loving daughter~

OVERVIEW

The Paradoxical Union

Category: Novel | Fiction (Spiritual Short-Story) with Religion/Inspirational message
Family & Relationships/Divorce

Manhattan, New York City Borough, primary setting beginning in the 1980s 'The Paradoxical Union'—follows the life of the main character named Paris Hope who powers through multiple trails, tribulation, and challenges growing up, then as a young woman enters a relationship seemly created by Heaven, but they were from opposite worlds. Instead, Paris soon learns that she entered into unhealthy and toxic matrimony that leads to a sheer pit of hell. The union gradually augments to a subtle intertwined ploy, extensive abuse, mental cruelty, aggression, and domestic violence. The character Paris has a loving spirit. She is intellectual, ambiguous, classy and has big aspirations and dreams, but; becomes stripped "TO" her joy—but not stripped of it. After devastating struggles and traumatization fostered by the twisted union, she finds a way "TO" escape finding survival through faith, shaping who she'd become, and accomplishing her dreams. Paris' intimate partner is a community, national and global figure who is self-exalted, grandiose and breeds narcissism. Dr. Melveena D. Edwards, the author, and therapist is the narrator of this short-story who has the birds-eye-view of all the goings-on from the perspective of Paris. Dr. Edwards is the outsider looking into Paris' life as she—pauses, revisits, and sojourns to impart her experience regarding the severe social epidemic issue of abusive and violence culture that plagues our society today. Paris shares her "must tell all" story—to help and motivate someone. In so telling the story, Dr. Edwards is educational and shares vital facts promoting awareness.

Prologue

Christt
"Husband ➼UNION➼Wife"
✝
Marriage a Divine Union

"Husbands, love your wives, even as Christ also loved the church,
and gave himself for it;" (Ephesians 5:25)
"Marriage is honourable in all, and the bed undefiled: but whoremongers
and adulterers God will judge" (Hebrews 13:4, KJV)

God intended for there to be marriage. In fact, Jesus Christ is the head of all marriages. The divine union or marriage consisting of a husband and wife becomes the nucleus or center of the family structure or cell division into the family's components.

Sadly enough, in my Christian counseling practice, I have conducted structured marriage counseling session comprising toxic relationships. Additionally, as a health care clinician caring for clients in the field of psychiatry/mental/behavioral health, and as an ordained clergywoman I have witnessed every form of domestic abuse that is not all equivalent. Thus, it is important to note, that there are variations in frequency, severity, purpose, and outcomes noteworthy to mention in this narrative. Domestic violence takes on several forms against a 'victim' including physical, psychological, verbal, emotional, economic, religious, reproductive, and sexual—abuse. More defined forms are physical aggression or assaults or threats; sexual assault/rape; controlling or domineering; intimidation; stalking; passive/covert abuse; neglect; traumas; and economic deprivation. Domestic violence abusive relationships can be described as endangerment even in instances, e.g. of harassment that can range from subtle progressing to coercion. This serious action can be as a result of deception, hypocrisy, anger, and exploitation that impact everyone.

The Paradoxical Union — is a novel with relatively comprehensive work of narrative fiction about imaginary people and events with expressed realism, and deals especially with human experience. While this writing is fiction, it is based upon the premise of real events through connected sequence witnessed in my counseling, nursing, and ministerial practices. Sit tight, while reading this literary genre consisting of a story beginning with some statistical facts stressing its seriousness, and possible life scenarios that may help you or someone that you know who is currently facing domestic violence or abuse!

One counselee expressed to me, that: "it is time to tell all" and gave consent—for me to do so in writing this book; so that others may experience HOPE and a way out of unexpected, paradoxical, or venomous unions. All names and locations have been changed to protect the identity of actual persons and venues.

As you travel through this storyline with me—know that as the author of this book I am a true advocate of the marital union and support the sacred intent that marriage brings. Also, I am an educator and counselor at heart and will impart and share facts, basic tips, methods, and techniques to assist the lay or professional Christian counselor—along the way. Unfortunately, I have learned through my counseling practice that some marriages fall into unexpected or expected turmoil based on an array of reasons; that may lead to destruction and its demise. Thus, leaving individuals wounded and in despair. The contents of this book will minister to the individual that has been traumatized by a relationship or suffered from divorce using the mechanism of Biblical counseling throughout this book to guide one into the cusps of healing, deliverance, and—into God's divine grace and mercy.

—*Melveena D. Edwards, Ph.D.*
Author

DISCLAIMER

The Paradoxical Union

Author's Note and Disclaimer:

The Paradoxical Union — is a Christian-based novel. As you read this work of fiction book, note as the author of this book, that it was created in my imagination; and I have been inspired by God to tell this story for deliverance and human preservation. Invents of the storyline encompasses made up characters, plots, dialogues, locations, dates; and sometimes even the settling are fiction. This fictional work does not claim to tell a true story. However, my counseling experiences, extensive research on the area of domestic violence or also named intimate partner violence (IPV) and relationship abuse are stated by truths to support criteria on this subject matter; and gauged statistical measurements used and cited throughout the context of this writing are real. In general, scenarios used are based on true events, typically representing character and action with some degree of global realism. Names and identities have been changed and are composites. The general purpose for and context of this novel is to serve humanity as a tool of awareness and education mechanism regarding the rising daunting global issue of "domestic violence or IPV—which is a pattern of behavior used by one partner to maintain power and control over another in an intimate relationship" (The National Domestic Violence Hotline, 2018).

What is more, this tool has been created to encourage individuals how to stand up with boldness, to become empowered, to be strengthened to endure, and survive domestic violence and abusive circumstances—by promoting awareness, and providing information, self-help resources, and practical interventions.

Throughout this storyline is interwoven educational components and emphasis on the subject matter of Christian Counseling. As the author of this book, my main aim for doing so is to share and impart tips for those actively involved in lay or the Christian Counseling practice, and desire to aid or support another regarding this subject matter.

INTRODUCTION

"There hath no temptation taken you but such as is common to man: but God is faithful, who will not suffer you to be tempted above that ye are able; but will with the temptation also make a way to escape, that ye may be able to bear it."
(I Corinthians 10:13, KJV)

"Toxicity of Domestic Violence"

Domestic Violence also called "Intimate Partner Violence –IPV" is real and is a significant problem in the United States. It cripples, it becomes increasingly toxic, it will rarely stop when started, it can impact a life forever and can have lasting harmful effects on individuals, families, and communities. Domestic Violence can exhibit "patterns of behaviors used by one partner to maintain **power** and **control** over another partner in an intimate relationship." Domestic violence or IPV as well can be described as an unhealthy power struggle that does not discriminate (infants to the elderly), and affects people of all stages of life. This behavior of "violence or abuse is by one person against another in a domestic setting, such as in marriage or cohabitation." (The National Domestic Violence Hotline, 2018).

Domestic violence occurs globally, in every culture, and affects people across society, at all levels of economic status. However, indicators of lower socioeconomic status have been shown to be risk factors for higher levels of domestic violence in several studies. In the United States, according to government statistics: Each year, four million domestic violence assaults occur nationally.

A healthy relationship is characterized by **freedom**, **safety,** and **equality**. Given the result of domestic violence, the traits represent a vast difference; and can occur in intimate relationships from all walks of life. "The most common victims of domestic violence are women and their children. Many times, it is difficult to tell if your relationship is abusive. Domestic violence results from an **abuse of power**" (United States Department of Justice, 2016).

Annuals of Epidemiology Statistics depict that, "on average, 24 people per minute are victims of rape, physical violence or stalking by an intimate partner in the United States—more than 12 million women and men over the course of a year" (The National Domestic Violence Hotline, 2018).

According to the Centers for Disease Control and Prevention—CDC (2018), "Domestic violence or Intimate Partner Violence –IPV is a serious, preventable public health problem that affects millions of Americans. The term 'intimate partner violence' describes physical, sexual, or psychological harm by a current or former partner or spouse. This type of violence can occur among heterosexual or same-sex couples and does not require sexual intimacy." The CDC also affirms that "More than 37 percent of US women and almost 31 percent of US men experienced intimate partner contact sexual violence, physical violence, and stalking during their lifetime" (CDC, 2018).

The Paradoxical Union is a short story about *SURVIVAL*. This story is primarily about a lady named PARIS HOPE who survives domestic violence. Her family name "Hope" is interesting as it is both a noun and verb. The word Hope in the Greek translation is *ELPIS* (Vine's 1981, p. 232) meaning favourable and confident expectation, correlated with the unseen, and the future according to Romans 8:24-25. This name also describes the happy anticipation of good; and the ground upon which hope is based.

Given Paris' family name and the charge upon her life, she made a bold decision to share her story, because she knew that she was not alone in dealing with domestic violence and abuse. Paris realized that her story needed to be told and referenced her experience as a "test or temptation." She would eventually learn that it is not uncommon for humanity, (woman or man alike) to be consumed with deep bondage and imprisonment in a relationship that is toxic and destructive. BUT KNEW from experience that "GOD, is faithful, who will not suffer you to be tempted above that ye are able, but will with the temptation also make a way to escape, that ye may be able to bear it" (I Corinthians 10:13, KJV).

Ending a marital relationship or divine union is globally controversial, especially as it relates to the church. While it took Paris 25 years to determine she would end her marital relationship, she eventually learned that in grossly negative instances where there is NO HOPE in the marital union; that one can depart and remain completely in the perfect will of God to reestablish NEW HOPE. Therefore, she vowed to "tell it all" about her survival story. Paris made a vital decision to share her story of survival that is compartmentalized into four components: (a.) *describing* the purpose for marriage and divine union, (b.) *discussing* the role of an elect lady as it relates to "the Body of Christ," and credence to marriage, (c.) *sharing* the root, core, essence, and spirit of her background and story, and (d.) *giving* simple survival self-help interventions for someone in need of a way out of an abusive situation.

Marriage will be briefly discussed in this book, as it is vital for you the reader to fully understand the framework of marriage; concepts of marriage; God's original purpose and plan for the marriage union; and to better understand this storyline.

Marriage is defined as the state of being married or a relationship between husband and wife in wedlock or Holy Matrimony. In marriage, it should be understood that every couple has a 100% chance of success in marriage. However, *both* individuals must want their marriage to be successful.

Today in our society statistics rates of successful marriages are falling at an astronomical rate. Statistical divorce rates are climbing in America and around the world. More than 50% of marital unions in America are ending in divorce, that most likely stems from poor communication, financial problems, poor decision-making, domestic violence, polysubstance abuse, infidelity, and the more—are sky-rocketing.

"*Divorce* is the legal ending of a marriage. The United States exhibits the highest rate of divorce in the civilized world. It is estimated that between 40% and 50% of current *first* marriages will end in divorce. Although the divorce rate has been steadily on the rise for the last one hundred years, it now appears that the divorce rate has leveled off beginning in the 1980s and continuing to the present" (Benner & Hill, 1999, pp. 359).

Moreover, the American Association for Marriage and Family Therapy—AAMFT (2018), statistics rates depict that: "Domestic violence is all too common in American families. In most 20 percent of all marriages, couples slap, shove, hit or otherwise assault each other. Emotional abuse—verbal threats, humiliating or degrading remarks, and controlling behavior—is even more common. Marital violence is especially common among young couples, and, without intervention, may escalate in intensity or frequency." In general, domestic violence "acts within a family unit that has threatening or violent aspects; that result in injury, whether physical or emotional; and that is excessive or inappropriate to the situation." Although there are many types of violence, "the most common types are violence by parents to children, violence by a husband to a wife, and violence by adult children to elderly parents" (Benner & Hill, 1999, pp. 363).

No one is exempt from domestic violence as it can affect everyone at any age. The CDC.gov Violent Prevention gives overview statistics that: "Nearly half of all women and men in the United States have experienced psychological aggression by an intimate partner in their lifetime—about 48.4% and 48.8%, respectively" (The National Domestic Violence Hotline, 2018).

According to an analytical study prepared and submitted to the *U.S. Department of Justice* by investigators Kelleher, Gardner, Coben, Barth, Edleson & Hazen (March, 2006), entitled: "Co-Occurring Intimate Partner Violence and Child Maltreatment: Local Policies/Practices and Relationships to Child Placement, Family Services and Residence," they assert that "Nearly 3 in 10 women (29%) and 1 in 10 men (10%) in the United States have experienced rape, physical violence and stalking by a partner and report a related impact on their functioning." The study does not necessarily reflect the official position or policies of the U.S. Department of Justice, however.

The preceding statistics are daunting, especially when God intended for marriages to be fruitful, successful, functional, and healthy. Divorce and ending a relationship can be devastating, detrimental, damaging, and disheartening to individuals involved. Domestic violence or abuse manifests in clusters (neglect, physical, sexual, and emotional) affecting a victim resulting in an array of emotions such as fear, anxiety, depression; and including feeling threatened. However, in such event, God can reverse your pain and disappointment to gain HOPE, strength, encouragement, freedom, liberty, and joy again in your life.

The Christian response to domestic violence is interesting and often taboo. This issue arises from the concern for human beings who have knowledge and experience of the repercussions of sin (missing the mark), but; need to understand God's forgiveness, His divine comfort, and Agape love. Sadly enough, the victims of domestic violence may carry scars and wounds throughout his or her life regardless of the lifespan. These scars from the trauma, and inflected mutilations, potentially could affect others with whom the victim of domestic violence or abuse may interact in his or her future within the context of their family, community or church. The feelings of rejection and dejection from the church is devastating. The process of generally learning to trust again from the sheer depths and pit experience of domestic violence or abuse for the victim is complex and challenging.

Journey with me as I discuss: what God intended marital relationships to become; what the elect lady was called to do; share a story of Paris Hope the main character of this novel along with her background, and turbulent marital relationship that became a paradoxical union—changing her life forever. In this story 'against all the odds,' Paris finds help, support, divine answers, and a godly "way *to* escape, that" she was able to endure all! (I Corinthians 10:13, KJV).

—Melveena D. Edwards, Ph.D.
Clinical Christian Psychology

The Paradoxical Union

Emotional Assault Defendant Marriage
Women Pain Verbal Children
Physical DOMESTIC Abuse Court
Argument Justice Grief VIOLENCE Defense
Cohabitation Psychological
Partner Alcohol Sexual Rage Anger
Help Victim Rights Threats
Safe House Spousal Social
Hotline Awareness Survivor

Contents

Chapter 1   **Marriage—A Divine Union** **23**
                 Biblical Perspective and Dimensions of Marriage **23**
                 Biblical Perspective and Dimensional Order of Marriage **31**
                 Biblical Perspective and Dimensional Order of Family **34**
                 Biblical Perspective and Dimensional Order of Man **38**

Chapter 2   **The Elect Lady | "Walking in Truth"** **40**
                 "Walking in Truth" **43**

Chapter 3   **Paris' Background and Story** **44**
                 "Favourable and Confident Expectation" **47**

Chapter 4   **"Taboo: The Contradictory Relationship"** **61**
                 A Stony Heart **121**
                 "Against All Odds" **136**
                 "No Box" **144**

Chapter 5   **Epilogue** **160**

About the Author **163**

Bibliography & References **169**

List of Tables

Table 1   Supporting Scriptures Relevant to Love 26

Table 2   Supporting Scriptures Relevant to Family 38

Table 3   Supporting Scriptures Relevant to Deliverance & Survival "No Box" 156

List of Illustrations

Figure 1   The box 147

Figure 2   Outer or surrounding the box.. 148

Figure 3   Outside the box 149

Figure 4   Inside the box 150

Figure 5   No box 151

Figure 6   The Model: Abuse & Domestic Violence Summary....................................... 152

Appendices

APPENDIX A: Helpful Tools for Marriages 175

APPENDIX B: Faith & Prayer 177

APPENDIX C: T.P.U. The Paradoxical Union 179

APPENDIX D: Abuse & Domestic Violence Model 183

APPENDIX E: The Model: Abuse & Domestic Violence Summary 185

APPENDIX F: The Virtuous Woman 187

APPENDIX G: There is a Way Out 189

APPENDIX H: HOPE: "October Domestic Violence Month" 191

APPENDIX I: Glossary 193

CHAPTER ONE

Marriage—A Divine Union

Marriage is a divine union and is a relationship of privilege. "Whoso findeth a wife findeth a good thing, and obtaineth favour of the Lord" (Proverbs 18:22, KJV).

Biblical Perspective and Dimensions of Marriage

The Lord and Savior Jesus Christ is the chief marriage counselor. Linked to His "Divine Agape Love," marriage cannot be destroyed. The "greatest" marriage is between individuals or believers who embrace Jesus Christ.

Marriage is defined in English as the state of being married a relationship between husband and wife in wedlock or Holy Matrimony. It is an intimate union between a man and a woman. Marriage from the Greek word, *gamos,* is translated "a marriage, a marriage feast, a wedding feast" (Miethe, 1998, p. 135).

The Christian view of marriage is that "a man and woman shall leave their families and become one flesh" according to Genesis 2:24, St. Matthews 19:5, and Ephesians 5:31, KJV. Marriage is a union resulting in intellectual, emotional, spiritual and physical oneness. Marriage is the deepest unity humanly possible and a unity God intends to endure for the lifetime of the couple according to St. Matthew 19:6. It was at the marriage feast at Cana of Galilee where Jesus performed His first miracle (St. John 2:1-11, I Corinthians 7:4, 11:11-12).

Counseling is defined in English as a mutual exchange of ideas, opinions, discussion, and deliberation. The counseling process is offering advice resulting from such an exchange. In the Greek translation counseling or council is *sumboulion* meaning a uniting in counsel, counsel, advice, or denotes counsel which is given and acted upon according to St. Matthew 12:14. Counseling means to have "took counsel." Counseling is also related to the term council, and assembly of counselors, or persons in consultation.

Biblical counseling is offering sound guidance or therapy that is inclusive of Holy Scripture, biblical criterion, and principles. Also, biblical counseling encompasses the understanding that "The Word of God" is a true source and foundation for a man to follow on a daily basis. Last, biblical counseling is not giving advice but remains Christ-centered in content and application demonstrating of empathy.

Love is—defined in English as a deep and tender feeling of affection, attachment or devotion to a person or persons. In Christian theology, the ability to love is a vital aspect of being "created in God's image" and "regenerated" by the Holy Ghost's power. In I John 4:7-11 it says:

> "Beloved, let us love one another, for love is from God; and everyone who loves is born of God and knows God. The one who does not love does not know God, for God is love. By this, the love of God was manifested in us, that God has sent His only begotten son into the world so that we might live through Him. In this is love, not that we loved God, but that He loved us and sent His Son to be the propitiation for our sins. Beloved, if God so loved us, we also ought to love one another."

For God is Love—Love is also one of God's most important attributes for us to follow. There are *four* common Greek words that describe the term love:

- *Philia*—translated "friendship, tendered affection" Example: love a mother has for her son or daughter.
- *Eros*—translated and often refers to the sexual or physical passion which is not utilized in the New Testament.

- *Storage*—translated "family affection" which is not found in the New Testament.
- *Agape*—translated the "best defined as intelligently, intentionally willing the best for another and the attitude of God toward His Son and toward us. God's unconditional love, self-less and God-type of love. Agape love is the most important type of love. Agape love is the kind of love that we want to possess, and that God wants us to encompass" (Vine, W. E., Unger, M. F., & White, Jr., W. (1996, pp.32).

Thus, the Agape love a Greek word simply means "love," distinctly a Christian term and has no counterpart in the Hebrew Old Testament. Various ways in the New Testament express ways to use Agape love:

1) Used to describe God's relationship to both individuals and groups according to St. John 17:26 and II Peter 1:17, toward Jesus in St. John 3:16 and Romans 5:8, toward the human race in St. John 14:21 toward those who believe.
2) Used to describe God's will concerning the attitude of His children in St. John 13:34 their attitude toward one another, in I Thessalonians 3:12, I Corinthians 16:14, and II Peter 1:17 their attitude toward all people.
3) Used to express God's essential nature according to I John 4:8.

The ultimate expression of agape is in the Lord Jesus Christ according to two Scripture references:

II Corinthians 5:14
Ephesians 2:4, 3:19, 5:2

Agape is through God's love and the gift of being His Son according to Scripture reference:

I John 4:9-10

Some other Scriptures used for people to further understand Agape love or to return this gift of love through obedience and self-denial are according to references:

St. John 14:15, 21, 23, 15:10
I John 2:5, 5:3
II John 6

Other supporting Scriptures relevant to *Love* passages are provided in **Table 1** below:

Table 1.

NEW TESTAMENT
St. Matthew 5:44-46
St John 3:16; 13:34-35; 14:21; 15:12-13; 17:26
Romans 5:8; 13:8-10
I Corinthian 13 Chapter is the *Love* Chapter
I Corinthians 16:14
Galatians 5:6, 22
I Thessalonians 3:12
II Peter 1:7
I John 4:7-20
Revelation 3:19

Christian love means more than a love for the giver of love. This type of love, is in action among God's children toward themselves, as well as those who do not yet know such love. Agape love is the standard that guides Christian's ethics. What is more, true Agape love, is the love that is the bases for all marriages.

In marriage, couples must develop the mind of Christ according to Philippians 2:5 where it says in the KJV… "Let this mind be in you, which was also in Christ Jesus." Those who accept the call of ministering must use Biblical Counsel and stay Christ-Centered. Christ, who is God manifested in the flesh and is the 'chief cognitive therapist' for *all*; His thoughts do not discriminate. Essentially, if the "root" of counseling is not sound "Biblically," little can be done to help the believer(s) to mature spiritually through the counseling process or experience. Therefore, this is the primary objective for Christ-Centered or marriage counseling.

The Christ-Centered lay or as a therapist should not merely attempt to provide assistance during some crisis in the life of the couple who are believers, but; should attempt to assist the couple to do the will of God in the midst of their crisis (e.g., related to this subject matter abuse, violence or divorce). There are essential counseling goals to meet in marital counseling to maintain a focus in the counseling process:

First, the *goals* of Christ-Centered/Biblical Counseling/Marital Counseling are to:

1) Provide assurance during in a life-crisis for a believer;
2) Assist believer to do God's will in the midst of the crisis;
3) Impart or teach appropriate decision-making skills, the appropriate attitude, or relevant behavioral modification;
4) Incorporate intercessory prayer/assisting in prayer.

Second, two vital elements exist in marriage and family guidance are:

- Reinforce that marriage was instituted by God as is the foundational unit of the family;
- Reinforce that marriage, and the act of sexual intercourse was created to be enjoyed and used for the procreation of humanity or mankind according to the Book of Genesis.

The lay counselor or therapist must be a minister of prayer concerning the couple that he or she is counseling with. The Holy Ghost/Spirit plays a major role in the counseling process. The role is the Holy Ghost/Spirit is to bring about the conviction of "missing the mark," or sin; facilitating "peace and restoration" to the counselees or couples. Most importantly, for the lay counselor or therapist, it becomes vital to know that what you are dealing with in marriage counseling will have a lasting effect on the salvation of both individuals.

For the advanced counselor, it becomes important to utilize the methodologies or counseling techniques in marriage or relationship counseling. There are simple methods that can be followed during any counseling process or session, and are listed below for your learning:

- **Data Collection**- (Listen, Observe Body Language, Questions and Assign Homework)
- **Comparison**- (Data that has linked and associated with Scripture)
- **Commitment**- (Need for change, true repentance indeed—not only word, and the need to change is for life)
- **The changing process**- (Discipleship, utilize Scriptural insight and direction)
- **Closure**- (Discharge or let a couple go gradually as a process over some time)

A marriage must be cultured or cultivated that it may grow like plants in a garden. Marriage is a relationship that takes time, communication, sharing and liking each other. Lack of *communication* and *financial difficulties* are the two most serious problems couples face in a relationship and must be overcome and placed under subjection before the enemy; Satin comes in the relationship to destroy. Couples must continue to stay sexually active and intimate, thus; the enemy cannot come between the couple. Even, if couples are having problems and are upset with one another, they should move forward, rising above the problems that they "come together" intimately to keep the devil out of their relationship.

The term *relationship* must be distinctly understood. Whenever two or more people come together, this process forms a relationship. As the author of this writing, what I deem as going up and down an adjustable "relationship continuum scale" of relationships types requires the commitment level to increase relevance. In relationship types, it is normal for the number of relationships to get smaller as you go up the levels. The highest level of relationship demands the most attention, anchor, and commitment. In increasing order of commitment, the levels may include, but; not limited. Relationship types or forms: acquaintances, casual, close friends, best friends, **Intimate/Marriage** and fellowship with God as in a "new birth" or "born-again" experience. Significant Scriptures to support this fact include I Corinthians 1:9; II Corinthians 6:14; Ephesians 3:9; Philippians 1:5 and I John 1:3.

In focus of the specific subject matter related to this novel, marriage is an *intimate relationship* the "one person in the closet relationship" or described as what "two people can have," and must build upon the element of *trust*. Erikson's stages of psychosocial development, as articulated by theorist Erik Erikson emphasis the element of trust. This first development task or stage that Erikson identifies is called: "Trust vs. Mistrust" that begins at infancy. Interesting enough, the stages' Virtues is HOPE: Trust vs. Mistrust (oral-sensory, Infancy, under two years). The element of trust, if not learned in this early time of life can carry over into adulthood. For instance, if there is abandonment, neglect, or unmet needs in this developmental task or stage of a relationship—trust will be violated. Thus, to correlate, in marriage sharing all aspects of life 'together' is essential in the relationship and there should not be any secrets between each other—causing a violation. Heretofore, trust is a must and becomes the foundation and anchor of a great marital relationship.

Since trust is established during this early developmental task or stage, learned at the beginning of life in early infancy, know that it stems from parenting and the family structure. This early task or stage is critical and can determine one's *trust factor* in adulthood. What is more, the term trust is a noun or action word that must be placed consistently in action and practice. The *trust factor* will determine the amount of depth the relationship will possess and fruitfulness. A violation of the *trust factor* can become serious and could strain any marital relationship.

Last regarding the relationship process in marriage, individuals must understand the "relationship continuum scale" or relationship level that is entered to appropriate the *level of trust*. However, in the intimate/marriage relationship trust becomes the foundation of relationships, and should become parallel to their faith. The *level of trust* will determine the amount of depth in a relationship will possess. Again, a violation of the *level of trust* can become serious and strain any marital relationship.

Communication and *forgiveness* are a must. We communicate words of life or words of death. Thus, our words are powerful when we speak a word into existence. Words of life build-up the marriage and bring the relationship into life. Then the words of death kill and destroy marriages and can lead to marital demise. The tongue can slash, kill, and can create a life-long damaging effect. A couple in their communication needs must commit to deal with the issues that are facing them. In life, we cannot allow or avoid issues by placing the blame on someone or something. There are times when one must take ownership when there becomes a lack of commitment or unfavorable actions. For instance, there were trust, communication, and unforgiveness issues superimposed concerning the "Garden of Eden," that is recorded in the Book of Genesis (1:24 through 5:32) between Adam and Eve that can be referenced as a reminder or in comparison to this area of discussion.

Communication and *forgiveness* also must be fully understood. As humans, we communicate words of life or words of death. In life, "our words are powerful." Words can kill, destroy, or bring forth death, and in comparison, words can bring forth life. The issues of Communication and forgiveness cannot be ducked or avoided, neither should there be the "pointing of the finger at the other," placing the *blame* on someone or something. The blame game does not work, in fact; this augments the issues. This is what Adam and Eve did in the "Garden of Eden," and the result got them nowhere! This couple's lack of commitment and actions resulted in sin and separation from God. They lost their fellowship/relationship or (in the Greek translation) *koinonia* with God.

Often in the heat of an argument, it is common for a couple to say, "I don't want to talk about it!" A delay that could be a way of trying to stop the argument, or not facing the issue. However, instead the couple should stop, take a break, walk away from the situation, and make a commitment to talk about the issues at hand later—but as soon as possible. Sometimes we try to be so right, that we are wrong in our attitudes. Often, a couple needs to forgive and forget. Forgiveness can be very difficult for individuals to do. However, the example that Apostle Paul gives, "Do not let the sun go down upon your wrath" becomes an outstanding path to follow. Also, biblical forgiveness is expressed all through the Bible. An example of "Biblical Forgiveness" for couples can also be applied in the context of five steps: a.) acknowledge, b.) confession, c.) conciliation, d.) commitment, and e.) cooperation. Therefore, in communication and forgiveness, it becomes essential to acknowledge the offense made and not hide from it.

Next, confess in your heart that unforgiveness is a sin process in the making. The conciliation in knowing that by working out the offense made could escalate into a planted "seed of bitterness" or "the spirit of bitterness," if not addressed could embed into a "root of bitterness." The "seed of bitterness," is a "pit of resentment and sourness." The "root of bitterness," grows deeper into an origin for divide, disharmony, criticism, control dominance, and eventually destructive behavior. Next, rise above the problem, committing to change the offensive behavior. Last, the general cooperation and coordination in asking your companion of relationship to assist you to change. That way, the issue and, problem become shared and, a framework of needing each other is priceless. Keep in mind, that humans are not born with insight, judgment, or skills to distinctly followed these steps of "Biblical Forgiveness," but; is a learned behavior that must be inquired and developed.

Another benefit for the believer, and inlay or professional counseling process is to possess empathy. The term empathy means an affection, passion, or Greek ***pathos***, meaning feeling: used to translate–a projection of one's personality into the personality of another to understand him or her better it is the ability to share in another's emotions or feelings. Empathy- it is the projection of one's personality into an object, with the attribution to the object of one's own emotions or responses. In other words, if possible, you the reader or a tip for the counselor must "see and feel the pain, situation, or condition," etc. of the counselees or couple involved. When the person or counselor has experienced the same situation personally himself or herself it is especially becoming more effective in the process. In other words, "Been there… done that!" slang if you will. As author of this book, in my view, the lack of empathy can become a lack of ineffectiveness. Therefore, there should be a self-analysis or self-evaluation regarding your ability to possess empathy.

The disadvantage can come when becoming too empathetic. It becomes a problem and can be very common. Then there becomes a need to control the empathy gift and or experience—creating balance. God uses the counselor to interact with clients, counselees, couples, but not to solve all their problems. Overall, ultimately God is the one who will guide marriage to solve their problems of communication and forgiveness.

Marriage—Aligning With the "Word of God"

When marriage aligns with the "Word of God," the union is fruitful. Faith is a gift that cannot be superimposed on someone else. Biblical guidance within the context of the "Word of God," primarily is applicable to the believer, but; can be used for anybody. Identifying a marital problem or taking ownership in wrongdoing in a marriage can occur through conviction. The process of conviction derives from the Holy Ghost/Spirit. In problem-solving, the solution is not, "jumping into the problem." In resolving a problem or effective decision-making in marital problems, one may need to remove himself or herself from a given environment, focus on claiming down, pray, and return fresh in attempts to resolve the conflict. The reason for this is at that given moment in a medium of anger or conflict setting may not be conducive for a resolution, and could result in harm.

As a believer, a married couple can plan and obligate themselves in advance that during any conflict to pause, pray, read a Scripture before revisiting the problem or issue. Couples will soon learn, that in following these simple steps can bring about a more peaceful resolution. In aligning with and acknowledging God's word can bring about praise, worship, and honoring Him in spiritual richness and joy. To *praise*, meaning to adore, respect, reverence, *worship*, and honor God—can bring about the right attitude or assist to re-set in talking things out with each other. To **Worship**, **(shacha/proskuneo)** in the Greek translation means [acknowledgment, praise, thanksgiving and service to God, (St. Matthew 4:10) who is to be worshiped in spirit and in truth, for He is Spirit and Truth (St. John 4:23-24), giving one's life in attitude and action as a "living sacrifice" (Romans 12:1-2), having the outward expression to the inward reality in Christ Jesus, it is a form of fruit, to worship prostrate or bowed down and a sweet smelling savor]. To **Praise**, **(halal)** in the Greek translation means [to celebrate, give glory, sing praise, boast in the Holy Ghost/Spirit, it is that which goes up to God]. God is looking for those two things from any believer. Once couples and believers possess these attributes, it can counteract what every problem that is presented. Together when aligning with the "Word of God," coupled with worship and praise—God will hear their prayers and hasten to assist in resolving the issues and strengthen the marital union.

Biblical Perspective and Dimensional Order of Marriage

In any marital relationship, it becomes essential to understand the order of marriage. If there is disorder in the union, this divide must be restored and bring order back into alignment with godly principles as soon as possible. By exploring the Holy Scriptures on this subject matter, helps to refocus, and restore relationship(s) the way God attended to be. For instance, reference the illustration below that further explains:

The Order in Marriage
GOD ➜ MAN ➜ WOMAN
CHRIST ➜ HUSBAND ➜ WIFE

In developing a balanced relationship, establish certain duties that the wife (mother) and husband (father) may have. There are some ascribed duties in every relationship. Example: call and lead prayer, laundry, budgeting, and cleaning, etc. These elements will bring back the relationship(s) to the point of equilibrium or balance. Then after the balance is restored, it must be continuously identified and kept focused. It is to be kept in mind that all problems are not identifiable and that sometimes there are only identified symptoms.

For this reason, in the marital relationship, it must be established if the symptoms are: Valid (a legitimate problem), Honest (a true problem), Workable (a problem with resolutions). In determining what type of symptoms or problems a couple is facing is what constitutes the essential resolution process. Also, it is important to understand the equation and structure for the human dimensions of man, marriage, family. For example, reference the illustration below that further explains:

The Formula for the Human Marriage and Family
God is Love + Marriage between male + female = the **two** shall become **one**

The following is an outline and summary regarding the Holy Institution created by God and should remain so today. Marriage has always been and remains today a Holy institution created and governed by God:

Outline of God's Word in Relationship to Marriage

Genesis 1:27-28
God's blueprint from which to build a marriage

Genesis 2:15-17
God's condition for man (humankind) to preserve the sanctity of marriage

Genesis 2:18
God's purpose of marriage is to eliminate the adverse impact of loneliness on humankind

There are Scriptures for couples to reference until help comes along restoring peace, resolution, and harmony:

- Psalm 23—allow God to be your shepherd and meet your needs
- Psalm 27:10—when the feeling of being forsaken, allow God to take you up
- Isaiah 41:10—know that God is with you
- St. Matthew 28:20—know that God goes with you to unlimited lengths
- Hebrews 13:5—be satisfied and content

There are Scriptures for couples to reference showing God's Love for Man that caused Him to bring Eve to Mankind:

- St. John 3:16
- St. John 15:19
- Romans 5:8, 38, 39
- I John 3:1, 2

God's love brought us, woman. It was unconditional love (Agape). It was a love that responds affectionately when we don't love back. Therefore, God expects us to reciprocate this same love as described in I Corinthians 13:1-13 that is often called the "Love Chapter" or the "way of love." The last verse of this chapter provides a unique summary regarding what Agape Love Is: "And now abideth faith, HOPE, charity, these three; but the greatest of these is charity" (I Corinthians 13:13, KJV).

God truly ordains marriage, it is sacred, and it is the strongest human relationship or institution on earth in which God honors. The essential elements for the growth of marriage are:

1) Family Prayer
2) Communication
3) Forgiveness

In married it is no longer "I" and "Me," but "We" and "Us." That marriage is symbolic of the church. The couple is at the center of creation on one accord, and that marriage is a reflection of who God is. A marriage vow is a contract between two people, and it is a holy institution of marriage that is not designed to be broken. Broken marriages send a negative message to the "world," because they are watching the believers. In marriage, if the couple allows Christ rule in their relationship, then marriage will last forever. Sadly enough, in the earlier statistical study result showed that more divorces are occurring in our society; and growing in number in churches.

There is a necessity in the marriage of continuing to stay on one accord. Sexual intercourse is sacred reviling a part of themselves and should be that person that will keep himself or herself until marriage. However, this choice is not true reality, and the individual may choose to have intercourse before marriage. Satan does not want couples to be in "marriage counseling," and does not like to see couples being on one accord; however, Jesus has a way of escape for us. For in the "Word of God," it says in Proverbs 11:14, KJV:

"Where no counsel is, the people fail: but in the multitude of counsellors there is safety."

Therefore, the "Word of God," instructs people to seek counsel when necessary providing a safe-haven for care and secure approach to guidance. In fact, Jesus is the great counselor and physician, and seeking Him wholly will produce results.

For the lay or professional counselor, confidentiality of marriage counseling is critical, what's discussed in a counseling setting "must stay in the room." A "release form" should be utilized for legal purposes and to provide written consent to counsel. As counselors, it is important to express that you are *only* giving guidance. Also, it is important to establish that there will be no recourse when the couple leaves their counseling session and that there should be "*no* hidden agendas."

Love with the emphasis of "Agape love" should be comprehensively discussed with couples, which will empower their relationship. Couples should be encouraged to "service in love," to continue to teach (family), and show God's love at all times; not only in marriage but at all times. It is significant to guide the counselees or couple to "keep the fire burning" in your marriage and that "it is up to the individual to make it work!" A marriage can work through sacrifice, and when they are committed to make it work!

Helping Biblical Scripture References for Marriages

Genesis 34:9

Exodus 21:10

Deuteronomy 7:3

Joshua 23:12

Psalms 78:63

Proverbs 18:21-24

St. Matthew 22:2-4

St. Matthew 22:9

St. Matthew 22:30

St. Matthew 24:38

St. Matthew 25:10

St. Mark 12:25

St. Luke 17:27

St. Luke 20:35

St. Luke 20:34

St. John 2:1-2

I Corinthians 7:38

Ephesians 5:25

Colossians 3:19

Hebrews 13:4

Revelation 19:7-9

Biblical Perspective and Dimensional Order of Family

From the being of time, God designed for there to be families. From the Scripture reference in Genesis 2:18-24 Eve was created to be a help meet for Adam:

> "And the Lord God said, It is not good that the man should be alone; I will make him an help meet for him. (The purpose for marriage) And out of the ground the Lord God formed every beast of the field, and every fowl of the air; and brought them unto Adam to see what he would call them: and whatsoever Adam called every living creature, that was the name thereof. And Adam gave names to all cattle, and to the fowl of the air, and to every beast of the field; but

for Adam there was not found an ***help meet*** for him. And the Lord God caused a deep sleep to fall upon Adam, and he slept: and he took one of his ribs, and closed up the flesh instead thereof; and the rib which the Lord God had taken from man, made he a woman, and brought her unto the man. And Adam said, This is now bone of my bones, and flesh of my flesh; she shall be called Woman, because she was taken out of Man. Therefore, shall a man leave his father and mother, and shall cleave unto his wife: and they shall be one flesh."

When Adam and Eve fell, they lost their sense of identity and a family unit. However, God had a plan to restore the family unit. The Scriptures unfold this plan of salvation and redemption, which culminates in the death, burial, resurrection, and ascension of Jesus Christ. God's search for man, His means of restoring human identity, begins with His question to Adam, "Where are thou?" and climaxes at the cross with Christ's atonement for our rebellion. Jesus gave back to us our sense of identity as a family unit by taking the punishment, rejection, and shame that we deserve. Through a response of faith to the person and work of Christ on the cross, human beings (families) can recover their lost identity. If there is no such response of faith, any attempt to recover human identity will prove futile or fruitless.

The "Word of God," establishes, that the man or husband is the head of the family and God ordained it to be so (I Corinthians 7:1-16 and Ephesians 5:21-33, KJV). The Bible says in Ephesians 5:21-23:

"Submitting yourselves one to another in the fear of God. Wives, submit yourselves unto your own husbands, as unto the Lord. For the husband is the head of the wife, even as Christ is the head of the church and he is the saviour of the body."

The remainder of the family lines-up after the husband and the wife or father and mother. Ephesians 6:1-2 says:

"Children, obey your parents in the Lord: for this is right. Honour thy father and mother; which is the first commandment with the promise."

Few people realize that being a parent entails an awesome responsibility and accountability, for the new life (bone of my bone and flesh of my flesh). To provide every physical necessity, along with a varying amount of luxuries; to give the best of education; and though he or she may rise to worldwide fame or amass a fortune, the parent has utterly failed if the reason for life and the accountability of God has not been taught. Ecclesiastes 12:13-14 says:

"Let us hear the conclusion of the whole matter: Fear God, and keep his
Commandments: for this is the whole duty of man. For God shall bring
Every work into judgment, with every secret thing, whether it be good,
Or whether it be evil."

The learning process starts early by copying the actions and repeating the words of those around, as well as taking on their thinking patterns. No child will ever respect a parent with word only saying: "Do as I say, not as I do." It is by setting an example indeed. The truth is setting Biblical examples and not going against God's law. To be successful, parents should sow a good seed by so ordering their own lives to be patterns for their children to follow, as they pattern their lives after Jesus Christ.

Unfortunately, due to the devices of Satan, the "gap" that he creates can cause division, disruption and, dysfunction in the family structure that God originally designed. He causes violence and death to the family nucleus. The Family is like a body cell that's held together by a membrane (controls what goes in and out). When there is damaged by invading properties that bring adversity, it can cause damage to the "cell" or "DNA" of the cell structure. When this happens, there may be situations for family counseling. It is then that the awesome task of the lay or professional counselor comes to assist in uniting and rebuilding the family structure causing it to function properly again. The family counseling process will bridge the gap to salvation for the family in need of counseling.

Only the husband and wife who have had a genuine experience of salvation and filling of the Holy Ghost/ Spirit will be able to stand the onslaught, sexually, emotionally, financially, morally and spiritually battles. The family should be united and put the training of their children in fear of the Lord, as their prime objective, for years pass so swiftly, and soon gone from the home.

Ernest B. Kidd (1987, p.69) the author of "The Master Counselor and Handbook," summarizes and supports this statement several Scriptures involving the family.

"Train up a child in the way he should go: and when he is old, he will
Not depart from it" (Proverbs 22:6).

"Children, obey your parents in the Lord: for this is right. Honour your
Father and mother; which is the first commandment with promise; that
It may be well with you and you may live long on the earth. And, you
Fathers, provoke not your children to wrath: but bring them up in the
Nurture and admonition of the Lord" (Ephesians 6:1-4).

This discussion has established the Biblical view of the family who may require spiritual guidance for family problems or issues. Family guidance could mean, that the entire family or part of the family may be involved in the counseling process, however; the primary focus should remain Christ-centered/Biblical in origin.

Some suggestion to incorporate in the family structure is the recipe for a happy family that includes *guidelines for a happy home, family prayer protocol for a happy home*, and *family scriptures for a happy home*. For example, reference the illustration below that further explains:

Guidelines for a Happy Home

Family guidelines consist of the following attributes:

Attributes

Love	Loyalty	Forgiveness	Kisses
Hope	Tenderness	Kindness	Faith
Laughter	Unity	Understanding	Hugs
Serving one another	Support	Wholeness	Friendship

Family Prayer Protocols for a Happy Home

Family protocols consist of the following functions:

Family Prayer Protocol

Prayer of the father
Prayer of the mother
Prayer of the sons or daughter
Prayer of extended family

Family Scriptures for a Happy Home

Other supporting Scriptures relevant to 𝓕𝓪𝓶𝓲𝓵𝔂 from the Old and New Testament passages are outlined in **Table 2** below:

Table 2.

FAMILY SCRIPTURES

Proverbs 1:7, 10	Proverbs 3: 6, 9	Proverbs 6: 1, 16
Proverbs 13:24	Proverbs 15:3, 15	Proverbs 16:32
Proverbs 17:21	Proverbs 20:1, 11	Proverbs 22:1, 6, 15
Proverbs 29:17	Ecclesiastes 12:13, 14	St Mark 8:36
Romans 12:21	Galatians 6:7	Philippians 3:14
Colossians 3:20	I Thessalonians 5:22	I Peter 5:8
I John 3:1	Revelations 2:10	Revelation 3:21

Finally, in understanding the family unit instituted by God, it is vital to know the basis for the family structure and Biblical views to stand and be strengthened during family problems and issues. The Christian family should be the example of the Family of God. The father has the great responsibility or demonstrating love, encouragement, and discipline in the family. The father should realize the magnitude of his role; not demanding respect by shouting commands to his children and exacting submission from his wife, but by so ordering his own life, showing sincere love and interest, that he wins respect, confidence and, love of his family. Thus, in essence, the father is winning his family closer to Christ and being an instrument as well as bridging the gap to salvation.

Biblical Perspective and Dimensional Order of Man

Man is a triune being (consisting of three in one). From a Biblical perspective, man has wholistic dimensions determining one's wholeness, health, and wellness: the whole-person consists of the components of the body, mind, and spirit—or the total man.

Wholistic health encompasses the whole person (mind-body-spirit). The term "holism" or "holistic" comes from the Greek root "*holos*" which means "whole." Holism is a philosophy that views everything regarding patterns or organization, relationships interactions, and processes that combine to form a whole. The whole person is one who seeks the inward journey of understanding the complexities of life.

In the Bible the *body* should be presented as a living sacrifice according to Romans 12:1 it says:

> "I beseech you therefore, brethren by the mercies of God, that you present your Bodies a living sacrifice, holy, acceptable unto God which is your reasonable service."

The Bible also tells us, that the *mind* can be kept in perfect peace whose mind is stayed upon Him and that God can give us a sound mind according to Isaiah 26:3 and II Timothy 1:7:

> "Thou wilt keep him in perfect peace, whose *mind* is stayed on thee: because he trusteth in thee:" (Isaiah 26:3)

> "For God hath not given us the *spirit* of fear, but of power and of love, and of a sound mind" (II Timothy 1:7).

God's desire is that man be whole. The "wholistic health and wellness" is expressed throughout the Bible, God ordains it for a man to understand the whole-person process. Below are three scriptures pertinent to the total-man in regards to the "Wholistic Health and Wellness:"

- I Corinthians 6:19-20
- I Thessalonians 5:23
- III John 2

Last, in this first chapter, the premise for this initial comprehensive discussion regarding marriage, love, relationships, family structure, and man is to provide a foundation for 'normality' or 'framework' of how God; intended each of these entities or units to function. As you, the reader progresses through this novel, you will experience a deeper delving into the dysfunctional process of each entity having a premise to compare the norm with the abnormal function of these units.

CHAPTER TWO

The Elect Lady | "Walking in Truth"

"The elder unto the **ELECT LADY** and her children, whom I love in the truth; and not I only, but also all they that have known the truth; For the truth's sake, which dwelleth in us, and shall be with us for ever. Grace be with you, mercy, and peace, from God the Father, and from the Lord Jesus Christ, the Son of the Father, in truth and love. I rejoiced greatly that I found of thy children walking in truth, as we have received a commandment from the father. And now I beseech thee, lady, not as though I wrote a new commandment unto thee, but that which we had from the beginning, that we love one another. An this is love, that we walk after his commandments. This is the commandment, That, as ye have heard from the beginning, ye should walk in it. For many deceivers are entered into the world, who confess not that Jesus Christ is come in the flesh. This is a deceiver and an antichrist. Look to yourselves, that we lose not those things which we have wrought, but that we receive a full reward. Whosoever transgresseth, and abideth not in the doctrine of Christ, hath not God. He that abideth in the doctrine of Christ, he hath both the Father and the Son. If there come any unto you, and bring not this doctrine, receive him not into your house, neither bid him God speed: For he that biddeth him God speed is partaker of his evil deeds. Having many things to write unto you, I would not write with paper and ink: but I trust to come unto you, and speak face to face, that our joy may be full. The children of the elect sister greet thee. Amen."

(II John 1:1-13, KJV)

Theoretical belief suggest that this brief epistle II John is anonymous, but the early church strongly affirmed that the Apostle John is the author, the youngest of the apostles; and a teacher at heart. The reason for this controversy is that the author identified himself at the beginning in this epistle as the "elder" or seasoned person suggesting a position of authority and honor. The actual date, place, and order are also unknown; however, scholars assert that John wrote this epistle after he wrote the Gospel which would date this letter at about A.D. 85-95. Scholars also believe that the setting for this epistle is believed to be Ephesus during the time he was ministering to the churches in Asia Minor. The author, John used the expression "the elect lady," and also addressed "her children" as recipients of this letter (verse 1). He also addresses the woman as "thy elect sister" (verse 13), as a sister congregation. Both of these descriptions have given rise to endless theologian discussion. In this case, the designation most likely referred to a particular woman or perhaps the "bride of Christ" or "the church" respectively, "her children" as the members—illustrated that he had spiritual authority. In other words, did the Apostle John write this letter to a particular prominent woman in the local church in the vicinity of Ephesus or was his precious letter addressing the local church representing a lady?

Nevertheless, his discussion in the letter is ascribed to a most worthy Christian character in his use of exhortatory language toward her. With John's dialogue, it was easy to concur that this Christian woman was of excellent character, well-known, and well-loved in the local church –who possessed more dignity than others. Even perhaps, like a princess in character or a woman of social distinction.

The term *elect* or *election* was used in the Old and New Testament history, and in the Greek translation is called *EKLEKTOS* that denotes someone picked out or chosen as mentioned in II John 1-13. What is interesting is that the source of the election is based on God's grace, and not by the will of man or humanity. The term *lady* in the Greek translation is *KURIA*. Also, the person addressed in II John 1-13 possibly giving a proper name in English as Cyria (Vine's, 1981, p. 306); that would be a person who demonstrated a special relationship with the local church. The foreknowledge view of these terms, one would need to understand that election was a sovereign act by God, in choosing certain individuals for His plan of salvation even before the foundation of the world. In other words, God knew aforetime what individuals would respond favorably and positively to His preordained Gospel message. The complete term Elect Lady denotes in the Greek translation as *eklekte kuria*, and Latin as "chosen lady." The term *Kuria* was rarely used during those times or in John's day—even to queens. The proper name, Kyria or Cyria where used in John's day. This term Elect Lady "may be refer to John's personification of a local congregation in verse 5, and elect sister in verse 13 would designate churches that knew each other. However, it is just likely that the designation may be referred to an esteemed friend" (Nelson, 1995, pp. 2092); or "chosen in the Lord" for His eternal purpose.

The *history* and *background* of the Scriptural passage is significant and brings commonalities to view that in the "picked out" or "chosen one" election demonstrates that: God's elects to be loving, God is glorified in the process, and the divine act becomes a product of individuals performing good works according to Ephesians 2:10; Colossians 3:12; and Romans 11:33-36.

One of the primary special features or emphases characterized in the epistle II John is that it is the shortest book in the New Testament. However, this Scriptural text layout content is phenomenal with an enormous message. II John is similar to John I and III in message and writing style and urging careful discernment before offering support to these false teachers. The purpose and message warn believers against receiving itinerant heretics teachings (Antichrist deceivers) in their homes; including those desiring to twist the "Word of God." These encounters occurred because the Roman Empire had an extensive network related to travel during that time with the average inn spread afar that was unsanitary, noisy, and often there were thieves. As a result, traveling ministers, teachers, evangelist, prophets, missionaries, or those who spread the gospel would receive hospitality from believers in an expression of Christian love (Roman 12:13; Hebrews 13:16). These believers willing to serve, would feed and offer lodging to those claiming to be spreading the gospel. However, unfortunately, there were some who took advantage of their kindness, and who had departed from the apostolic truth. Some of these travelers may have even spread false teaching. The Elect Lady may have found herself in this scenario, and John got wind to this and sent this letter to warn her. At the end of this epistle Apostle John concluded with great anticipation of his upcoming face-to-face visit according to II John 10-12, KJV saying: "If there come any unto you, and bring not this doctrine, receive him not into your house, neither bid him God speed: For he that biddeth him God speed is partaker of his evil deeds. Having many things to write unto you, I would not write with paper and ink: but I trust to come unto you, and speak face to face, that our joy may be full." Apostle John expressed hope in meeting with them again, and that this would be their joy satisfied."

Within the context of his message John asserts himself with authority speaking firmly about a core aim or theme of the book: "Agape Love & Hospitality." The word love is reiterated four times in this Scriptural passage. Also, he speaks about "truth," which is mention five times. John exhorted the Elect Lady to continue in love and truth offering balanced hospitality, but; admonishes her to look out for deceivers. What is more, John sends her a message to safeguard her against the abuse and taking advantage of Christian fellowship. The context of love and truth is a common command in the Bible and is also intertwined in John's message in I John 5:3; II John 6; I John 4:3; II John 7; II John 10-11. Therefore, this act of kindness was customary.

"Walking in Truth"

Walking in Truth—Apostle John wrote this epistle to the Elect Lady and her Children (II John 1-3); on behalf of the "truth." The general theme of this epistle is "Walking in Truth." John was exhorting in his letter for the elect lady, the bride of Christ or the church to maintain their strong stance of "walking in truth" and expressing this truth through the practice of love toward one another. However, in doing, he wanted the believers to be cognizant of others who were not adhering to the doctrine of Christ' Incarnation according to II John 7. Therefore, he cautioned the believers not to offer shelter or housing to false teachers (II John 10). Instead, John commanded action from them. He gave counsel and warning to recognize false teachers, to beware of being negatively influenced by them; and refuse them any use of their home. Yet, he encouraged them to remain faithful in love; and in conclusion expressed his desire to see them again (II John 4, 12).

In summary, the Apostle John introduces the Elect Lady in II John in many facets of truth, love, hospitality, as exemplary, and a privileged lady. John did not mince his words against the peril of these deceivers who were guilty of intellectual errors and leading people astray in ungodly conduct. In so doing, John protected her spiritual integrity and community status. There is persuasion within the context of John's epistle that the Elect Lady valued the spiritual advice from her aged friend and teacher, and adhered to the doctrine. She no doubt followed his wise counsel and practice of keeping near to Christ and walking in His truth.

Today and in modern times the titles "First Lady" or "Elect Lady" are often used to address the wife of a husband that is in the office of a minister, pastor, or bishop. In the secular world or politics, a "First Lady" is used to ascribe to the wife of a major, governor, presidential levels or of male elected for an office.

In this novel, the main character Paris Hope was a woman of excellent character, highly esteemed, whose godly influence touched the lives of those around her, and her child. She had many spiritual daughters and sons who looked up to her. Paris' desires, roles, views, and experience as a First Lady or Elect Lady brought about extensive passion, compassion, and commitment regarding her role as an Elect Lady, in ministry, in the body of Christ, and community. Quite the contrary to one's thinking, due to Paris' love for all of these roles often than not, she would overlook and ignore the fact that she was overwhelmed with emotional grief, torment, abuse, domestic violence that existed in her marriage of 30 years.

CHAPTER THREE

Paris' Background and Story

Most of us have or will inevitability experience ups and downs in life. This story is about Lady Paris Hope who truly loved the Lord. Her whole life was centered around the reverent fear of God, having compassion for those in need; and the will of serving others. Without controversy, Paris' story was also full of mountains and valleys. Like many have experienced, Paris' background involved marriage, family dysfunction, abuse, and divorce, and those who have triumphed over these adversities. Paris had a strong faith that by sharing her story can serve to support, enlighten, and heighten awareness—as well as promoting hope, healing, wholeness, deliverance, and inspiration surrounding family, relationships, and divorce.

One winter evening while praying the "Spirit of the Lord" moved upon Paris, and she began to praise and worship God. During this supernatural encounter, God placed in Paris' heart to tell her story regarding her pain and heartbreak. Meanwhile, as she continued to pray and worship God Paris could strongly feel the presences of the Lord upon her. There was a compelling force to release, let go, and let God move in her life by using her for His glory. The primary mission and goal for sharing her story were birthed during this encounter with a supernatural assurance that someone would be helped and liberated. More specific, it was fully evident that God intended for Paris to share her life story and experience to benefit a hurting world filled with tumultuous times involving marriage, family and, relationships.

Along life's journey sometimes God allows His people to endure grief, and suffering wrongfully—and we must take it patiently because this is acceptable with God and glorifies Him. God also allows tests, trials, and adversity to come your way to seek him wholeheartedly for His help and that others may witness God's power of deliverance in your life. For instance, the Holy Bible tells us that:

> "For this is thankworthy, if a man for conscience toward God endure grief, suffering wrongfully. For what glory is it, if, when ye be buffeted for your faults, ye shall take it patiently? But if, when ye do well and suffer for it, ye take it patiently, this is acceptable with God. For even hereunto were ye called: because Christ also suffered for us, leaving us an example, that ye should follow his steps" (I Peter 2:19-21).

Paris' story of survival, begins with her birth, background, life's journey, wounds, and her experience with damaged emotions. The pathway to her life leads to travel that is full of multifaceted trials, and tribulations encompassing deep: pain, pressures, sufferings, and distresses. Undoubtedly, looking back without these pivotal experiences in her life she would not be the spiritually empowered person that she became. Still, Paris can proclaim that—through her sufferings, she found blessed hope and divine empowerment. Ultimately, she desired to share a glimpse of her life with you offering hope, healing, encouragement, and empowerment through Biblical counsel by delving into areas of life-truths, with the purpose of edifying the *Body of Christ*, and for the advancement and upbuilding of God's Kingdom.

Paris' personal story involved much pain and suffering surrounding her immediate family, inter/intrapersonal relationships, and social orientation. Elements of her inborn temperament, her past life chapters, her physical afflictions since birth, and her life experience with her *first* love (childhood sweetheart, and beloved husband) whose name is "Lamont" throughout this story becomes the framework for her survival. Paris' background will be shared in hopes to encourage the wounded heart. Within her story, Parish will share intricate levels of a second marriage, her personal life as it was, feelings, pain, sufferings, and pressures endured—that changed her life forever.

Having a life surrounding suffering, Paris relied upon a few Scriptural references that the Holy Ghost/Spirit guided her to, in addressing her pain and suffering. To begin, the following three Scriptures are some passages that God lead her to read *initially* during her sufferings:

> "STAND FAST therefore in the liberty wherewith Christ hath made us free, and be not entangled again with the yoke of bondage" (Galatians 5:1).

"Blessed be God, even the Father of our Lord Jesus Christ, the Father of mercies, and the God of all comfort; Who comforteth us in all our tribulation, that we may be able to comfort them which are in any trouble, by the comfort wherewith we ourselves are comforted of God. For as the sufferings of Christ abound in us, so our consolation also aboundeth by Christ. And whether we be afflicted, it is for your consolation and salvation, which is effectual in the enduring of the same sufferings which we also suffer: or whether we be comforted, it is for your consolation and salvation. And our hope of you is stedfast, knowing, that as ye are partakers of the sufferings, so shall ye be also of the consolation. For we would not, brethren, have you ignorant of our trouble which came to us in Asia, that we were pressed out of measure, above strength, insomuch that we despaired even of life: But we have the sentence of death in ourselves, that we should not trust in ourselves, but in God which raiseth the dead: Who delivered us from so great a death, and doth deliver: in whom we trust that he will yet deliver us; Ye also helping together by prayer for us, that for the gift bestowed upon us by the means of by many persons thanks may be given by many on our behalf" (II Corinthians 1:3-11).

"My brethren, count it all joy when ye fall into divers temptations; (test) Knowing *this*, that the trying of your faith worketh patience. But let patience have her perfect work, that you may be perfect and entire, wanting nothing. If any of you lack wisdom, let him ask of God, that giveth to all *men* liberally, and upbraideth not; and it shall be given him" (James 1:2-4).

To note here from these passages of Scripture we can find great comfort during any pain and suffering circumstances of life. From this divine comfort through "The Word of God," we then can be liberated for Kingdom living, liberated for the advancement of God's Kingdom, and liberated through empowerment in any situation.

Last, before beginning Paris' story, in the conclusion of this book, you will become illuminated by her miracle and life transformation through "***survival***." It is Paris' belief, that enduring "***suffering***" has been the result of her reward from her pain and sufferings, and she now knows this process was in God's divine plan for her life.

In the Epilogue, as the author of this book, I will affirm my final view on the theory, theology, empowerment, belief, and hypothesis *related to* Paris' area of pain, suffering, from domestic violence, abuse, and eventually divorce.

Marriage—A Divine Union

Paris vowed to devote her life fully to God by becoming goal-directed with
a vision and mission to help the hurting globally~ preliminary

Preliminary question: Before you begin reading this story, how would you vow today?

"A way to escape!"

Your Vow ~

"Favourable and Confident Expectation"

Paris was born on June 20th in New York at a community hospital following severe maternal complications and as a neonate a life-threatening delivery. Both Paris and her mother escaped death by a divine miracle. Paris' mother and father were natives from a small village in New York, who both are deceased. This small community was a place where both of her parents grew up. This city was considered a historical village with 383 acres and was a community where everyone knows one another. For Paris, the village always reminded her of a type of "Peyton-Place" when she would go and visit during her childhood. What is intriguing about this community is that it is a place where strong and powerful leadership evolved, and where "everybody is somebody," and a community known for "working together in unity."

Paris' parents married in the year of 1940 and moved to Manhattan and started their family. Paris' father was always a hard worker and an excellent provider throughout his life and retired from engineering. Paris' mother was a housewife, a virtuous woman (Proverbs 31) throughout their marriage, and exceptionally gifted and talented with her hands. Together they had four children two sons and two girls including Paris in which, she was the youngest of the four with a ten-year age gap in contrasts to the oldest. Paris' family was Christ-centered and raised as devout Christians, so it seemed; and faithful churchgoers.

Paris' and her three siblings were not very close, however; it was understood that they all loved one another. Perhaps this was due to the gaps in ages between them. Finding common interests between each other became challenging as Paris and her three siblings were in different growth, development, and social phases of life.

What dominated Paris' remote memory regarding 'family' were multiple conflicts and dysfunction between them, which would have a huge emotional impact growing up. For Paris, the family conflicts, dysfunction, and relationships consisted of undeserving or unavoidable pain and suffering for her. Therefore, some of her pain and suffering experience, she did not deserve and in most cases was avoidable.

In the world of Christian counseling and psychology, it is understood that all families are dysfunctional. According to Dr. David Stoop (Stoop, 2005, pp. 241-255). in his profound writing on *Family Systems: Breaking the Unhealthy Patterns*, he illustrates a profound work and analogy of healthy and unhealthy family patterns. Stoop's analogy focuses on the fact that there is no "perfect family" and all families are "dysfunctional" and not working the way God designed families to be.

Indeed, Paris' family structure was not perfect! Her family was moderately dysfunctional and did not originally work the way God intended her family to be. Moreover, she didn't claim to have been a passive bystander in all of this. During her upbringing, many family issues produced serious pain, suffering, pressure, and distress over the years that generated negative family behavior.

For Paris, it seemed that when they were all together as a family unit, her parents showed love to her and her siblings in their way. However, her parents hardly ever showed love to each other. Frankly, Paris could only remember seeing her parents faintly hug one another, but; never a kiss. Paris' parent's relationship was rather cold, however; they functioned somewhat normally as a family unit in a general sense relevant to daily routines, holidays, events, and birthdays, etc. Growing up Paris would sometime question the presence of genuine love (**Storage**—translated "family affection") between her sibling truly existed. In fact, at best Paris' memory of "family" was consistent with discord, arguments, and fighting each other especially when her parents were not home. Sadly enough, this behavior continued throughout Paris' lives as a family unit and even through adulthood. Unfortunately, for Paris, she witnessed intense arguments and fighting between her siblings when they were all together, especially during holidays.

Paris believed that her father always favored her oldest sibling the most, which seemed to cause interpersonal conflict between them. This process of favoritism behavior by her father especially created intense sibling rivalry between her three older siblings. As a result of the favoritism displayed by her father overtime, Paris witnessed severely damaged emotions expressed by her siblings in their growing up; and that the genuine healing process between her sibling failed to take place. Instead, the behavior and damaged emotions would pass down to each family generation.

For Paris, growing up she was told by her family, that she almost died at birth due to high-risk prenatal pregnancy, maternal complication, and traumatic labor and delivery process. Paris learned while she was 'in utero' or 'in the womb' pregnancy became quite challenging for her mother because she was afflicted during each trimester. In addition to this, during her mother pregnancy, her parents were experiencing marital problems. There were serious marital issues that lead to several separations, and sometimes there was a threat of divorce. However, her father would eventually return home. Still, even Paris' father would return home; her parents would ongoing have frequent unhealthy arguments, and extensive fall outs lasting for months.

In growing up, it was periodically conveyed by her father that Paris was an "unwanted" child. To further exclaim, Paris was told by her father that from her conception in her mother's womb and subsequent pregnancy she was an unexpected or unwanted child *initially*. Throughout Paris' life, she was told that she was a "diaphragm baby" or a "mistake." There was an improper use of their choice of contraceptive at that time of conception. Nevertheless, Paris knew that she was formed in her mother's womb and was fearfully and wonderfully made (Psalms 139:13-14) according to Scripture. Fortunately, Paris knew that she was a child of God in His divine care, guidance, and supporting strength. Also, she realized that God was with her in all situations, in whatever status or what the future brings. Paris believed while she was in her mother's womb, that God creatively covered her and kept her. Ultimately, Paris had a clear understanding that God personally cares for the unborn baby from the moment of its conception, and His regard for a fetus extends to a plan for his or her life and divine purpose.

Throughout Paris' mother's pregnancy, she was extremely ill with a prenatal disorder called gravidarum hyperemesis [Greek *hyper*, above, + *emesis*, vomiting], or excessive vomiting. Hyperemesis is nausea and vomiting during pregnancy of such severity and duration that systemic effects such as acidosis and weight loss occur. Hyperemesis is pernicious vomiting of pregnancy, which may develop during the first trimester or three months of pregnancy. Her mother stated she couldn't keep any food down; she experienced nausea, vomiting, stomach pain, hiccups, gastric pyrosis (heartburn) and severe thirst and dehydration. The etiology or cause occurs most frequently in highly sensitive, neurotic individuals. Although it may begin on a neurotic basis, the constant vomiting brings on pathological changes, producing nutritional deficiency, dehydration, ketosis, jaundice, fever, peripheral neuritis or death from hepatorental [both liver and kidneys] failure. In other words: it was an extreme form of "morning sickness" that causes severe nausea and vomiting during pregnancy. Paris' mother was admitted to the hospital for necessary treatment and survival.

In the third trimester of Paris' mother's pregnancy, she developed severe preeclampsia that progressed to eclampsia. Preeclampsia is a life-threatening disorder causing complications in pregnancy; in which there are high blood pressure and either large amounts of protein in the urine or other organ dysfunction. The onset may be before, during, or after delivery. Most often it is during the second half of pregnancy. The seizures are of the tonic–clonic type and typically last about a minute. Eclampsia usually develops after a previous diagnosis with preeclampsia with the onset high blood pressure and proteinuria (protein in the urine), that can progress to developing seizures or coma. The exact cause of eclampsia is not known, but certain risk factors have been identified that include: (first- time pregnancy, vascular diseases such as diabetes and nephropathy, obesity, high blood pressure, malnutrition or poor diet, family history, and age below 20 or above 35). During this condition, the woman may also have low clotting factors (platelets) in the blood or indicators of kidney or liver trouble. This condition is also called 'toxemia' or pregnancy-induced hypertension (PIH).

Fortunately, by divine will Paris and her mother survived these severe complications. Still, through all of the life-threatening events, Paris was born one sunny day in June, although she and her mother almost died. At birth, Paris was diagnosed with septicemia [*haima*, meaning blood]. Simply put, Septicemia is a serious blood infection. Septicemia is a morbid condition of absorption of septic products into the blood and tissues or of pathogenic bacteria, which may rapidly multiply there or is called a type of blood poisoning. Symptoms and signs, usually, include chills, fever, petechiae, purpuric pustules, and abscesses. Paris' first months of life were in the neonatal intensive care unit or NICU at the community hospital. In this place, was where Paris fought for her life for several months. When Paris finally improved enough to go home, her mother described Paris as a frail baby with numerous "needle picks," at the bottom of her feet. During this time, also was when her mother was finally able to bond and hold her for the first time without hospital devices attached.

Despite the unexpected and unwanted pregnancy issue, Paris' mother, and she shared one of the most fruitful and beautiful lives until the end of her life on earth or until she passed away. Paris' relationship with her mother grew to be the most loving, special, sweet, and powerful mother-daughter relationship that she cherished.

In Paris' home growing up, there were times that her mother and father did not speak to each other for months, and sometimes even up to a year. As a result of this, Paris became an in-between messenger for her parents when something essential needed to be conveyed. Simply there was a dysfunctional gap that existed between them both, and Paris became that advocate filling in the gap of communication. This dysfunction within a family is called a *triangle communication*, especially in alcoholic families. Communication is characteristic by sending messages through someone else or a third party. Triangles become a three-person emotional configuration, which is considered the basic building block of the family system. When anxiety becomes escalated between two family members, a third person is brought in to form a triangle. Therefore, triangles are dysfunctional in that they offer relief from anxiety through diversion rather than through resolution of the issue. Paris grew on to believe that her parents did not get the proper level of parenting that demonstrated a healthy communication system, and this negative style of communication carried over into their adulthood.

By this time Paris' sibling were adults, had moved out of the home, and were now married, and starting their own families. Paris was the only child in the home experiencing the escalation of dysfunction and abuse. In any event, from the source of triangle communication there became a plan for a summer family vacation to travel together across the country from New York to Oakland, California. At the age of ten Paris began to see the demise of her parent's relationship after this nearly 3,500-mile trip across the country. Paris remembered that this vacation became an intense one when her parents drove non-stop from New York to Oakland. The duration of this trip was three and one-half days where they only stopped once to sleep overnight in Denver,

Colorado. The next two days resulted in continued travel until they reached Oakland. Paris remembered having a cold can of pork-and-beans that they shared in the motel one night as a means to save money for the trip ahead. They arrived safely to Oakland in one piece, and enjoyed sight-seeing and were able to connect with some of their extended family members who lived in the city.

The return home was in the same nonstop manner. Upon reaching New York, Paris remembered that her father got out of their brand-new automobile and kissed the ground of their front sidewalk because they had arrived home safely. The Irony of this was that Paris had never seen her parents kiss and only a hug once. Paris was perplexed by this fact that her father found a way to kiss the dirty ground easily as a symbolic trophy of a 'safe' travel home about 7,000 miles round trip on a family vacation, but; was unable to show love toward her mother.

In looking back, no doubt, there is an understanding that *all* families have some level of a dysfunctional nature. Paris learned that this family vacation took dysfunction to another level, and she knew something wasn't quite right regarding her parent's relationship. When Paris and her parents returned from California, she noticed that her parent's relationship was becoming progressively more abusive and dysfunctional. Her parents rarely interacted or communicated with one another. Marital discord was apparent through destructive arguments, verbal aggression, and mental cruelty exhibited by her father toward her mother. Later on, in adulthood, Paris' mother shared with her how aggressive and abusive her father was toward her. For instance, her mother shared with Paris that her father would often demean her; and he would kick her out of their bed after having intercourse.

Paris needed divine intervention at this point in her life due to this severe family dysfunction. She began to seek God for help earnestly and grew closer to Him. She realized that God was omniscient (all-knowing, knows everything) and that God knew what her future would hold. As she spiritual grew in God, at the age of 11-years-old, she became a 'born again Christian.' This spiritual encounter changed Paris' life forever. God gave her a new spiritual direction, and in looking back, she understood that God was ordering her steps.

During that same year was when Paris' parents' relationship began to die and resulted in an *ugly* divorce. The divorce would result in her mother and Paris moving out of their home. Her father would only allow them to take the bare minimum furniture items, and resources for them to begin their new life. Although her mother was a housewife during her marriage, she was a virtuous woman, a faithful member of the church and sincerely loved the Lord. She was extremely talented and gifted with her hands in the areas of sewing, crafts, painting, arts, gardening, and an expert in cooking. Paris' mother was skilled in catering, organized classy parties for special events, banquet dinners, and was well-known for her pound cakes and fruitcakes during the Christmas Holidays. Therefore, throughout the years, Paris' mother started a new life and worked hard after the divorce. Her mother used her gifts to re-establish herself and to raise Paris as a single mother resulting in many past, present, and intense years of pain and suffering for them both. The experience strengthened them both, and they spiritually grow to depend upon God for everything.

Paris grew proud of her mother, admired her strength and viewed her as a strong "woman of God" full of love, faith, and commitment to God and His promises. Amazingly, through all her mother's pain and suffering, she utilized the supernatural empowerment of the Holy Ghost/Spirit (the indwelling Spirit of God) given by God to survive the abuse, mental cruelty, and aggression. Her mother was born and raised in the church and was a firm believer in her doctrinal faith.

The next twenty–five years would prove to be the most important years in Paris' life. She and Paris developed one of the most beautiful mother-daughter relationships and emotionally supported one another. Paris learned so much from her mother, mostly through observing her mother's faith, obedience, and submission to God's will. From this learning process, Paris experienced a spiritual impartation by living with and witnessing her mother progressively press forward after her divorce. Overall, Paris felt her mother represented a yielding and holy vessel of God with unwavering faith.

On the other hand, Paris and her father grew very distant, and their relationship was vague after her parents' divorce. Eventually, she learned her father had many internal emotional problems, intra/interpersonal conflicts, and unhealthy social conditions in his life, which resulted in alcoholism. Deep down, Paris knew her father loved her and her siblings in his own way. However, she believed that her father did not know how to express his love without imparting gifts or "things." Her father was extremely handsome, appeared to be well liked, and socially accepted by his enter circle. However, in looking back, Paris believed that her father demonstrated loneliness based on his ongoing behavior after the divorce. Assuredly, Paris knew that her father had extensive inner emotional pain, sufferings, and exhibited distress in his life. He was difficult to reach out to and connect with his inter-spirit (inner man) to help him. Sadly, to say, Paris personally believed, but; have no way of validating her thoughts—that his emotional issues were related to an unhappy childhood in which he deeply suffered. Unfortunately, her father was unable to express what he endured growing up to her or anyone in the immediate family. Mostly, though, Paris believed her father's outward behavior evolved from a place of deep generational brokenness, bondage, and strongholds—which resulted in his alcohol abuse and later alcoholism.

Paris would progress to understand her father's frustration when she thought about the facets of strongholds. The term strongholds according to the Greek word *OCHURŌMA* is translated fortress or to make firm of those things in which mere human confidence is imposed. Strongholds become Satan's solidified devices that come to destroy and paralyze humanity against the knowledge and will of God. Our warfare is against the spiritual forces of wickedness according to Ephesians 6:12. Heretofore, carnal weapons such as human ingenuity, talent, wealth, organizing ability, charisma, eloquence, and personality are inadequate to pull down the strongholds of Satan. The only weaponry adequate to destroy or annihilate the fortresses of Satan, degrees of unrighteousness, and chicanery are godly "weapons of our warfare" that are not carnal (fleshly). We know that Apostle Paul defends this fact in II Corinthians 10:4-6:

"(For the weapons of our warfare are not carnal, but mighty through God to the pulling down of strong holds;) Casting down imaginations, and every high thing that exalteth itself against the knowledge of God, and bringing into captivity every thought to the obedience of Christ; And having in a readiness to revenge all disobedience, when your obedience is fulfilled."

Paris' father's alcoholism had a vastly negative impact on her. She believed that the condition of alcoholism led their family into a series of trauma and destruction that she at sometimes, personally continued to emotionally battle but with a perspective. Later in Paris' life, she would learn that being an adult child of an alcoholic parent or substance abuse disorder can have a negative impact. This condition is under microscopy of evaluation in the mental health arena, as a medical diagnosis among the American Psychiatric Association— (APA). This condition is being considered as a Diagnostic Classification in the field of psychiatry, and for the Diagnostic and Statistical Manual of Mental Disorders—(DSM-IV-TR), a Multiaxial Classification and Evaluation Tool of the American Psychiatric Association—(APA). This tool provides a complete numerical listing of codes and diagnoses and allows mental health professionals to assess various axes (components-Axis I through Axis V). This healthcare tool "provides information on different domains assisting in planning interventions, identifying outcomes" in psychiatry, and attempts to address the whole person. Thus, a person is viewed in a variety of perspectives. More specific, the Axis IV references the "Psychosocial/Environmental" in which this diagnosis would best align. In the area of psychiatry, it is evident that children growing up in the home of an alcoholic can have grave emotional trauma from this devastating issue. Below is a complete clinical model of what a mental health axis model encompasses (Pedersen, 2005, pp. 40-41):

"Components

- o   Axis I: Clinical Disorder (symptom or focus of clinical attention)
- o   Axis II: Personality Disorders/Mental Retardation
- o   Axis III: General Medical Conditions
- o   **Axis IV: Psychosocial and Environmental Stressors**
- o   Axis V: Global Assessment of Functioning Scale (GAF)
- o   Current:
- o   Past Year, highest level:
- o   Admission:
- o   Discharge:"

From this assessment, it becomes important to note that these psychosocial or environmental stressors do play out in clinical settings varying from acute on chronic; and from mild to severe cases. These stressors may be related to an individual's primary support group, social environment, educational problems, occupation, housing, financial issues, access to health care, legal matter, medical conditions, or traumatic exposure.

For Paris as a young child, her father told her that she "was a mistake." Hearing this vastly hurt Paris and created emotional damage. Also growing up, Paris' father frequently told her that she was adopted, which made her feel inadequate. He sometimes stated that she was "dumb." This feeling of inadequacy fostered a "low self-esteem" for Paris. This consistent negative reinforcement from her father affected Paris' academics in elementary, junior high, and high school causing mediocrity.

Paris struggled through her childhood, teenage years, and young adulthood with—inner anger, sadness, and severe depression that later involved nearly 38 years of her life. She was unhappy at school and often fought which resulted in suspension and unpopularity. She was an average student with limited support and motivation to learn or study. Paris had no parental guidance in academic support and learning process which is pivotal during school age years. Paris was unaware that she had a wealth of wisdom and knowledge within her, just waiting to evolve and manifest. Overall, Paris would not even apply herself to anything that she did wholeheartedly, because; she just wanted to "get by" or be the "average student." Unfortunately, Paris was never pushed or motivated *academically* by her parents or by the surrounding environment most of her young life. When Paris became an adult, she would frequently pray and ask God to give her the wisdom and knowledge that He gave Solomon. Later in life, Paris was drawn to the Holy Scripture in James 1:5 where it says:

> "If any of you lack wisdom, let him ask of God, that giveth to all men liberally, and unbraideth not; and it shall be given him."

In essence, what was meant to cause harm or hurt to Paris diabolically became empowerment to help her exceed. Instead, Paris supernaturally became an achiever, and she developed an unending drive for education and to succeed in her life.

According to Clinton, Hart & Ohlschlager (2005, pp. 6), "50% of child abuse and neglect cases are connected with the alcohol or drug use of a guardian, two-thirds of domestic violence victims report the involvement of alcohol."

As it relates to this fact, Paris was one of these children who grow up exposed to this environmental stressor. She was plagued with the memories of this serious issue most of her life and throughout her adulthood. Sadly, the parental alcoholism that she experienced had an adverse impact on her life and caused her trauma and destruction regarding the smallest things of life. Paris could not remember a period *growing up* during the holidays without memories of verbal abuse, alcoholism, and exhibited domestic violence. Additionally, she would experience significant anxiety and depression when the holidays would approach due to this associated experience. Paris' father tended to drink heavily during holidays, especially on Christmas days that caused him to become extremely agitated, abusive, verbally and physically aggressive; and demonstrated out of control behavior. Often, he would instigate arguments between Paris' siblings that created violent fighting. For instance, Paris father would deliberately purchase more expensive gifts for one of the siblings, as opposed to the another that created havoc and jealousy at Christmas. Paris became a living witness to this fact that these types of family issues can affect a child for a lifetime; without divine help from God and godly intervention.

After the divorce of Paris' parents, she would learn about many skeletons in the closet related to her family over the subsequent years that would change her perception regarding life in general. During this period, at her age of twelve Paris would encounter an incidence of sexual abuse/molestation and the aftermath for her was quite traumatizing. After the incidence of sexual abuse, she made a decision not to share this devastating experience with anyone. Instead, Paris repressed and suppressed the event until her early adulthood. In looking back after this traumatic event, Paris endorsed the fact that between the ages of 12-19 years-old she became progressively bitter, moody, didn't make many friends, and was deemed an introvert over the years. Paris believed that these overall feeling stemmed from her attempts to process all that had occurred in her past life, and realizing that her defense mechanisms were in play. These emotional feelings were costly and created much pain and suffering in her young life. The thought process of this incident did not resurface until she was in her early twenty's since she had blocked the trauma. In actuality, the life crisis event was an act of sexual assault or abuse of a person, especially a woman or a child.

Paris was extremely close to her mother, and they had a relationship of which they could share anything. One evening Paris's mother had an incident that occurred in her driveway that resurfaced all. One evening when her mother was getting out of her automobile to go into her home, a male came from behind entered her automobile and grabbed her purse and ran off. Fortunately, there was no physical harm to Paris's mother. During this emotional discussion with her mother, Paris recalled her traumatic event of sexual abuse/molestation and finally shared the sexual abuse incidence with her mother. When Paris' mother listened and learned of this traumatic encounter, she was initially quiet, then became muted. Paris and her mother never spoke of this matter again.

Later in Paris' adulthood divine help came her way. One way that God helped her was through divine intervention and healing by learning her temperament. He created a path through spiritual networking from the premise of learning about her inborn (God created) temperament—or "who God created you to be!" Through a Christ-centered generated profile system she learned this life-changing fact. In knowing her temperament-type provided answers to many of the perplexing thoughts, she had experienced, and about her character traits.

What's more, learning who she was and what God created or called her to be, would become a turning point in her life. This insight greatly enhanced her outlook on life, and her healing process began. During Paris' younger years, she had a disconnect or was fully unaware of her call, purpose, and destiny ahead. Instead, up to this point in her life, she was attempting to process events related to her birth, childhood, and past trauma. Indeed, from this new beginning, Paris realized her "need-areas," found within the temperament was *not* being met in her home, the environment, and life issues. Learning her unborn temperament lead Paris to the reality that even though she knew her family loved and cared for her—that her temperament needs were *not* being met (e.g., love, affection, and approval) from parenting, family or significant other(s), etc. Nevertheless, Paris loved her parents and family for what they were able to give or share with her in the elements of love, and emotional needs, despite their past negative issues.

Looking back, Paris knew that her psychosocial and environmental stressors were a medium that catapulted her weaknesses stemming from her inborn temperament causing ungodly traits to surface. As the author of this novel, it is important to reiterate that our inborn temperament is *not* our personality or character. First, personality is our—self-selected behavior. Second, the character is our—learned behavior as we all have, is known as the "*masks*" that we wear daily as a self –learned response to our environment (Arno, 1993). Thus, for Paris throughout years, it took a supernatural encounter with God to guide, lead, and teach her his ways channeling her God-given strengths in positive ways or into a godly way for divine use.

During junior high school when Paris was in the eighth grade at the age of fourteen, she met a young man named "Lamont" who changed her life forever. Lamont, for the most part, was very popular, was an all-sports star, especially in track and field, basketball, and football. Lamont played sports and had excellent athleticism in junior high and high school, and played with athletes who eventually became celebrity athletes. However, Lamont became acutely ill and was unable to play sports after high school.

Lamont was extremely intelligent, an honor student, and was very attractive. He had charisma and was quite charming. Paris' thoughts were that Lamont was an extrovert and friendly. Over time, they became very attracted to each other at the young age of fourteen. Eventually, they became childhood sweethearts and were inseparable. He filled many roles in her life. Paris' temperament needs were being met through his love, affection, and approval. At the age of 14-years-old Lamont became Paris' best friend, boyfriend, and was like a father-figure. Paris believed that "Lamont taught her everything she knew about life, romance, and in having a loving relationship." Lamont proposed to Paris at the age of fifteen, and they committed to each other. While attending junior high school, Lamont worked part-time and gave Paris a pre-engagement diamond ring that year. Lamont later became her future husband. Their love grew strong and developed into a stated long-life commitment and marriage.

Strangely enough, at the age of fifteen Lamont became seriously ill and was diagnosed with a rare disease. Lamont was hospitalized in the pediatric hospital for further workup, evaluation, and treatment. Over a month time frame, Lamont stabilized and was discharged from the hospital with a plan to closely monitor his condition. Once recovered, Lamont was provided with instructions, education, and precautions to follow regarding how to take care of himself. Lamont stabilized for several years with little to no symptoms.

Lamont remained active in sports and successfully made it through high school despite rough times and racial associated high school riots. Paris graduated from high school. However, had to graduate outside in the rain that year due to the ethnic rioting within the school walls that year and reported police brutality. That year, Lamont and Paris eloped to a small city in Kentucky and were married three months before graduation from high school. Lamont and Paris truly loved each other and couldn't wait to be married. Lamont began working in a steel factory, and Paris became a dedicated housewife. Within months of their marriage, Paris noticed the same signs and symptoms that Lamont was having in years prior. However, Lamont's symptoms were worse than before. During this time frame, Paris was now pregnant with their first child, in the midst of this health crisis. Instead, Lamont had just turned eighteen years of age with a baby on the way. For Lamont and Paris this became a devastating life-crisis event; and a road toward much suffering.

In all of this turmoil, one of the happiest days and life-changing events was about to happen for Lamont and Paris. With mixed feeling, they were going to have a baby! Paris decided to be that perfect mother and followed all the prenatal instructions from her obstetrician. Ironically, Paris delivered on the exact day that she predicted in the same community hospital that she had fought for her life at birth. Lamont and Paris decided to name the baby girl "Stella." Lamont and Paris believed that their baby was beautiful and a precious jewel—like a ruby! Despite Lamont's health crisis, Stella brought them so much joy and gave more meaning to their lives in the midst of crisis.

Over the next 25 years, Lamont became chronically ill and suffered greatly. The account of Lamont's general illness was surmountable. Paris became fully aware that his illness brought him sheer pain, sufferings, pressures, torment, distresses, disappointments, and frustration. During Lamont's chronic illness, he managed to be one of the bravest and empowering men that Paris had ever met. Lamont always managed to smile, show love, and affection toward all his family. He continued to take care of his family, and always showed a godly witnessed to others during his illness and on his deathbed. Throughout Lamont's chronic illness Paris stood by his side, beamed, and learned from Lamont's strength.

Although, Paris learned that during chronic illnesses individuals might have a complete sense of feeling "out of control," and sometimes can resort to manipulative behaviors. As Lamont's wife, this was one of the most challenging areas for her, and she honestly struggled with being manipulated and controlled at times. Fortunately, Paris had insight regarding this factor and realized that being manipulated and controlled is, in fact, conflict with her temperament. Still, Paris understood Lamont's behavior. Paris realized that she was his wife, the closest person to him, usually got the brunt of it all and suffered with him as well.

Shortly after Lamont's illness Paris began working for an insurance company, continued to care for Lamont, and daughter who was now attending preschool. During this period, Lamont's health continued declining, and he had undergone numerous surgeries. Somehow during all of this, Paris was drawn to attend college. At this time, this didn't even add up with all of the stress and responsibility on Paris as a "breadwinner," mother, wife and now "student." Nevertheless, she found a way through the help of God, His supernatural power, and significant support from her mother to obtain a higher level of education. Over time Paris attended college for a total of six years while working and caring for her family.

To convey the degree of pain, pressures, sufferings, and distress that Lamont endured, Paris created a diary journal of events regarding what Lamont physically endured. Paris believed that Lamont was able to turn his suffering into empowerment by giving God His glory. On Lamont's deathbed, he withstood hardness as a good soldier and was an example of someone who endured pain and 'suffering of the righteous.' He became light and witness for Jesus when anyone would be in his company. When Lamont's family and friends would visit him often, they would experience apprehension in seeking ways to encourage, yield Scripture, or comfort him. However, in contrast, when individuals would walk in his hospital room or his home most often it was Lamont who "in-turn" would comfort the visitor, and he would speak hope into their life.

Lamont was a believer who had a relationship with God, he understood the purpose for his afflictions and sufferings, and he sometimes felt "pressed out of measure, above strength, insomuch that he despaired even of life" (II Corinthians 1:8-10). However, he did *not* feel forsaken and knew he had the overcoming victory within himself. Lamont understood the premise of his suffering and became empowered by God's comfort, consolation, and salvation. He knew his pain and suffering was for the cause of Christ and His Glory. He realized that the outcome of his pain and suffering would strengthen, establish, perfect and settle him for a set purpose and meaning in his short life. God redeemed Lamont through his divine word because he knew he was not exempt from the issue of pain and suffering. Also, Lamont knew it was universal, inevitable, and he left this earth empowered by the Holy Ghost/Spirit.

Closely to this same time frame Paris' mother passed away and lost from a long battle of cancer. Paris received comfort in knowing that her mother was no longer suffering, and moved on to be with the Lord eternally. Nevertheless, Paris took her passing hard and grieved for months.

For Paris, the overall period of when she met Lamont was pivotal; and the total experience was a critical turning point in her young life. Lamont became Paris' true love, friend and life support. Their marital union of 25-years was precious and ordained of God. Lamont's chronic illness became a powerful learning experience for Paris, and as she moved forward in life what she learned became a premise for a HOPE in hell. The same coping skills that Lamont used during his affliction; Paris would later use for her survival in her life ahead.

Several years *before* Lamont passed away God called Paris into the ministry. One summer day God placed in Paris' spirit to begin ministering to the hurting, sick and afflicted. This call to ministry became an expansion of her lifetime commitment to serving humanity, and a vision and mission were birthed.

During one week of fasting and consecration, God revealed to Paris further that she was called to the "healing ministry." Shortly afterward, Paris was instructed by God to position and prepare herself for this ministry. That fall, Paris enrolled in seminary to prepare for a successful ministry. This preparation became the beginning of twenty-years studying theology. After a seven-day fast and consecration, she opened her Bible, and God guided her to a life-changing Scripture in St. Luke that further showed His will for her life; her purpose and destiny:

> "The Spirit of the Lord is upon me, because he hath anointed me to preach the gospel to the poor; he hath sent me to heal the broken-hearted, to preach deliverance to the captives, and recovering of sight to the blind, to set at liberty them that are bruised, To preach the acceptable year of the Lord" (St. Luke 4:16-19).

This encounter with God changed Paris' life forever, and she humbly accepted her divine charge to serve God's people. As a new widow, she dedicated her life to God and began preparing herself for serving God's and His people.

From a teenager to young adulthood, Paris lived her life with her childhood sweetheart; full of tribulations. Although, she faced much grief from her loss and became challenged by the fact that she was now a single mother with a teenage daughter. Through this life experience, she knew that God was her refuge and strength. Lamont asked God to allow him to live to see his daughter make it through high school, and the Lord honored Lamont's request. When Stella graduated from high school, Lamont was able to attend her graduation, helped organize her graduation celebration, and paid cash a new automobile as her graduation gift. Lamont lived two years and three months after Stella graduated, and Stella beamed and learned immensely from her father surround life values. The last ten years of Paris' life with Lamont were extremely difficult. Still, she counted the experience, relationship, and marriage with Lamont would always be cherished. Paris deemed Lamont as her hero of humanity and a great example of endurance. In total, he suffered 25-years during the entire time of their marriage. His suffering experience taught Paris early on life-skills of survival and how to trust in God. For Paris, this unforgettable experience eventually helped condition and prepared me for the bumpy road of life ahead.

After the passing of Paris' mother and husband within the same year, and following her sore grief process she sought the Lord with her whole heart for help and delivery from emotional anguish from her losses. She prayed a prayer of commitment to Him, vowed to service God humbly; and in ministry. *PARIS HOPE*, in keeping with the Greek meaning of her name HOPE 'favourable and confident expectation,' correlated with the unseen—became the basic foundation upon which her new hope and faith evolved. Given Paris' family name and the charge upon her life to carry the family baton, she poised herself to always— (a.) live godly remaining in God's perfect will and favor, (b.) remain self-assured and strong in life battles, and (c.) have a hope and expectation that God will always deliver in the time of need and trouble. Paris believed in the Holy Scriptures and knew through faith and the "Word of God" that:

"In God is my salvation and my glory: the rock of my strength, and my refuge, is in God" (Psalms 62:7, KJV).

"God is our refuge and strength, a very present help in trouble" (Psalms 46:1, KJV).

"But, I will sing of thy power; yea, I will sing aloud of thy mercy in the morning: for thou hast been my defence and refuge in the day of my trouble" (Psalms 59:16, KJV).

CHAPTER FOUR

"Taboo: The Contradictory Relationship"

NOTHING could prepare Paris for the next chapter of her life. Before this time for Paris in looking back on her life, what she thought was the "trial of her faith and life,"—related to the long sufferings with Lamont, her *first* love; became a light affliction. The circumstances that Paris would experience in her next phase of life would stir up the very essence and quintessence in the existence of her salvation. The subsequent events of Paris' life relevant to her second marriage would become progressively daunting, and what she faced in the next thirty years would try her faith to the utmost. What is more, Paris learned in this union that a reflection in the mirror might not emulate the same image. Also, she quickly realized a known fact that—"you cannot judge a book by its cover." So, it was, Paris would meet and marry someone adorned in sheep's clothing, but; inward in the like of a ravening wolf. Just as the Apostle John warned the Elect Lady regarding false prophets or abusers who would take advantage of Christian fellowship; he would send a message to remain cautious of who she should entertain—Paris would bear the same. For the Bible says: "Beware of false prophets, which come to you in sheep's clothing, but inwardly they are ravening wolves" (St. Matthew 7:15, KJV).

Following the passing of Lamont, Paris felt an imbalance in her life becoming a widow. She became lonely since Stella was away at college in another city. Paris continued her education in theological studies and seminary, remaining faithful to God, and in her church attendance. Howbeit, though Paris believed that she would not marry again or find another spouse, and she became reasonably isolated. Paris moved forward in her life, and was financially stable and worked three jobs. The major problem Paris faced after losing Lamont was that she was extremely vulnerable. Also, she was filled with grief, pain, sufferings, and distress at a relatively young age.

Paris was a lifetime member at a growing local church in New York. Shortly before Lamont's passing away, there was an evangelist and his wife who relocated to New York and became members of her local church. The evangelist later became one of the active ministers at the church. His wife had a terminal illness and was sickly most of the time. Paris would often listen to the church announcements requesting prayer for other individuals, including herself who were undergoing family crisis, losses, grief, and sufferings—and Paris felt a sense of compassion toward their pains. This evangelist was one of them, who was going through a crisis caring for his wife while doing the work of the ministry. On an early winter morning, the evangelist's wife passed away after a long chronic illness.

Before this evangelist's wife passed away, she gave him final encouragement to find a future wife. The night before she passed, he and she had a sincere conversation about what he should do in his future, and she gave him instructions about finding a specific type of wife. The beauty of it all is that she released this evangelist to remarry before she died. When Paris would later learn about this, she felt that she was so unselfish for not allowing him to continue to suffer without her. These instructions would play out just as she instructed without him realizing it was happening. For this evangelist, he believed that he was guided by God to find her. This evangelist would eventually say often that his wife said to him before her passing that: "you will know that it is her when you first see her." He knew that when she stated this that she was referencing a virtuous woman.

As time moved on, Paris would be that "wife." When the union was formed, she felt so blessed that God sent a "minister" to be her husband, and she felt so humbly grateful to God. Paris believed that God was blessing her for the past years of sufferings and felt blessed after all that she'd been through since birth. In the beginning, this evangelist would often say that: "when I found Paris, I found the woman declared in Proverbs 31." Also, he would say, that Paris was the woman described by his wife before she passed away: "Who can find a virtuous woman? for her price is far above rubies (verse 10). "Her husband is known in the gates, when he sitteth among the elders of the land" (verse 23).

"Her Price is Far Above Rubies" …

These words became repetitive by this evangelist who would also often say: "that meeting and marrying Paris was a continuation of an unending love that I cannot explain." In the beginning, Paris felt beyond a shadow of a doubt that their meeting was of a "divine appointment," and that their marriage was by a "destined union." Together they declared that the prophecy was truly of God and that God had brought them together to do greater works!

Jacob was his name, of whom he will be referred as in this short story! Although their courtship was brief, Paris and Jacob felt they were meant to be with one another and didn't feel a long courtship was needed. They had both just lost their spouses, were a great support to one another and were both ministers. Thus, their thoughts were—why wait? Over the next two years, Paris grew to learn more about Jacob, her new husband, his background, and family structure in which proved to be astonishing.

One early spring day Jacob and Paris began discussing his background. She learned more about his parents and siblings. His parents met in the early 1920s and were married in 1928. Together they had six children: three sons and three daughters. Jacob was the youngest child of the family, and there were eighteen years between him and the oldest sibling. Jacob described his family as a loving and beautiful family. He remembered that they always would have dinner together, and this was such a special time for their family.

Interestingly enough, he portrayed that his family often attended church, however; his father would not attend with them. The reason for this was when his father was a young man he witnessed "abuse and domestic violence by the pastor of the church." Jacob believed that this scenario had a negative impact on his father and later affected his entire family, as they would not attend church together. Jacob believed that this issue became the root problems of their family dysfunction. Jacob would often express that his father was a hard-working man who worked in a factory when he was growing up. Amazingly his father never had a car or drove a car, but managed to get around the city without difficulty. His mother also was a hard worker who ironically worked at the same factory as well. His mother continued to work until her childbearing years, however; became a full-time housewife when his oldest brother was born. He depicted that his mother was gifted in music and could play the piano well. All of this is how Jacob *initially* remembered his family.

As Paris and Jacob continued to discuss his background, she learned that Jacob's perception, regarding the dysfunction in his family, began to progress when he was eight years old. At that time Jacob's grandmother was found dead in her home by his mother. Before this time, Jacob's mother and grandmother were extremely close, and her death altered his mother's life greatly. This particular time vastly affected Jacob as well. After Jacob's grandmother's death, he felt that his mother began rejecting him from that day forward. He would often describe that he would go to his mother, but she didn't want to have anything to do with him, and he felt rejected by her throughout the rest of her life. Jacob felt isolated after his grandmother's funeral. However, Jacob claimed that he had some comfort from his mother's brother who would come to visit shortly after his grandmother's death offering him support. Jacob's uncle would spend time with him, talk, and play with him. Jacob further exclaimed to Paris that although this time with his uncle seemed to provide him temporary comfort and helped to cope with the rejection from his mother, however, didn't replace the need for his mother's love.

Perceived parental rejection is one of the most arduous forms of rejections that individuals can face in life. Ultimately, individuals who experience parental rejection can have an enormous negative effect and can explain aggressive behaviors throughout a person's lifetime. There are numerous studies, and researches conducted that suggest individuals with a mental illness have often experienced parental rejection.

The long-term effect on parental rejection in childhood causes trauma and demands recovery. The trauma may consist of mental health conditions such as Major Depressive Disorder—MDD, Complex Post Traumatic Stress Disorder—PTSD and Borderline Personality Disorder—BPD, etc. For instance, author David Hosier, M.S.C. (2014) in his outstanding work on *Childhood Trauma Recovery*, personally experienced childhood rejection beginning about the age of eight. Hosier in quoting significantly affirms this subject matter:

> "Being rejected by parent/s can have an enormously negative effect upon— (a) how a child's personality develops, (b) self-image, (c) self-esteem, and (d) how he or she learns and relates to others. Not only can these effects last throughout childhood, but, without therapy, can extend years and years into adulthood; in fact, they can last a lifetime" (Hosier, 2014, p. 1).

Hosier expounds upon the work of Ronald Rohner of the University of Connecticut, an expert on the effects of "Parental acceptance-rejection theory—(PARTheory), a theory of socialization that aims to predict and explain major causes, consequences, and correlation of parental acceptance and rejection within the United States and worldwide" (Rohner & Khaleque, 2002, p. 3). Khaleque & Rohner (2002, pp. 54-64) conducted a "meta-analysis of cross-cultural and intracultural studies" of about 10,000 participants of research significantly affirming this subject matter.

The results of these studies are staggering to learn. First, *pain* from parental rejection during childhood tends to extend into adulthood. Second, those who have *suffered* parental rejection during childhood tend to have difficulties in trusting relationships in adulthood. Last, "neurological studies (studies of the physical brain) suggest that parental rejection activates the same part of the brain which is activated by the experience of physical *pain*" (Hosier, 2014, p. 1 & Rohner & Khaleque, 2002, pp. 1-10).

According to the *Psychology Dictionary and "World's Most Comprehensive Online Psychology Dictionary"* (2014, p.1), it is defined that parental rejection is a: "continual denial of acceptance, affection, or care by one or both parents, at times, hidden beneath a cover of over-indulgence or over-protection." They also assert that: "when parental rejection is faced the most probable cause for feelings of low self-worth as an adult and is compensated for with a grandiose and narcissistic attitude" (Psychology Dictionary, 2014, p. 1).

These philosophies and theories regarding parental rejection correlate with Jacob's background, and later prove to be the premise for Jacobs own behavior. During Jacob's childhood experience and state of parental rejection, he believed that his mother's mental status and behavior was the core root of his family falling apart.

Subsequently, Jacob described to Paris that his mother's condition progressed into a severe mental illness with various bizarre behaviors over those next four years. Jacob continued describing in detail the progression of his mother's mental illness with her often having amnesic episodes with unexplained or unaccounted disappearance causing serious alarm to the family. Amnesic episode refers to the sudden unexpected travel away from one's customary place of daily activities, with the inability to recall some or all of one's past. Initially, there was some consideration that the disappearance may have been related to medical factors or that this may have been causing and contributing to these symptoms. However, as time moved on it was not medical factors. Instead, her symptoms turned out to be serious mental health issues and a crisis for Jacob's family. Jacobs exclaimed that his mother would go missing and would wander off in the neighborhood with her night clothes on and created panic for the entire family. Then, his family would need to go searching for her only finding her on the streets laughing inappropriately, responding to internal stimuli; and talking to herself, etc. During that time, he'd remember that law enforcement would often find his mother, and brought her home when she would wander off from their home.

Jacob's oldest brother enlisted into the military and served for 25 years. When his older brother returned home from active duty and retired over a period, he became an alcoholic. Jacob's second oldest brother became involved in a love triangle, brutally assaulted his girlfriend after learning about her unfaithfulness; and resulted in the second-degree murder of the other man. As a result, this brother served twenty years in prison, and he was released from the penitentiary after serving his full sentence. His three sisters graduated from high school and completed college. Also, his three sisters married and moved on building their own families. His father began to daily drink beer and wine and developed hepatic complications and cirrhosis of the liver at the age of 45. Jacobs goes on to describe that his mother's mental condition worsened, and at his age of nine through twenty-five, his mother was placed in a psychiatric hospital in his hometown.

When Jacob was 15 years old, still, after surgery and treatment his father passed away at the age of 59 years old due to alcoholism. After the passing of Jacob's father and his mother was committed to a psychiatric hospital, he went to live with his oldest sister and family. He still had not adjusted to both losing his father and from the childhood rejection of his mother. Jacob's oldest sister essentially assumed rising him. However, Jacob perceived that his sister began to abuse her authority with him, and it became uncomfortable in their home for him. Therefore, when Jacob would go to school, he didn't want to return home; feeling further neglected. Instead, he would find as an outlet in going to bars and joined forces with neighborhood gangs. As time passed, he felt that his oldest sister and brother-in-law didn't want him in their home. From this point on, he progressively began to live in the streets, malingering and picked up the habit of smoking two and one-half packs of cigarettes a day and smoking along with heavy Cannabis use (marijuana). Jacob resorted to homelessness for one year even though he somehow continued to attend high school. He elected to never return to his sister's home at a very young age.

Jacob expressed that between the ages 17 –21 years old, that he had no fear of God, and became an atheist and later an agnostic. On the streets, he learned how to survive, and amazingly he believed that "family values could work on the street." He described his condition as 'a hell situation.' While living on the streets, Jacob experienced abuse, violence (e.g., guns to his head and various threats were made upon his life). Jacob endorsed needing to steal food or sold off sidewalk grills that were aligned on the downtown streets, restaurants, and diners for his survival. Jacob developed a severe tobacco/nicotine dependence, a smoking habit that became desperate enough to smoke cigarettes off the street and left on bar counters.

Later as he was describing his background to Paris, he'd compare his life to the likeness of Jonah; because he felt that he was in a 'hell situation' and had a call upon his life—and that Jonah was destined to come to God. Likewise, Jacob later believed that he was predestined to be saved by God's grace and mercy. One day he met a woman walking down the street who witnessed to him about God. His initial response to her was that: he "didn't need Jesus for a crutch," and felt that: he "was God himself." This lady offered a kind gesture and stated that she would pray for him and walked away.

Not long after the encounter of meeting this lady, Jacob's local community developed a program for the less fortunate to achieve vocational training. Thus, this program struck an interest with Jacob, and he took advantage of the opportunity. He signed up for that program and selected a vocational training in auto mechanics. Fortunately, for Jacob he was accepted into this program, eventually received a certificate in basic automobile mechanics, and was able to secure a job for the first time as an adult. During his educational training, he runs into the same lady that witnessed to him about God that he saw on the street some weeks prior; who was also enrolled in a vocational program. When Jacob spotted this lady once again, he viewed her differently. Thus, Jacob pursued to get her name and make friends with her.

During his training, Jacob and this lady developed a courtship, fell in love over the year, and later were married. Jacob proclaimed that this lady—now his wife was raised in a foster home on and off because her parents were having marital problems. She attended church when she lived in one of the foster homes, and this was where she came to know Christianity. She was baptized and became a 'born again' Christian at the age of 15-years-old. However, through her emotional pain and suffering became angry with God. Soon after they married his wife returned to being faithful in church, to begin a new life with Jacob. When Jacob's new wife recommitted her life to Christ, he felt like he had lost a friend, and the feelings of rejection and loneliness resurfaced. He became rebellious, aggressive, abusive, began to drink heavily, and started "running the streets" again. As Jacob was sharing his story with Paris, he expressed that he was once again feeling a sense of rejection.

As time went on, despite his rebellion and aggression—to appease his wife, Jacob agreed to be baptized at a storefront church by her pastor in a horse trough. However, after Jacob was baptized, he was unwilling to give up nicotine and alcohol use; and resumed smoking and drinking heavily. His wife would continue to bring prayer meetings in their home that would make Jacob extremely angry and uncomfortable. The church began to intercede in prayer for Jacob. However, due to Jacobs ongoing abusive behavior, anger, and aggression forced them out of his home when they'd arrive to pray. Later in Jacob's conversation in explaining all to Paris about his background, he admitted that the prayer meetings began to change him.

Over some time, the pastor continued to pray, witness, and minister to Jacob even though he remained fearful of attending church. He would always remember his father's behavior, rationale, and fear of not attending church. Later Jacob would describe that he believed that this was a "transfer spirit" from his father. Several months would pass when Jacob left a nightclub at 3:00 A.M. he began to weep uncontrollably when he looked back over his life. Nevertheless, Jacob proceeded to another after-hours nightclub from there but stated he "couldn't find rest." He came out of the nightclub and looked into the sky speaking to God saying: "What do you want from me?" Then Jacob returned to his automobile and continued to drink on his way home. He stated it was then that he had an encounter with God. Jacob further claimed that the last thing he could distinctly remember on this night was "going over a bridge and embankment into the river. However, the steering wheel began to turn on its own at a point where he should have gone over an embankment and died." Jacob then described that he did not know how he got home safely that morning, but; he believed that "there was an angelic being that drove me home."

For Jacob, that spiritual encounter became the beginning of closing the gap of unbelief toward seeking God and His salvation. He further described to Paris that a 'spirit of convention and repentance' evolved, and there became a desire for him to live for God. In Jacob's mind, he thought to himself: "I'm tired of living like this…and I need a change," and continued to repeat this in his mind. He then asked his wife to give him her pastor's telephone number to obtain prayer and help. When he telephoned the pastor, Jacob began to open up to him and told him he couldn't stop crying; and that he didn't know what to do. The pastor began to further witness to him and explained that God was calling him to salvation. Jacob told the pastor that he couldn't come to church because he didn't have any clean clothes to wear. However, the pastor's reply was: "you have tried everything… this morning give Jesus a try, and wear what you have!" Jacob's response was: "Okay, I'll try him this morning, but if He fails me, I will not try him again!"

One spring Sunday morning, on that same day of Jacob's encounter with God, he went to the church door and took a puff from his cigarette—and tossed it away. Before he went into the church, Jacob stated: "If God is real deliver me from these cigarettes, alcohol, and smoking marijuana!" He then went into the church crying and listened to the pastoral message, and the gospel of Jesus Christ was preached to him that morning. During the time the pastor called those to receive God, Jacob ran to the altar and fell on his knees crying, and the pastor proceeded to minister to him. That day he accepted Jesus Christ as his Lord and savior—and Jacob received the infilling of God's spirit.

Jacob described his marriage as wonderful and became active in the church. They began to have a ministry of caring for foster children throughout five years and raised about twelve-five foster children. Jacob described their ministry as an emergency home for foster children, which meant that the city would select their home for any children in a crisis, abuse or domestic violence cases. Jacob became faithful in church and answered his call by serving in the capacity of 'the gift of helps,' as a deacon, and later he was appointed the chairman of the deacon board. Soon after this time, their pastor moved to another state, and the church acquired a new pastor. Shortly, after that time he accepted his call to service as a minister and claimed after that period his life greatly changed.

Several years would pass when Jacob's wife began having signs and symptoms of a serious illness. Jacob took his wife to a local hospital for medical evaluation and treatment. However, he claimed after her initial medical evaluation that providers could not determine a medical diagnosis. After several outpatient diagnostic testing, procedures, and blood work a diagnosis was determined. Unfortunately, Jacob's wife was diagnosed with a terminal illness.

For Jacob, after learning his wife's diagnosis, he was devastated, and he expressed that his and her life drastically changed. Their faith became challenged but did not waver. They remained faithful to God, fasted, prayed, and sought God for help and direction. Shortly, after her diagnosis, she became home-bound for one year needing round-the-clock caregiving. Intermittently, his wife's illness would stabilize showing some improvement off and on. Time of stabilization would give them both a glimmer of hope.

Shortly, before his wife's illness, they changed their church membership since their first pastor moved to another state. At this new church home, was where Jacob learned the elements of deliverance ministry and studied demonology. This area of demonology opened up his scope in ministry, and he developed a deep interest and understanding in this area. As a result of this learning experience, it became a turning point of Jacob's ministry and subsequent numerous healing and deliverance episodes for his wife through faith. In years to come, he would eventually teach demonology and became an expert in this area. As a result of the leading of God, in attending this church, Jacob gains an educational experience that richly enhanced his ministry. Additionally, he continued to study, research, and maintained devotion to this area and began teaching demonology in his ministerial travels. At this new church, Jacob moved on to become one of the church's treasures, and later an ordained elder.

The next several years became one of the biggest trials of Jacob's life that resulted in many trials, tests, and suffering for both he and his wife. This life crisis truly became "the trying of his faith…working patience." As Jacob continued to explain to Paris about his past life, he proclaimed that his suffering was not just physical; however, they both experienced rejection and isolation from others. For him, he believed, sadly enough, that most of the rejection and isolation came from the faith-based community. He claimed their experience was somewhat of a "Job experience," because many people came with the mentality that Jacob and his wife were in sin. Others assumed that the "sin" was the reason for her affliction. However, Jacob stated that he was not going to be defeated by these feelings and was reminded about the Scriptural passage James 1:4 where it says: "But let patience have her perfect work, that ye may be perfect and entire, wanting nothing."

During this discussion with Paris, Jacob claimed that these negative experiences lead his ministry to evangelism due to the rejection of the faith-based community and at his local church. Jacob voiced that he needed to "get out of New York." For that reason, he began traveling across the country evangelizing. During that course of travel time, it seemed that his wife got somewhat better and went into remission. Jacob primarily believed that the illness improved due to prayer, their faith, a change in health habits, alternative medicine (herbs); and improved medical treatment over time.

He believed that he had truly been in a "hope in a hell situation." However, what he was about to learn was, that the past situation was only the beginning and that it was the tip of the iceberg in his and her sufferings. Jacob began describing to Paris, that over the next series of events as a "faith on trial." This saying became one of Jacob's classic homiletic messages that he would preach ongoing during his evangelistic travels. Jacob asserted during the interview that for him that during the trial he and his wife experienced much pain and suffering, and indeed, would go on to perfect him in Christ Jesus.

As the author of this short story, it becomes vital to note here that the "Word of God" informs us that to establish patience or completeness, "patience must have its perfect work." In the Greek translation, *teleios* means completion and maturity, and that patience must "have her perfect work, that ye (you) may be perfect and entire, wanting nothing."

Over the years, Jacob's wife underwent much suffering that indeed became a trial of their faith. Her illness was challenging for them both. The medical history became extensive consisting of multiple complications. During this time, his wife experienced numerous inpatient hospitalizations, rehabilitation; and several episodes with near-death experiences. Toward the end of her life, she progressed toward needing palliative care, and extensive total caregiving by Jacob. Eventually, Jacob's wife insisted that he promise her that if she would ever progress to another near-death experience to let her perish. Reluctantly, he agreed with her request—however never had intentions to do so. Despite his plan, Jacobs' wife passed away when he dozed off to sleep one morning while at her bedside. However, before her death, she released Jacob to marriage again.

As Jacob continues to tell Paris his story, he described his deceased wife's last few days of life in detail. Jacob stated that: "Through it all, she was a true vessel of God and left a spiritual imprint on many lives with her testimonies. Throughout her life, illness, and deathbed she was used of God and ministered prophetically to many." Paris could only listen and reflect on her own caregiving experience, and sincerely understood Jacob's grief. Jacob went on to conveyed that many years of her illness and near-death episodes seemed hopeless or negative. However, these episodes were turned into something positive through empowerment by the Holy Ghost/Spirit from that life experience.

As Jacob concluded in telling Paris his story, she began to correlate, compare, and contrast the similarities between the two past marriages. For Paris, she believed that she and Jacob had undergone a common suffering experience, could truly relate to one another—in a demonstration of true care, faith, and empowerment that could only enhance their future ministry together. Jacob expressed that the experience he had with his wife and caregiving changed his life.

During this in-depth discussion, Jacob stated to Paris that: "I thank God that our paths crossed because she led me to God, and I give God all the Glory for this. Although I grew up in a strained life as a young child and had many afflictions myself in childhood, I never saw such suffering as I did with her. Mentally I had much pain and suffering from losing my mother so young in my life due to her mental illness as a child until adulthood. My wife was a great comfort to me in this area because she was like a mother, friend, and a wife to me."

The Paradox—As Paris begin to share her life surrounding her second marriage to Jacob, it is vital to note that she provided these initial graphic details of Jacob's life because these circumstances eventually correlate with destructive behavior in the marriage and surrounding relationships for over thirty years. Looking back on all, it eventually became Paris' belief that when she married Jacob, he had never recovered from his childhood emotional traumas in his life surrounding his parents, parental acceptance–rejection factor, family structure, nor the loss of his first wife. Paris conjectured that throughout their marriage Jacob continued to suffer from the bondage of negative personality disorder, low self-image, low self-esteem, and exhibited difficulty in trusting relationships with others.

When Jacob and Paris were dating, he told her that he had a disability for many years; however, that he worked full-time doing the work of evangelism. Therefore, during their 30 years of marriage, Jacob did not work in the secular arena and took pride in the fact that he didn't. When there were financial difficulties, Jacob would often use his disability as a scapegoat as a means to justify that Paris was the only breadwinner of their household and that he could not work. The paradox of his and her ongoing financial situation during that time frame was that Jacob could do everything, and anything, he would put his mind to do—when he wanted to. However, working and caring for Paris never became an option during their marriage. In looking back on the marriage, Jacob was comfortable with not working. Instead, his comfort lied with Paris taking caring of him for 30 years.

Soon after their marriage, Parish learned that Jacob came from a family with a strong history of mental health issues. From a total family of eight members including Jacob's parents, half of his immediate family were diagnosed with a serious mental illness. Mostly, though, the biggest impact for Jacob was that his mother was diagnosed with mental illness when he was eight-years-old leaving him feeling rejected; and he had yet to overcome from the traumatic childhood event.

Within a year of their marriage, Paris learned that Jacob was a man of Grandiosity, Narcissism, and demonstrated borderline personality features. Reflecting on the 30 years of marriage it was revealed that delusional thoughts were intertwined throughout their relationship, and only to learn at the end of their marriage that Paris was living with vain untruths. Over time, eventually, there would be a frightening discovery as life would slowly reveal to Paris, that the intricate details surrounding Jacob's background, family structure, and his first wife—may have represented fabrications, falsehoods, and untruths. Instead, their marriage would prove to be consumed with multiple-level distinct types of abuse and domestic violence: (physical, mental, emotional, sexual, social, spiritual, and neglect); which caused Paris much-unexpected pain and sufferings for thirty years.

As fate would have it, major problems began to seriously manifest within Jacob's and Paris' marriage when there was financial instability. Within a few years of their marriage, Paris became incapacitated and was not able to work on a consistent basis due to physical afflictions to substantiate their lifestyle. Paris began to notice an escalation in negative behavior exhibited by Jacob, and the relationship slowly began to collapse.

When Jacob and Paris first met, she truly believed that their meeting was "the destined union," and according to Romans 8:28-31 that God had truly blessed her due to past sufferings. The term *destined* is defined as "intended for." In the Latin translation, it means to fasten down or secure. Generally speaking, it is fate, usually in a passive sense — destined means to head for, to be bound for, and to be set apart for a certain purpose or intent. Destined also means to be destined for leadership. The term *predestinate* in the Greek is *Proorizō* and is a verb, which is translated as "determine." This verb is distinguished from *proginōskō*, which means to "foreknow;" the latter has special reference to a person's foreknown by God.

At first, Paris was overwhelmed with joy, and God ordained the union. She paralleled their prior life experiences as a godly strength and empowered witness. *Paris believed*, that their meeting was by divine appointment and that their marriage was by the destined union. *Paris believed* that they were set apart for a divine purpose. *Paris believed,* that as a result of his and her past pain and suffering that they were "called," and justified—for "such a time as this" to be used by God in a mighty way! *Paris believed* that they were born to be leaders of God's people as in a type of "Queen Esther," and "King Ahasuerus," for the upbuilding and advancement of God's Kingdom on earth and in heaven (Esther 1:1-10:3). *Paris also believed*, that according to the Holy Scripture that all things were working for good in their lives:

"And we know that all things work together for good to them that love God, to them who are the called according to *his* purpose. For whom he did foreknow, he also did predestinate to be conformed to the image of his Son, that he might be the firstborn among many brethren. (Preordained) Moreover whom he did predestinate, them he also called: and whom he called, them he also justified: and
whom he justified, them he also glorified. What shall we then say to these things? If God be for us, who can be against us?" (Romans 8:28-3, KJV).

Thus, how perfect, logical and consistent can this be? How could anything go wrong with this scenario? Of course, it would appear that this union was meant to be!

So, how did Jacob and Paris meet? And how were they united as one?

During Paris' caregiving years with Lamont's pain and suffering—she believed that she suffered as well, but in different ways. Perhaps one would say Paris was in the prime of her life during this time, and she was questioned by many during her caregiving: "How do you do it?" or some would say "I couldn't do it … I would need to leave my husband if that were me!" This type of thought never entered Paris' mind during that time, and the only thing Paris knew to do was to care for her husband, and "to do the right Christian thing." Paris continued to work and take care of "Lamont" and young daughter Stella during this time, and there was no other option for Paris!

One fall season, Paris went on an extended fast and consecration (solemn assembly) collectively with the entire church according to Joel 2:15. The Lord dealt with Paris during that week of solemn assembly and led her to a new Spiritual realm and encounter. During this consecration God leads Paris to the Scripture passage found in St. Luke 4:1-19 and this "Word of God," became a time in which the divine call to ministry was upon her life. Paris remembered going to the hospital to see Lamont one evening and shared her encounter with him. Paris remembers Lamont's smile, the support that he gave, and the encouragement he offered to attend seminary. Paris began seminary in New York that same year. Shortly after this event, Lamont started to deteriorate. During this time-frame, Paris unconsciously began grieving. She believed that most of the family members and friends did not begin their grief process until after Lamont's passing. However, Paris' experienced an early grief process, which was difficult for some to understand. Lamont had undergone about 20 years of suffering and experienced a long-term chronic illness, and Paris was right there with him during his suffering process.

In the last few years of Lamont's life, he had multiple intermittent hospitalizations, and he had routine visits from their local church ministers and pastors at that time. At the same time, Jacob's wife was also experiencing multiple intermittent hospitalizations and hospitalized in the same hospital. Therefore, the same ministers would visit both Lamont and Jacob's wife since they were both hospitalized in the same place. Jacob at the time was an "elder of the church" and was considered part of the ministerial team of the local church. However, would not leave his wife's bedside unless he was forced to do so. Before this time, Jacob had been evangelizing across the country for numerous years, thus; he was on sabbatical leave from his ministry, so he thought. One of the ministers from their church insisted that Jacob come along to do hospital visitations. The ministerial team did this to get Jacob out of his wife's hospital room. Several of those visits would be to visit Lamont, and in one instance, Jacob left his business card at Lamont's bedside for him to have access to contact him if he needed future prayer. The irony was that Paris and Jacob's paths never cross during those visitations, and they never saw each other during this period.

One fall day after Lamont's passing Paris progressed through her grief feeling lost and empty. Of course, Paris knew that God was there to comfort her and essentially all she needed. However, she also knew that God places within us the natural need and feelings of wanting to be loved, experience affection, approval, and belonging to someone. Stella was away at college in her junior year by the time of Lamont's passing. Therefore, Paris was confronted for the first time in her life with complete loneliness and vulnerability. Paris firmly believed that even at her fairly young age that she would be a widow for the rest of her life. Paris and Stella had a close mother-daughter relationship and bonded even closer during the caregiving years of her father. Naturally, Paris was feeling much grief and emptiness in her life during this time. Thus, Paris prayed to God for help. As Paris prayed, she said to God: "You made and created me to have these feelings, and it hurts… God, you be my husband or take these feelings away."

The church that Paris attended had a membership of about 2000 parishioners and continued to be her spiritual support for the most part. There were only a few people that comforted her during this time or perhaps even knew how Paris was hurting on the inside from her loss. Paris believed that no one knew how to reach out to her during her grief process. She remained faithful to God, continued to attend seminary school, and go to church as she usually did. During church services, she continued hearing the church announcements for over a year requesting prayer for Jacob's wife, who continued to decline physically in the hospital. Often, during church announcements, Lamont's and Jacob's wife's names were frequently 'called out' requesting parishioners to pray for them both due to their simultaneously failing conditions. As Paris listened to the announcements, her thoughts were: "I know what he is going through." Somehow Paris felt (later to learn, Jacob's) pain, suffering, and had surmountable compassion and concern for him that she couldn't explain.

Paris' thoughts were at that time, even in her grief that: "if I would ever see him, I would tell him that I understood his hurt and pain." Before this time, Paris did not personally know Jacob until their pastor began to ask him to preach at their church on some Sunday evenings. Initially, during the time Jacob began preaching at their church, Paris viewed him as presenting differently. Paris thought that Jacobs mannerism seemed humble and that he would preach on a level that parishioner could easily understand. Jacob also would minister to the church members and pray for every individual that God directed him to pray and minister. Ironically, out of all the 2000 parishioners in the congregation Jacob never ministered and prayed for Paris directly. Paris would go home and ask God "why?" She then would say: "Lord, you see me suffering and in pain," why did I not get ministered to?" Paris got no answer from God.

On that cold winter morning Jacob's wife passed away, there was an announcement made at the local church regarding her passing. Paris felt that Jacob was going through the same grief phases as she was in life. So, Paris prayed for him with concern and compassion. After Jacob wife's funeral service, eulogy, and internment he was surrounded by many families, friends, church members, and a group of ministers. Additionally, Jacob became surrounded with an entourage (a group of associates or attendants; retinue for his protection). Paris later learned that this group of ministers were assigned to watch over him to protect him from women and comfort him during his grieving process. However, on the other hand, this group moved in his home, made themselves comfortable, sleeping, and eating up all the food that came in from the bereavement process, e.g., turkeys, covered dishes, cakes, pies, and cookies, etc. Jacob would later proclaim that most of the bereavement meals came mainly from females wanting his attention. During that time, Jacob was grieving and was attempting to adapt to his loss. With Jacob's unbeknownst and lack of full awareness; other male friends and ministers moved in with him having a mission to protect him from other women. Jacob planned to take a small sabbatical from the community and travel to Texas to spend an extended time with his former pastor who first led him to God. However, he was advised that he needed to remain in town to complete some legal matters concerning his wife passing. Therefore, unlike his usual activity of evangelizing, and having the opportunity of getting things off his mind; Jacob's plans had changed for him to stay in town until legal matters were complete.

After the funeral, Jacob remained in the city and began attending church at his local community on a regular base instead of evangelizing. Jacob came to church one early spring Sunday morning followed by his entourage of friends and ministers. Before this time, Paris was perceived by parishioners as quiet, shy, an introvert, and non-gossiper. Parishioners once depicted Paris as a typical person who was always faithful coming to church with her daughter Stella, and who was always the first one to leave the church after the benediction. Stella was still away at college, thus; Paris was going to church alone. In the past Paris, Stella, and her mother would always meet and sit together in church. However, now Paris was feeling alone having lost her mother, husband, and her daughter was away at school. Still, Paris continued to attend church faithfully, but; was somewhat depressed with an ongoing grieving process.

One Sunday morning in the early spring Paris came to church and assumed her usual pew space, which was on the third row from the front, the end seat on the far-left pew section adjacent to the pulpit. As the service progressed, Jacob walks in with his entourage (about seven men) to the front and center pew section just in front of the pulpit. The praise and worship service began, and the anointing of God was flowing within the sanctuary. As the service began, Paris looked up briefly over toward the pulpit her eyes focused on the left lateral and posterior aspect of Jacob's head. Looking back, Paris believed later that the encounter was the 'Spirit of the Lord,' revealed to her foreknowledge of what would take place in her future. Paris affirmed that she heard the voice of God say: "*That is your husband.*" Paris trembled in her seat and suppressed this encounter in her mind and within her spirit. However, somehow didn't recall that encounter for many months later.

When the service began to end, Paris' heart began pounding; and she felt a compelling force to approach Jacob to express her sympathy. Paris walked up to Jacob trembling as she'd never done this type of thing before. When Paris got about five feet away from Jacob, she witnessed multiple women surrounding him, and she decided to wait a few minutes before she proceeded to approach him, however; it seemed like hours—until the line dwindled to a few persons surrounding Jacob. Paris walked toward Jacob until she got an arm's length away, and when she offered her condolences, expressed words of empathy; and sympathy to Jacob. Looking back, Paris remembered that she was so afraid, began to tremble again, and felt her heart continued to pound rapidly. For a person who was shy, an introvert, and who usually left church immediately after the benediction this was a big step and challenging. In actuality, Paris was certainly going out of her comfort zone! After service, the church remained full of parishioners, who were in fellowship, and greeting one another as usual.

Paris' slow and steady walk from the third-row-pews seemed like a mile long. However, somehow Paris made it up to the front and center roll about two feet from this evangelist. When Paris reached her destination what she witnessed in this long appearing walk, was what she would describe as a mob of people mainly women surrounding him as well as his entourage. Jacob was being pulled from every direction with handshakes and condolences. Paris then thought to herself: "What am I doing here?" At that time, she wanted to run off so badly, but somehow, she couldn't. But she slowly guided her hand through the crowd in front of her and lightly tapped him on his right forearm. This motion seemed like a lifetime, but Jacob turned slightly, finally looked toward his right, down toward Paris. Then, Paris began to say to Jacob these words: "My name is Paris. You have my deepest sympathy in the passing of your wife. Somehow, I know what you are going through. I feel your hurt and pain. I wish to thank you for visiting my husband Lamont in the hospital, and praying from him." He in turned stated to Paris and stated: "Who? …Who? … I don't know a Lamont. I don't remember praying for your husband." When Paris heard this, she immediately, felt so embarrassed; and wondered if she had gotten her facts wrong regarding his hospital visitations. Paris began to think that Jacob was the wrong person who came to visit and pray for her husband. Initially, she felt panicky and wanted to run away. Still, Paris did not run away, she then said to him: "I am sorry, I thought that was you, however; you have my sympathy." At this point, Paris felt like she must have "come down from the Spirit." Instead, in her shyness, Paris felt an urgency to leave and left the church walking extremely fast.

Paris walked rapidly to get in her automobile and drove to a local restaurant to eat dinner, and she began to feel so senseless and silly for what she'd just done. Initially, Paris felt that her actions were a carnal part of her or the "flesh," that was in operation. However, Paris later found out that it was not, and she learned that the encounter was ordained of God; and the 'Spirit of God' did move upon her. While at the restaurant and waiting for her meal, Paris noticed so many couples and families eating and that they were having so much fun together. After all, the day was Sunday, a typically considered a family day after church, and was a traditional thing for people to eat out with family and friends. While Paris was at the restaurant, she began to talk to God and asked him to be her husband and take away her pain, suffering from grief; and loneliness. She began to deposit what had just happened at her church way in the back of her mind—to move on.

After this Sunday encounter and dining at the restaurant, Paris drove home still feeling somewhat embarrassed for approaching "the minister." Unfortunately, she didn't go to church that evening due to her embarrassment. That evening Paris felt so alone, left the lights off in her home, and as she would lay in bed praying. Paris felt embarrassed not recognizing or remembering the message that she received from the "Spirit of God:" "*That is your husband.*" Perhaps, this was related to Paris' low-self-esteem or because she had not experienced a "Spiritual realm" on that level before. Perhaps, Paris was allowing her flesh to interfere with a great "Spiritual Blessing" that was to occur from all of her previous pain and suffering. Instead, there were thoughts that the enemy was perhaps attempting to rob Paris of a blessing due to the flesh and fear.

That evening Paris called her daughter Stella who was now living on campus at a university dorm. Paris began to share with Stella about her experience that Sunday morning. Stella listened and expressed to Paris that perhaps it was not a good idea for her to go to places like restaurants where couples or people were until she was healed from her grief. Paris agreed, and ended up praying herself to sleep that night; not knowing what truly was transpiring. Before Paris fell asleep that night, she made a plan and commitment that she would never do anything like this again. Paris felt like she had made a mistake, and if an opportunity were given to her, that would apologize for mistaking Jacob for the person who was visiting Lamont. In turn, she planned if she ever saw Jacob again that she would re-empathize her deepest sympathy regarding his loss.

On that unusual day, Paris later would learn that Jacob's experience was quite the opposite. After that Sunday morning service, Jacob would later convey that he was confronted with many female parishioners. However, Jacob remembered that one woman stood out to him, and had made a compassionate statement to him on that Sunday after church service. Jacob had remembered this one woman saying to him: "I thank God for you coming to the hospital, and praying for my husband before he passed away." Then he'd remember saying: "Who?… Who?," Then she replied: "My Husband." Jacob asserted that he didn't remember Paris saying her husband's name— "Lamont." The next thing Jacob stated he remembered, was that another member of the church pulled his left hand, and began talking to him, which caused this woman's hand, (who he would later learn was Paris); that slip off his right forearm. Jacob would later assert that as he was standing with his back to the pulpit and looking into the crowd, he felt the anointing of the Holy Ghost/Spirit moving up his right arm to his face as Paris' hand slipped off his right arm. When that happened, Jacob looked to see whose hand was on his right arm, but Paris' hand quickly lifted off his right forearm as she began walking quickly away. Jacob later claimed that he had a very brief glimpse of this woman before to walked away; and that he would always remember. Jacob would remember that this woman had a small hand with gold around the wrist with a gray sleeve and that she wore a unique dangling gold barrette in the back of her hair.

After the encounter, Jacob stated that he leaned forward to pick through the crowd for that one particular "woman" who had just touched him—to see if he could find that woman. To do so, he backed straight back all the way to the altar to get a good view of the sanctuary and those who were surrounding him. Jacob was 6 foot and 8 inches tall and, it did not take much for him to look over and beyond other people. When he could not find or identify this "woman," Jacob then turned to his entourage circle and asked: "Who, was that woman who touched me on my right arm?" They all would like at one another, and said to Jacob: "How could we tell who touched you with all those "women" standing around you?" Then he looked at one of the entourage group members and said: "Come on, we have got to find her!" Then one of the group members said: "What woman? … Do you know what she looks like?" Then Jacob said: "No, but; I saw the back of her head and her left arm sleeve." Then one of the group members said: "That is going to be like looking for a needle in a haystack!" At that time, their church was the second largest church in the city with the square footage of about 50,000. However, Jacob and his entourage began looking over the entire church premises including the church library and parking lot for this "woman." Unfortunately, their search would be to no avail. As Paris, "the woman," was long gone from the church grounds Jacob and his entourage circle were unsuccessful in finding Paris since she had left so abruptly from sheer embarrassment. Once they realized that they couldn't find this "woman" they finally left the church as well.

Later that Sunday evening Jacob and his entourage decided to attend another church in northern New York which was a two-and-one-half-hour commute. During that travel time, Jacob always asserted that he had a supernatural encounter with God. He began to ask the Lord: "Who…was that woman *you* sent to touch me?" Jacob claimed that as he was talking with God, he began to say that: "I knew the anointing that I felt, and I know *you* sent her to me." He then said to the Lord: "Lord what is her name?" Then he proclaimed that the Lord replied and said: "Her name is Paris." With excitement, he began shouting to those in the car with him, and said: "The Lord just gave me her name!" Then one of the entourage members said: "What is it?" After he thought about the entourage's agenda, and assignment, he decided to ponder the answer in his heart and said to the member, "No, I will not tell you her name!"

After the church service was over, they all traveled back home, mystified by the encounter. That same evening when he returned home, Jacob was compelled to telephone one of the associate pastors of their home church. Jacob asked the question: "Do you know a Paris?" Jacob continued to reassert that he loved his first wife and did not want to see her go. However, when he realized that God was going to take her from him after she passed away that he began to discuss with God what type of woman he wanted if he would marry again. Thus, he made his petition known to God and requested a virtuous woman according to (Proverbs 31:10-31). The associate pastor asked him: "Where did you get her name?" Jacob replied and said that the Lord gave him the name. Then the associate pastor began to describe who Paris was and said: "She has been in church all of her life and was filled with the Holy Ghost/Spirit at a very young age. Her whole life is centered around a reverent fear of God and compassion for those in need. Her mother was saved, I know her, and the family well. She would be a good wife. Her husband recently passed away about a year ago. Don't you remember when I took you to her husband's hospital room to pray for him?" He then said: "What was his name?" The associate pastor said: "Lamont." Then he said: "Oh' now I remember. Can you point her out to me?" The associate pastor then said to him: "Don't you know what she looks like?" Then he said: "No, I never seen her only a glimpse of her arm sleeve and the back of her head." Then the associate pastor said: "Come to Bible study on Wednesday night, and I'll point her out to you. The only problem is that she leaves the church promptly, so you will need to come up to me as soon as the benediction is over." Jacob declared that he had a sense of satisfaction after this conversation with the associate pastor; however, he was feeling perhaps it might be too soon to be feeling that way he was regarding this "woman." Based on these feelings Jacob wanted to be sure it was the Lord. Thus, he continued to desire the mind of Christ and wanted to be sure that it wasn't his flesh. Therefore, Jacob decided to fast and pray for two days before the upcoming Wednesday evening Bible study.

Jacob always professed that he was committed to staying in the city post bereavement of the loss of his wife, and complete all the pending legal matters before evangelizing again. However, he was not planning on attending Wednesday Bible studies. However, Jacob endorsed that he had a different mission in mind on that particular Bible study service. That mission was to find that "woman." Before he went to Bible study, he decided to obtain counseling regarding this matter. Therefore, he confided with a close friend that he had planned to meet someone, and he needed them to pray with him. Indeed, Jacob went to Bible study on that Wednesday evening again with his entourage circle and sat in the front pew as before. Later Jacob would always say, he felt that the Bible study message was excellent and informative; however, he was concentrating on the task at hand—and what he needed to accomplish at the end of the service. The Bible study message that evening was to be "spiritual-minded" to obtaining help for deciding disputes. Also, the Bible study message was to know that there is comfort found in the Holy Scripture. Jacob proclaimed that he agreed, but was thinking about these following Holy Scriptures on that one Bible study evening:

> "He *that is* first in his cause *seemeth* just; but his neighbour cometh and searcheth him. The lot causeth contentions to cease, and parteth between the mighty. A brother offended is *harder to be won* than a strong city: and *their* contentions are like the bars of a castle. A man's belly shall be satisfied with the fruit of his mouth; *and* with the increase of his lips shall he be filled.

Death and life *are* in the power of the tongue: and they that love it shall eat the fruit thereof. **Whoso, findeth a wife findeth a good *thing*, and obtaineth favour of the Lord**. The poor useth entreaties; but he rich answereth roughly. A man *that hath* friends must show himself friendly: and there is a friend *that* sticketh closer than a brother" (Proverbs 18:17-24).

Jacob also related this Scriptural passage to have a wife is like contrasting wealth versus poverty:

"House and riches *are* the inheritance of fathers: and a prudent [Prudent: *careful, wise, cautious, discreet in conduct, circumspect and not rash, capable of exercising sound judgment in practical matters*] wife *is* from the LORD" (Proverbs 19:14).

After the Bible study service, Jacob did as the associate pastor instructed him and quickly went down to where the associate pastor was ministering to other parishioners. While he was waiting to speak to the associate pastor, a particular woman was standing directly in front of him waiting as well to speak with the associate pastor. Jacob stated that he grew impatience progressively, and was thinking to himself: "God forgive me, but; I need this woman standing in front of me to go away." So, Jacob began to pray that the parishioners in front of him would soon go away so that the associate pastor could point out the other "woman." The irony was that the "woman" who was standing in front of Jacob was Paris, and who was requesting prayer. Finally, the crowd narrowed down, and the "woman" in front of him left.

In reiteration, Paris normally would leave the church immediately after any service, and would not be one to fellowship or socialize afterward. But this time was different. On that particular Bible study evening Paris walked away from receiving prayer by the associate pastor, she was detained by a classmate from the seminary they were both attending. Paris and her classmate began discussing one of their homework assignments. As a result, this conversation held Paris up about fifteen minutes that seemed like a record for her stay after service was over. In the meantime, the associate pastor engaged with Jacob regarding their plan after service. When Jacob approached the associate pastor, he pointed his hands upward and outward toward Paris, the "woman" and said: "That was her standing just in front of you one moment ago!" For him, Jacob felt that the funniest thing about this particular story was that the woman that he was praying away to move so that he could speak with the associate pastor; just happened to be Paris—the woman he was attempting to find. He then beckoned the associate pastor to put his hand down, because he didn't wish for anyone to know that he was looking for someone that soon. Jacob viewed that this situation was odd and that he knew at this point in his bereavement process that others would not have understood what was happening to him so soon. Therefore, he was attempting to be discrete with his actions and with his initial contact with this woman "Paris."

Shortly after Jacob sighted Paris, as usual, she was making her way out of the church. Paris had just stepped out of the lateral north double doors of the sanctuary leading to the parking lot when Jacob proceeded to catch up with her. Unusually, Paris proceeded to continue talking with her classmate as they both walked out the door. It was then that Jacob approached Paris for the first time and said: "Excuse me, can I talk with you?" The classmate said, "Me?" and then Jacob said: "No, Paris." The classmate department and Paris stood almost paralyzed on the sidewalk of the church parking lot, as he and she both simultaneously began speaking. At first and as Paris committed, she would do, began to apologize to Jacob for being out of place, and coming up to speak with him on that prior Sunday morning. Paris stated: "I'm sorry, I thought that you were the man and minister that came up to pray for my husband." Instead, Jacob hastily exclaimed: "No, No, I'm the man! Yes, I'm the man that visited your husband and prayed for him at the hospital!"

Undoubtedly, Paris had some anxiety. However, spiritual boldness came upon her again, and she began to minister to Jacob regarding his grief, pain, and suffering process and shared with him that she truly understood what he was feeling. Additionally, Paris began to impart and educate Jacob on the five stages of bereavement or the "death and dying cycle:" (denial, anger, bargaining, depression, and acceptance). Paris began to support Jacob and explained to him that individuals who suffer a loss of a loved one often go through these stages of grief as well and that individuals must learn to recognize these stages, so they can: (a) be aware of the stages, (b) be helped through them, (c) be careful not to fall prey to them, and (d) heal. Paris shared with him that he would experience these five bereavement stages involuntarily. In other words, she explained that in grief, pain, and suffering process it is universal and inevitable as well could sometimes be undeserved, and unavoidable to experience grief from a significant loss. Howbeit strange, and for someone that Paris didn't know, that she began to coach him on the church parking lot to accept and prepare Jacob for these stages.

Later, Jacob would describe this encounter as "enlightening with truth and spiritual comfort" and stated that he'd never heard of this fact about grief before. After their discussion on the church parking lot, Jacob then asked Paris for her telephone number. Paris then reached into her purse and obtained one of her checking account deposit slips and tore off her telephone number and gave it to him. Jacob always claimed that he kept this torn deposit slip with him afterward for years. Symbolically, when Paris thought back on this experience, the encounter was similar to a "deposit slip" in her "spiritual life" that was arranged by God. To further clarify, during their conversation on that church parking lot God was dealing and talking to the both of them during the encounter. Jacob and Paris later learned this, and began sharing with each other, numerous couples, people, during public speaking engagements, conferences, and revivals, etc. when they would tell their story regarding "how we met"—that while they were talking to each other on the church parking lot, they both had a supernatural experience—and God was speaking to them. God was telling Jacob, "that is your wife." Paris believed that she had heard the voice of God on the Sunday prior saying: "*That is your husband*," and was feeling unexplainable love for him at first sight and contact.

At the about an hour, and end of their conversation on the parking lot, Jacob asked Paris if he could walk me to her automobile. Jacob would always say, that the most amazing thing Paris said was: "yes!" However, her automobile was only a few feet away from where they were standing. During his sabbatical time of caring for his wife, he stated that the Lord directed him to have a business of selling perfume oils when he traveled. Therefore, he was very familiar with perfumes and fragrances. As he walked Paris to her automobile just a few feet away, he noticed her perfume fragrance in which was one that he was not familiar. The last thing Jacob asked Paris was what fragrance are you wearing? Paris stated: "Victory Secrets." They parted and went their separate ways.

After this encounter, Jacob always claimed that when he went home that Wednesday evening that his house was full of people. When he arrived, he stated that many people there wanted to converse with him and one minister began to "give him a word." That word was: "You are to stay single and to make your life as a eunuch." Of course, Jacob concluded that: "this word was not of God," and that this word did not agree with his spirit and what he had experienced that evening. Therefore, Jacob dismissed what was said to him, and turned in.

When Paris got in her automobile that Wednesday evening her heart was pounding, but; in a different way. The experience felt like a dream. However, Paris was not going to allow herself to be misled. Instead, Paris counted the experience at that time as a wonderful fellowship after church and the opportunity to minister to someone. Additionally, Paris resorted to the fact that if Jacob never telephoned her, that the experienced served a godly purpose that day.

At that time, Paris continued to work long hours on the night shift. On the next morning, when she got home from work, there was a telephone message on her voice mail from Jacob. The message was a request for her to call him, and he left his telephone number on the voice mail. Frankly, Paris was surprised to hear from him the next day, and she returned a call to him. Jacob and Paris talked on the telephone for nearly five hours that evening, primarily about the Holy Bible, and they ministered to one another. During that time, Paris continued in seminary/college and was stimulated and illuminated with the "Word of God." As a result, even though Jacob claimed to be well seasoned in the "Word of God," this provoked Jacob to study. Thus, for weeks between work and daily activities Jacob and Paris would talk on the telephone intermittently for months, but; never saw each other. These conversations would become cyclic, and Paris would become sleep-deprived due to frequent conversations with Jacob.

On one Friday evening, there was a special event at their church of appointing a new pastor. Surprisingly, when Paris stepped into the church lobby to cast her vote for a new pastor, Jacob was the first-person Paris she saw standing in the line to cast his ballot. Paris would go on to remember this day so clearly and vividly. She could even remember what Jacob was wearing in every detail—cream and a light brown sweater over his tie and white dress shirt.

Over the next several months Jacob and Paris would continue to daily converse for long hours by telephone, ministered to each other, and essentially courted this way for several weeks. For months, they never dated outside their homes, but only had telephone contact with one another. The only time Jacob and Paris would see each other was when passing each other at church services.

Unknowingly, they both began to fleece or "to pluck out whence" God regarding their relationship. They both began seeking God for special events to occur, or that specific thing would be stated related to their personal needs for security, and related to a possible future companionship. For instance, Paris always viewed herself as a serious, focused, meticulous, and somewhat picky in certain areas. Paris was notorious for being finicky, to say the least, and was a true introvert. Paris asked the Lord to allow Jacob to say without her prompting that he would: understand, respected, and loved her. Shortly afterward this divine request, one evening when they were talking on the telephone, and without prompting Jacob, made a clear statement: "Paris, I don't quite understand it. But I feel like I love you just like my first wife. The feeling seems like a continuation of a love that I had for her. Paris, I don't know why I am saying this, but; I understand you and respect you. I don't know when… but, one day will you marry me?" Paris was somewhat in shock, however with much ease and no hesitation answered softly: "Of course!" Paris would later learn that after her response to Jacob's question: "of course" in his mind he was thinking: "O´ my God what am I going to do?" Shortly, after her response to this question, he stated: "The only thing…. I am very possessive!" Initially, Paris found this to be flattering and that the act of possessiveness would become a type of security in her life. At that time, Paris didn't realize how true of a statement that would be or how much of an understatement that would become. Eventually, she would learn that this statement meant that he wanted me all for himself; and that he was not willing to share.

On the other hand, Jacob had purchased for his first wife an expensive full-length mink coat that ended up being too small for her, and she never wore the coat. This mink coat still had the original price tag hanging on it, and Jacob made a declaration. Jacob prayed to God saying: "God I am going to give Paris this coat, and in doing so this would be worth it all if I learn in advance, that she is materialistic—the evidence would be her keeping her eyes on this coat when I give it to her, rather than me. That way, I will know she's not for me." Jacob decided that if Paris kept her eyes on the coat when he gave it to her, then that would be a sign she would not be for him. During the days of their ongoing telephone courtship, they would learn that Jacob's entourage circle who had moved in with him to keep him safe and protect him during his bereavement, was listening in on all of their conversation's downstairs on another telephone, while Jacob was upstairs in his bedroom conversing with Paris.

Nevertheless, Jacob eventually wrapped the mink coat in a large sheet to conceal and get the coat to pass his entourage, who were watching every move he was making; and supposedly guarding him. He then hoisted the load over his shoulder and carried the coat out of his home. Jacob planned to take the mink coat to Paris as an engagement gift and noting that her response would determine the future outcome. Later Jacob would learn, that his protection team came to a complete panic when they found the mink coat was missing. For Jacob's entourage when the coat went missing, they believed that their mission had failed in protecting him during his grief, vulnerability, or from women seeking to get his attention as a new widower.

On that day Jacob took the coat to Paris' home as planned. When Jacob handed Paris the mink coat, she accepted the coat and thanked him. She turned slightly to place the coat on a nearby chair. Paris was unaware that she was being discerned and monitored by Jacob on her response to receiving the coat; and if she appeared materialistic or not. Instead, Paris maintained persistent and direct eye contact with Jacob and not the coat. The coat was so heavy that it began to slide off the chair to the floor, and Jacob quickly jumps to catch the coat from falling to the floor several times. At that time, he went to his right knee and officially purposed marriage to Paris. Jacob asked the question: "Will *you* marry me Paris?" Paris repeated a second time: "Of Course."

Contrary to many, this evolving relationship became extremely difficult to understand. Jacob and Paris both had dearly loved their deceased spouses, however, had undergone numerous years suffering from a chronic illness and long-term caregiving. In actuality, they both had already experienced an extensive grief process. Jacob and Paris believed that they had sought God for His comfort in their situation and that God had answered. They both knew their marriage was a gift from God encompassing divine approval, a divine assignment, and for a divine union doing "greater works." During that time, they both believed that this was happening from the "Spiritual Realm." They know that there was a process for their divine purpose in the future, and knew that God had a plan for their future lives together in ministry. Despite that fact, there were those who would reject the marriage. Instead, they accepted, moved forward, and understand their position in God. As a result of this, Jacob and Paris became very selective with who they would associate with and share while continuing to court over the telephone.

Shortly after Jacob give Paris the mink coat, they both made a major decision to marry. They believed and trusted God and that this was His perfect will. Once married they experienced much joy in being together as husband and wife. Jacob and Paris believed that coming together in marriage was a destined divine union.

After they were married, Paris was so happy, and it seemed as she was living a wonderful dream. She was humbled and took great pride in becoming a minister's wife. Mostly, though, Parish believed that she was experiencing the will of God in her life in doing the work of the ministry; and in fulfilling her new role. Paris truly loved her new husband, honored, and cherished their union, and knew that she had married him for the appropriate reasons. Paris also did not minimize the higher call, duty, and the new role upon her life as a new "minister's wife," and sought diligently to learn more and fulfill this call as unto the Lord.

The first several years of Jacob's and Paris' marriage were described as a true honey-moon life-style and filled with love for each other—so it seemed. Jacob began evangelizing once again, and Paris was humbly honored to travel alongside him. As a whole, Jacob and Paris enjoyed the ministry and witnessing the great move of God in their ministerial travels. What is more, they valued their experience of being used by God in evangelism, preaching, teaching, spiritual conferences, and the healing and deliverance ministry nationally and internationally.

Though Paris' temperament, personality, and character together created a tendency to cause her to stay focused and diligent in her Elect Lady tasks, and responsibilities at hand; she was in denial and not acknowledging the serious dysfunction surrounding her marriage. Indeed, that was what happened throughout the thirty years of their marriage, which seems unimaginable! When they married Paris' daughter was away a college during that time. Paris continued to work three jobs and surrounded the rest of her life traveling in ministry with her new husband. Jacob and Paris were continuing to learn of one another, as they prepared to merge soon to buy a home together. Once they settled in their new home, it did not take long for Paris to learn that there was sobering "baggage" coming along with them that was not related to the moving process. The "baggage" consisted of generational strongholds, deep emotional wounds, demons from the effects of unresolved parental acceptance-rejection trauma, and the more.

Occasionally, Paris began noticing a change in Jacob's behavioral patterns, however, stayed focused on her everyday tasks, responsibilities, and never addressed them. During this time, the true meaning of Jacob's possessiveness came in to play. Once they were married, he insisted and established with her that he was going to take her everywhere she needed to go. Taking her everywhere inclusive of work, professional hair designer, doctor appoints, personal errands, and just anywhere that Paris had to go. Jacob would often say on a daily basis: "Where are we going today?" Initially, Paris felt pampered and believe it was his way to show his love. In actuality, if anything, his demanding, possessive behavior should have become a "red flag" that something wasn't quite right with Jacob's behavior.

Still, Paris flatly did not acknowledge this behavior and looking back she was in gross denial. Very soon after their marriage, Paris noticed that there was one intense habit that Jacob had, which was that he talked on the telephone most of his free time. He was always adamant to explain that when he was talking to others on the telephone that he was: "ministering to others" and stated that: "this is part of my ministry!" When Jacob was on the telephone, his discussions were primarily with women or "sisters" as he would call it. Jacob would often state, that he was ministering on the telephone when he was talking to other women whether they were (marriage or not). At that time, Paris found this activity to be strange, and Jacob was extremely sensitive about being questioned regarding these telephone discussions. However, for some reason, Paris never felt insecure about this type of activity and was unable to control Jacob's serious cravings, desires, and possessiveness in excessively talking on the telephone and taking Paris everywhere she needed to go. His over possessiveness and excessive talking on the telephone continued throughout their marriage, and it became detrimental. In time, Paris would eventually be ostracized from her family; and as devastating as it was, even from her daughter.

Paris and Stella were extremely close because they had been through so much together and especially due to them providing care to her father Lamont for so many years. Before the marriage, she and Stella would always do everything together, e.g., take walks, ride their bicycles in the park, go shopping, and sometimes dressing alike. Additionally, it was Paris' delight and pleasure to take care of her financially, and supporting her while she was away at college. However, due to Jacob's jealousy, all of this would come to a complete halt once he came into the picture, and became aware of this. After Jacob learned of this supporting fact, this financially spiraled into Stella, needing to take a break from college, and came home to live with them for a while.

When Stella came home from college her life became a "living hell" due to Jacob's aggressive behavior and conduct. In looking back, to Paris' regret and eventually guilt, she did not learn about serious multiple abusive scenarios surrounding what her daughter endured, until toward the end of their marriage. The reason for this is that Stella feared for her mother's safety, and she did not want to be wedged or forced her mother further apart from her. However, Jacob's mindset was that Paris' daughter was unwanted in the home at all. Often Jacob would seize the moments when Paris was away at work to become verbally threatening toward Stella. Jacob would taunt her, bully her, and postured himself in positions in attempts to intimidate; and hit her. Jacob's conduct was quite scary for Stella—as Jacob is 6 foot 8 inches, and she is 5 foot 2 inches, and his behavior was unpredictable to say the less.

Sadly enough, Jacob behaved in this manner hopes to force Stella to leave their home. Paris later would learn, that he also had an agenda not to share Paris with Stella or anyone else. That fact of the matter was, *initially* at that time Jacob was abusive with a pattern of behaviors to maintain power and control over Paris demonstrated in possessiveness, aggression, and intimidation. When Paris came home from work or any place Jacob was not that intimidating person as described when she was away from home. Moreover, Paris could not understand Stella's strange behavior around her when she was home. All awhile, Jacob would be attempting to demonize Stella  endeavoring to convince Paris that her daughter had inner demons. Stella became very depressed and became isolative and predominately stay in her room and the basement when possible. Paris' guilt feelings would eventually be evidence regarding these circumstances later in life, however; occurred due to her lack of discernment, sheer denial, and naïve notion at that time.

To Paris' unbeknownst, Jacob continued his unacceptable and aggressive behaviors toward Stella when Paris was not home that became unbearable for her. Therefore, to keep out of the picture, she began staying and living in the basement most of the time, which became concerning to Paris. One weekend Jacob and Paris went out of town for a five-day revival. Without Paris knowing, before they departed from the home on their ministerial travel Jacob deliberately locked the basement door knowingly while Stella was down in the basement sleeping on their way out the door. The basement was where Stella would stay most of the time to isolate due to her emotional despair, distress, grief, and pain from verbal and threatening abuse from Jacob. Fortunately, and by the grace of God, the revival ended early that week. Thank God, instead of five-days away, it became a 72-hours weekend trip. Normally, Stella used the portable telephone in the basement most of the time, and when Jacob and Paris left that morning, the battery would soon die. Therefore, during the time they were out of town she was trapped in the basement without food, water, bathroom access, and sheer necessities. When Jacob and Paris came in the garage door, Stella began pounding vigorously on the basement door and yelling loudly. When Paris opened the basement door, Stella ran up to her room without saying a word. The fact was, Stella had been trapped in the basement for 72-hours. Initially, Paris did not compute that essentially her daughter had been deliberately trapped in the basement for three complete days. For Stella, this episode became a turning point of her life regarding her life and need for survival. Looking back on all of this conduct, Paris' would later declare that she was in gross denial. Paris did not discern the demonic activity entering into their life, and the level of abuse and destruction happening within the home.

Somehow soon after this frightening event, Stella courageously managed to pull herself together despite all odds, and found a job that she through time maintained for over twenty years after this event. Still, despite the emotional trauma she eventually rose to the top in leadership and account management at this company. Immediately, after the terrifying basement episode, she rented an apartment with two of her long-term friends and gained peer support. After Stella moved out of their home, even this wasn't enough for Jacob, and he had further intent to hurt and damage. Therefore, he began to assassinate Stella's character and began making derogatory statements to others about her that was not true. Then, Jacob made the worse mistake by beginning gossip to others that he "put Stella out of the house." Fortunately, for him, Paris did not learn about this overall conduct until years later in her life—five years before the end of their marriage. Numerous years later—Paris learned the complete details, truths of the basement matter, and the demeaning untrue statements Jacob was making to others regarding Stella's character. The irony here, the time when Paris learned about these facts nearly 15 years later, she was experiencing despair and pressure above measure regarding her relationship with Jacob. Fifteen years later, Jacob also would, in turn, become—"verbally threatening toward Paris, would taunt her, bully her, and postured himself in positions in attempts to intimidate and hit her" throughout their marriage. Thus, Paris' relationship with him at that time took a gross spiraling downward with a turn for the worse. Discovering this truth would eventually turn Paris' heart into sheer bitterness toward Jacob, and it became the factor that stemmed from their days growing further apart. Paris began to see Jacob for what he *was* and was *not*. Despite the cost and woundedness, when Stella moved out of the home, Jacob and Paris' relationship stabilized for a while—so it seemed.

Over the next eight years, Jacob and Paris remained extremely active in ministry, and Paris continued to work full-time in her professional field. In keeping note of the discussion in chapter one regarding marriage, two factors that become the most critical elements of a successful marriage are maintaining an open channel of communication; and financial stability. Both of these elements began to crumble and challenged their relationship due to Paris' surfaced health problems. What is more, Paris began to suffer intensely mentally, physically, emotionally, and spiritually which made the trials regarding her first spouse 'Lamont' seem like a light affliction.

In keeping with the time, it is critical to note that Jacob never knew Paris' mother, however; during this time-frame, her father was still living when Jacob and Paris married. Paris' father lived a long time after her mother's passing. However, the father-figure or role model needs were limited after her parent's divorce. Paris' father was extremely close to and had a stronger relationship with her oldest sibling. Paris' and her father were not close after her parents' divorce, yet deep down, Paris believed her father desired a relationship with her. However, her father didn't exactly know how to return his love to Paris and others. There were times that Paris didn't even see her father or talk to him for years. Paris became completely shut out of her father's life, which became emotionally damaging. Paris later became more emotionally damaged when on one occasion unexpectedly she received a telephone call from her father after several years had passed. Out of nowhere, her father began yelling and screaming at her on the telephone and hung up on her not allowing her to respond. Paris would never learn the reason for this angry outburst she experienced or didn't understand the reason for her father's behavior. After this perplexing telephone conversation call from her father, she would never see or have contact with him for well over a year.

In looking back on all, Paris realizes, that the turbulent relationship that she had with her father was the premise for many of her own broken relationship/friendships, social separations, unpopularity in school, and negative wedges in her life growing up. She contributed her childhood issues, life experience with her father, and her association with an alcoholic father as part of her codependency problem as it related to her relationship with Jacob.

Codependency is a serious psychosocial problem, psychological condition, or a "relationship addiction" in which a person is controlled or manipulated by another. According to the Mental Health America (2014, p. 1), they assert that:

> "Codependency is a learned behavior that can be passed down from one generation to another.
> It is an emotional and behavioral condition that affects an individual's ability to have a healthy,

mutually satisfying relationship. It is also known as "relationship addiction" because people with codependency often form or maintain relationships that are one-sided, emotionally destructive and abusive. The disorder was first identified about ten years ago as the result of years of studying interpersonal relationships in families of alcoholics. Codependent behavior is learned by watching and imitating other family members who display this type of behavior."

Today, however, "Codependency has broadened to describe any codependent person from any dysfunctional family." As family dysfunction was discussed earlier in this book, the Mental Health America (2014, p. 1) provides a profound outline of this area of mental health. They proclaim that a: "dysfunctional family is one in which members suffer from fear, anger, pain, or shame that is ignored or denied." In this case of Codependency, "dysfunctional families do not acknowledge that this problem exists." What becomes the deep lingering problem "is that families do not talk about or confront them." As a result, "family members learn to repress emotions and disregard their own needs." They become "survivors."

Additionally, codependent individuals "develop behaviors that help them deny, ignore, or avoid difficult emotions" Codependent individuals have a tendency to have "low-self esteem and look for others to make them feel better. They have good intentions. They try to take care of a person who is experiencing difficulty, but the caretaking becomes compulsive and defeating" (Mental Health America, 2014, p. 1).

Codependency then becomes a "relational style characterized by unhealthy bonding, repression, compulsions, poor social image, and a sense of duty and obligation." This type of lifestyle is also "an irrational involvement with another party where denial, imbalance, disruptive behaviors, and low self-esteem shape the relationship." Also, "the codependent person is usually driven by an intense need to connect with and a deep desire to belong to a significant other (person, object, system, or entity)." However, at "the same time is compelled by an unconscious motive to control the outcomes of that relationship" (Benner & Hill, 1999, p. 212).

In correlating these factors regarding Paris' second marriage, and while she always demonstrated good intentions of being a "caring wife," concerning Jacob, this later became emotionally destructive for her. The phenomenon of codependence was evident in Paris' life, and she had fallen into a codependency pattern associated with a typical dysfunctional family. This realm of behavior originating from her childhood issues, that was characterized by a compulsive tendency to make a difficult relationship work for many years. Over the years, this focused behavioral pattern was exhibited in Paris' life after her marriage to Jacob and played out grossly in a massive clinging to a toxic and unhealthy relationship. Paris made numerous attempts to keep the peace or harmony at any price. Paris would begin to repress and suppress events that were occurring in her marriage. She would dismiss serious character flaws and covered up destructive patterns of behaviors demonstrated by Jacob, thus; contributing indirectly to the relationship addiction, acting out, or allowed the psychopathology of Jacob's behavior. In fact, this habitual system of thinking, feeling, and behaving was somewhat one-sided. Paris developed an exaggerated sense of taking responsibility for his actions, tended to do more than her share, unhealthy dependence in this relationship, and often covering-up or justifying Jacob's sometimes bizarre, and radical behavior over time, and throughout their marriage. The codependent behavior was an unhealthy attachment and symbiotic relationship stemming from her irrational expectations in which Jacob was unable to deliver.

Soon after this time, Paris would learn that her father's health was failing, and he passed away. Still, in providing closure regarding her parents, through it, all her parents managed to become friends eventually numerous years after their divorce. Amazingly, Paris' parents found a way to visit each other periodically and often had many telephone conversations before their demise. In their way, Paris believed that it wasn't until the latter years of their lives that they showed openly any love and concern for each other. In the end, Paris believed that her father made his peace with God before he left this world. Paris was able to release and forgive her father and several years before his passing, Paris' talked with her father in-depth and ministered to him regarding spiritual matters. Having the opportunity to minister to her father was extremely gratifying, however; Paris was certain that they did not touch the deepest chambers of his woundedness. Paris healed and had closure from the belief that they had gain peace with each other before he passed away.

After the death of Paris' father, they continued to have an active life in ministry traveling the country. One year there was one particular preaching engagement that always stood out that they participated in which was a thirty-day crusade in southern, Florida. During this crusade, there was a great move a God and many souls were saved. The crusade was powerful! God used Jacob in miracles, healing, and deliverance during the week he was asked to minister. Jacob and Paris began developing strong spiritual bonds, connections, relationships, and fellowships with many of the parishioners in southern Florida and grow to love it there. Paris never felt so alive, loved the work in the ministry and cherished the fellowship. This crusade experience turned out to be one of the highlights of Paris' life and during her union with Jacob. The reason for this was that Paris experienced a powerful move of God, she observed many souls coming to know God, and witnessed the manifestation of many who were healed by God.

Additionally, Paris took part in the demonstration of spiritual deliverance and, the encounter was glorious to behold. This overall crusade was life-changing for Paris, and the spiritual event became pivotal in her ministry, and she further grew to realize how vital her call and role in ministry had become. This crusade would open a door for many trips to southern Florida for Jacob to minister and evangelize.

As fate would have it, during one of their trips to southern Florida Jacob and Paris met a young man named Paul, a parishioner and who was in the military. Paul was also one of the musicians and minister of music at the church Jacob ministered during the powerful crusade. As a customary after Sunday service and church fellowship, one of the parishioner's families invited Jacob and Paris over to their home for dinner after one of the Sunday morning evangelistic services. Ironically, this was the same home where Paul the young military man lived. After dinner and during the fellowship, this young man asked Jacob if he could see a picture of his stepdaughter Stella. Jacob chuckled, and readily reached for his wallet and took out a photo of Stella, and in fact, showed Paul her picture.

That Sunday evening was the last day of the evangelistic revival, and again God mightily used Jacob in the ministry, while Paris sat attentively with the congregation witnessing another great move of God. When the service was over, and before Jacob and Paris left church traveling back to New York, Paul walked up to Paris knowing this would be the last time to do, asked Lady Paris for her daughter's telephone number. Paris thought nothing of this request, was always known to be a very strict parent, without hesitation gave Paul Stella's telephone number. Looking back, Paris' could never understand how she so readily offered up her daughter's telephone number; when she had always guarded her in the past. However, this time she didn't see any reason not to give this young man that she had met her daughter's number. Paris truly thought that would be the end of it! However, for months Jacob and Paris did not know that this young man began calling their daughter immediately from southern Florida, and for months after that.

Shortly after Jacob and Paris returned to New York, Jacob accepted his call to pastor. Paris readily and humbly accepted her call and role as first 'elect' lady and eventually co-pastor. Once Jacob accepted his call to pastor it seemed the warfare and dysfunction intensified. Life suddenly appeared like things were falling apart, and Jacob developed many physical, mental, emotional, and spiritual attacks upon his life. Jacob developed several medical problems within months after they started to pastor the new church. These medical issues during that time were truly the trying of Jacob's faith. However, he always proclaimed that from his experience with his first wife that he was well conditioned, equipped, prepared, and empowered to be victorious in Christ Jesus despite the afflictions. Thus, Jacob vowed to live a normal life despite these disease processes and move forward in his ministry. For Jacob, he believed that witnessing his first wife's chronic illness had enabled him to be more sensitive to what was happening to him, and the life-crisis would not hinder him from continuing to minister to others. For Paris, although the situation was quite challenging, she remained steadfast in loving and supporting Jacob through all of the crisis events. In time, Jacob would stabilize and, all would seem well and, hand—and they began to adjust with their new roles in pastoring. For Jacob, this was a huge adjustment as he had been evangelizing for nearly two decades. Therefore, his travel became minimal.

In Paris' view, the only time that there was any decent relationship between Jacob, Stella, and Paris was when we decided to celebrate one Christmas in Orlando, Florida at Disney World. Once there, Paris noticed that Stella stayed most of the time in her hotel room around most sight-seeing activities. Shortly after noticing this, Paris learned Stella was in her room talking to the young man in the navy from southern Florida. The fact that Stella and already began receiving multiple telephone calls from this military man was such a surprise for Paris. In the end, Paris believed that the overall trip to Orlando was wonderful. However, Stella had an extremely different view of family travel. Stella later expressed to Paris that the only reason that she decided to come along was to spend time with her and that she had developed a mindset that whenever she could spend time with her mother, she would seize the moment. Stella knew deep down that Jacob didn't really want her around and that he was progressively becoming verbally abusive toward her behind Paris' back—and this was the only reason why she would travel with them both.

During this time, Paris' physical health became challenging. By January of the next year, Paris was suffering from severe back pain and had difficulty walking. After undergoing an MRI scan, she was diagnosed with Degenerative Disc Disease—DDD at $L_4 L_5 S_1$ with multilevel bulging disc protrusions, severe spinal stenosis, and she learned that she had scoliosis since birth. The results of this diagnostic testing became the answer to why she suffered from back pain early-on as a teenager. By early spring Paris' back pain became pronounced during her attempts to work, and this condition became the premise for suffering from severe back pain. However, during this time in Paris' life, this condition became debilitating. Suffering in this manner began to threaten her livelihood and caused a strain on their marriage. There was not much traveling in ministry during this time, and Paris continued to be diligent in her duties as a first lady. Paris remembers working so hard in wearing so many hats conducting: e.g., church administration, developing bulletins, establishing church announcements, leading praise and worship, preparing herself to teach Sunday school, Bible studies, sometimes preaching, and the more.

By mid-spring, Paris developed a right breast mass that was quickly surgically removed. When Paris learned of the results, she readily gave God all the glory, as the breast mass was benign. During all of this, Paris' back condition continued to worsen, and her income status declined drastically. Boy did their lives and marriage ever change from this point due to limited income. Paris continued to be on and off work from severe back pain, and eventually ended up having to be placed on medication and underwent numerous series of physical therapy treatments. Although it was quite difficult, she managed to get back on her feet and return to work as soon as she could to maintain their financial commitments and to help sustain the church expenses.

During this time, Paul the young military man in the air force of whom Jacob and Paris met in Florida, continued telephoning Stella on a regular basis to Paris' and Jacob's unbeknownst. In their ongoing telephone discussion, Paul was making plans to travel to New York to finally meet Stella. To this point, he only had a picture of Stella to think about and view. In time, Paul traveled to New York, and their meeting became "love at first sight!" Their adventure involved a long-distance courtship via telephone, and premarital counseling in southern Florida eventually would prove to be turbulent and to no avail.

The chaotic and confusion medium was predominantly because Jacob would daily continue to taunt Stella severely, and it would be deemed to be described as "domestic verbal abuse." The abuse was aggressive in pattern especially when Paris was working or not at home. At this point, in this storyline, it becomes vital to mention here that Jacob had a conspiracy in becoming progressively verbally abusive toward Stella also— undermind, to facilitate a callous mission, to uproot from home, and to destroy her reputation. The rationale for this devious behavior demonstrated by Jacob was that he did not want to share Paris with anyone; which became persistently evident throughout their marriage.

Soon after this time of Stella's and Paul's, meeting each other, Jacob concocted vicious lies surrounding Stella depicting that she was a promiscuous woman, someone who persistently indulged in spiritual harlotry or Jezebel (Revelation 2:20-23) lifestyle. What was even more detrimental was that Jacob was communicating this to Paul's pastor and numerous key church members in Florida; in an attempt to break up their relationship. When in fact, Jacob's deceitful tale could not be beyond the truth! In actuality, this was a mythical untruth and methodically planned out action by Jacob! Stella was well-mannered, well-grounded, well-behaved in her upbringing, and had never been in trouble, a lady of class with a huge potential for success; and most importantly–still was a virgin who had kept herself from any sexual activity at her current age.

Despite this damaging fib, Paul and Stella courted long distance, flying back and forth between Florida and New York to spend time with one another. Stella was brilliant in her courtship and would carry her herbs and spices on the aircraft to Florida to prepare gourmet meals for Paul that she had learned from her maternal grandmother growing up. While Stella was in Florida, there were several episodes of pastoral counseling with Paul's pastor and even to the arrangement of a bridal party arranged for Stella by some of Paul's home church members. Unfortunately, their relationship would not survive the nasty rhetoric, gossiping, haughtiness and grandiloquence conversations that Jacob would plot out to deliver to various people associated with Paul's church. Jacob was driven at most, to continue the quandary, undermining, and plight in destroying Stella's character.

These falsehoods resulted in Paul ending the relationship with Stella, because; he did not want her lifestyle to interfere with his status or reputation as a gifted musician; and, the plot had created a "spirit of confusion" established by Jacob. Sequentially, this devious action was associated with the break-up. Based on the premise of the concocted lies or "unknown falsification," Paul felt the need to separate from Stella due to the complex scenario of turmoil and confusion that he was facing from all of this.

For Stella, the break-up was devastating. However, she stayed strong in moving forward in her life. During that time, Stella moved out of the home to her apartment, and she needed to drop out of her junior year in college as Jacob "cold turkey" would not allow Paris to support Stella any longer while attending school. Stella began working as a banker, attempted to move on in her life meeting Samuel, a new boyfriend on her job who had one year of college left in medical school. After nine months, Stella and Samuel were engaged to be married. Stella, seemly was happy, and with a wedding date planned for January 15th. However, Stella's happiness was not the case. Deep down Stella was suffering severely and devastated from multiple losses. Stella progressed to major depression and occasionally would contemplate suicide from the obvious disruption and destruction factors brewing and looming in her and her mother's lives. Besides, Stella had not fully grieved her biological father's passing due to her altered new life. Instead, Stella felt she had lost her mother Paris as well. Therefore, she was grieving losses of both parents, the break-up with her fiancé in Florida, and being uprooted from her stable home.

About one year passed, Stella remained engaged to be married to Samuel with a date set for January 15th. Jacob routinely behaved in excessive gossiping and consistently called around the country stirring up fallacies and confusion primarily among the churches he was affiliated. Through a mutual friend of Jacob and Paris, Paul was informed that Stella was engaged to be married. In despair, Paul began praying and asking God for direction, if Stella was meant to be his, and needing God's divine intervention. At this point, Jacob never believed that Paul could regain Stella's love—however, he led him on the path to try. Shortly after this, Paul made the conscious decision and risk flying into New York to see Stella and to gauge whether or not Stella still cared and loved him. What a risk for Paul to take! Paul knew with his decision to return to New York was taking a huge chance, heretofore, he prepared himself for possible impact and rejection.

In all of this state of confusion, Jacob arranged and allowed Paul to stay with Paris and him when he flew in from Florida with a plan and strategy to re-connect with Stella. Over that next four days would become the trial of Paul's faith and indeed serious rejection from Stella, Jacob and even Paris' as they hadn't gotten over the level of pain that he had caused Stella. Interesting enough there were multiple church events scheduled during those four days he was in New York in which Jacob seized the moment to use Paul's musical talents to back Jacob with musical compliment while he was preaching out of town on that Saturday, and at the Sunday morning church service that weekend. The irony was that Samuel, Stella's fiancé needed to work and study for his finals during these four days while Paul was in New York. Therefore, whenever they were all together, Paul had plenty of time to attempt in re-connecting with Stella. Everywhere they went Stella found herself reluctantly in the company of Paul. However, Stella remained cold toward Paul. Despite all of this, Paul asked Stella could they go out to dinner one evening to talk. Stella reluctantly accepted and, their primary discussion was based upon that fact that she had moved on and had developed another relationship with Samuel. Over dinner, Stella reiterated on multiple occasions that she was happy and soon to be married to Samuel on January 15th. She reinforced with Jacob that it was over between them and that his coming was in vain.

On that Sunday morning and the last day of Paul's stay in New York, this rejection would begin to dissipate and melt away. During that morning church service, Paul played the organ and sang a song: "God is Just a Prayer Away." Paul sang the song with all his might! While the congregation was packed-out and full—somehow what stood out in the mists of the congregation were Jacob, Paris, Stella, Samuel, and Paul. In the sanctuary, you could "cut the tension with a knife," but; also needed a tissue while Paul was singing. There was not a dry eye in the church and, as Paris gazed over at Samuel, she noted that he was in shock from what was supernaturally happening in the atmosphere. The church was highly uplifted and began praising and worshiping God supernaturally.

The last stop and chance for Paul to make his final move to win Stella's heart back again would come with dinner after church that Sunday afternoon. They all ended up going to an elegant restaurant to finally socialize and fellowship which is fairly normal for members of the church to do on Sundays after service. AT THE TABLE, the social conversation was generally cautious and superficial. While at the table, Paris noticed that Stella was muted, and she had a very sad affect. Stella soon got up from the table and went to the lady's room—after about 45 minutes in the bathroom Paris went to the lady's room to inquire and check on Stella. When she walked in the lady's room, she didn't initially see Stella and called her name out: "Stella." There was no answer. Paris then stooped down and looked to the floor of the stall/cubicle and saw Stella's beautiful long satin bronze skirt, and called her name again. Paris said: "Stella," as she preceded to ask her to open the stall/cubicle door—she opened the door to Paris' sheer jolting shock experiences. Stella was sitting on top of the commode (not using), but; she was crying profusely. Paris said: "Oh Stella, what's wrong?" Again, Stella was somewhat muted and didn't initially respond.

In the middle of Paris asking Stella a second time, "What's wrong?" All clicked at the same time. Finally, Stella said: "I don't want to hurt Samuel." Then, Paris almost collapsed realizing what was happening and said: "Oh my God!........He (meaning Samuel) will understand!" Just as Paris was embracing Stella and attempting to reassure her that all would be "okay" and that she had nothing to feel guilty about; there was a knock at the lady's room door. By this time, this lady's room encounter was going on one-hour and counting. Paris went to the door, and it was Samuel asking if Stella and everything were alright. Paris politely stated to Samuel, "Stella's is not feeling well… but, she's coming out in a minute." When Paris and Stella came out of the lady's room, they all soon wrapped up their dining out. However, Stella went straight home from the lady's room to soul search. That evening it would be easy to conclude that Paul's mission to win Stella's heart back would not take place. After dinner, they all went their separate ways, and Paul went to Paris' and Jacob's home to pack his bags to fly back to Florida on the next day.

As Paul arrived at the airport somehow, he believed God for a miracle that Stella would somehow be there, as he had shared his departure time, gate, and airline information with Stella before he left to travel back to Florida on that Monday. While in actuality, at that same time Stella was indeed in her automobile running late, speeding, as she traveled to the airport feeling emotional, frantic, and crying. The chances of Stella arriving at the airport was slim to none. As she approached the gate, she did not see Paul and quickly ran to the terminal screen to ascertain the status of his flight—seemingly that she had missed him entirely. Stella began to sob and weep profusely while she was looking up at the terminal steadfast in the middle of a busy New York airport terminal corridor; when simultaneously she felt two arms come from behind and passionately embraced her and hearing the words: "So, you do still love me!" Feeling somewhat embarrassed, Stella turned around, gained her composure, control her emotions, put her guard up, and looked Paul directly in his eyes. That moment and time would prove to be pivotal and life-changing for them both. At that point, the dialogue was precise and brief and, there was an attentive agreement to think about their relationship for a possible reunion once again over that next week.

Over that next seven days, Stella engaged in a serious shut-in with God and remained in her room. She did not eat, sleep, talk to anyone over that next week—and would not even see or talk with Samuel. During that week she fasted, prayed, and sought the Lord with her complete heart for His guidance, help, and divine direction. What is so critical here was all of her heart-brake and confusion resulted from Jacob's diabolical plan to create pain for her and Paul, and in which was deemed domestic emotional abuse.

After her week of consecration and seeking the Lord, Stella made a life-change decision. At the same time, Samuel was having prophetic dreams and could not interpret the message or meaning of the dreams. Samuel came to Jacob's and Paris' home in concern that he'd not been able to connect with Stella and was feeling somewhat distraught regarding a repeating dream. Paris had a gift of interpretation of dreams, and Samuel was aware of this asking her to interpret. Howbeit strange, as Samuel began to share his dream to Paris—she was supernaturally about to interpret the components of the dream as he rolled it out. The content of the dream was spiritual; and conveyed to Samuel in peace that his marriage would not take place. This dream agreed with Samuel emotionally in a way that calmly offered him comfort and harmony in spirit.

After this encounter Paul and Stella's relationship progressed and resulted in marriage exactly on the same day, she'd plan to marry Samuel—on January 15th in New York. While at first before they broke up Stella agreed to move to Florida to start their lives together. This time, the marriage engagement would be contingent upon Paul's willingness to move to New York beginning their lives together verses Florida—proving his love to her. Paul decided on New York! This reunion Paradoxical, yes! Every element of Stella's plans for her wedding with Samuel was converted to another 'groom' at the very last minute. In other words, Stella used the same date, church, wedding dress, invitations with only a groom name change, bridal party, and wedding ceremony rehearsal, reception arrangements, and last but not least the honeymoon arrangements to Jamaica— BUT SWITCHED THE GROOM! Many were shook-up and could not understand what had happened. The wedding coordinator could not get over the last-minute groom switch around. Needless to mention Paul and Stella's union was deemed miraculous, and how they finally came together is an enormous story by itself. The situation seemed like a happy ending to a fairy tale story—and all should be happy. Unhappily, they would soon learn over time that their marriage would be grossly challenged and strained due to Jacob's unpredictable and erratic behavior would nearly destroy all of their lives.

Paris proudly walked her daughter down the aisle and "gave Stella away." Jacob and Paris officiated, performed the ceremony, or solemnized them. After their marriage Paul now Paris' son-in-law, moved to New York and became a member of their church, and it was a great relief for Paris as Paul became the minister of music and musician at their church in New York. Shortly after their marriage, there was an incident when Jacob grew extremely agitated which lead to an intense argument between them, and it ended with Jacob physically assaulting Paris. After the incident, Jacob immediately left their house, and without thinking Stella frantically called her daughter and son-in-law. They lived in an apartment at least fifteen minutes away from their home, however somehow Paul and Stella arrived at the house within minutes in their nightwear—Paul was in his onesie. It seemed like a breaking point for Stella, and she was quite angry. Paul later conveyed that the trip to their home took them only a few minutes to get there, and was a nightmare. Paul further exclaimed that it took 'the power from above' to calm Stella down as she was furious! Afterward, Paul, Stella, and Paris talked about the incident, and they all calmed down some. Paris strongly encouraged Paul and Stella to go back home before Jacob would return to prevent possible repercussions for their being there. Feeling emotionally threatened, Paris thought about everything, and she realized that there could be more potential physical harm for her if they were present when Jacob returned home. Therefore, Paris insisted that they leave. Reluctantly Paul and Stella did leave the house, but; they were severely affected by the encounter with domestic abuse. Mostly, Stella became increasingly depressed knowing and discerning that her mother was entangled in bondage and that there was a festering toxic situation forming. Stella believed that there was nothing she could do and felt hopeless and helpless.

Contrary to one's thinking, soon after this episode of assault, Jacob had the opportunity to be consecrated to the office of a bishopric. Jacob decided to accept the call to the office of a bishop. Paris worked diligently to organize the ceremony and published the event in the local newspaper. The event was open to the public, and he was indeed consecrated to this office one Sunday morning. Initially, Paris was so proud of him. However, shortly afterward his arrogance intensified to all those surrounding him. Jacob's expectations of Paris became augmented coupled with manipulation, control, and narcissism. The vanities and egotism would soon become apparent, and this elevation in ministerial office of a bishop was a new title firmly established by Jacob. Early on, he asserted that Paris was to call him 'bishop' and honor him as such.

After his consecration to the bishopric, Paris was rebuked often by Jacob if she did not address him as "bishop." She would verbally threaten, and he would be aggressive toward her if she did not address him as "bishop," especially in public. To prevent any issues, Paris made sure that she didn't. The sad piece here was that Paris did not recognize at this point or was in gross denial that this was not a healthy situation. Instead, Paris' desired to move ahead to do the work of the ministry. In all, Paris' choices and actions were based on the premise that: she truly loved the Lord; she loved ministry; she loved her role as the "elect lady;" she honored her salvation and current position in the church community; she loved God's people, and she loved and wanted to please her husband. Instead, by the end of the year after this ecclesiastical elevation, Paris became perplexed about "why" the church was not growing and in keeping up with the expense incurred by the church was becoming a burden for Paris financially.

During this time frame, there was an incident that occurred at their home that Paris ended up suppressing for numerous years, and the incident resurfaced when she thought about sharing her story in "telling all" about her life experience. Jacob became bitterly angry with Paris, and physically assaulted her, but this time resulted in him giving her two black eyes. Looking back, Paris did not realize it at that time, that she was a victim of domestic violence or intimate partner violence—IPV. At that point Paris never missed a church service, therefore; she decided to attend the service wearing sunglasses thinking no one would notice. Of course, wearing sunglasses didn't hide anything! Stella became inquisitive and removed the glasses cautiously off her face, and questioned Paris how she got the black eye. Needless to say, after she thought about it, Paris didn't need to say one word. Unfortunately, Paris later learned and validated from many parishioners that the abrasive conduct and behavior by Jacob was running members away. He continued to be

verbally abusive and disrespectful toward Stella, especially Paul, Paris' son-in-law, and their friends whenever the opportunity would arise. Jacob grew to hate Paul viciously, with any cause or rationale.

In actuality, Jacob's unpredictable behavior was the premise of why their church congregation wouldn't grow. Looking back, Paris always remembers attempting to patch-up things or episodes behind his unpredictable behavior. Often, such behavior would occur at their local church between members, conventions, convocations, conferences, revivals, church services, and Jacob's counseling sessions more often than not. This behavior stemmed from his arrogance, grandiosity, and narcissistic behaviors and borderline personality features. What became most disheartening for Paris, was that Jacob brutally counseled one of the ministers of their church. Subsequently, this member left the church and eventually the faith for a long period due to the inflicted verbal abuse and emotional trauma. Fortunately, over time this minister eventually returned to God and faith. However, after multiple pastoral encounters for this parishioner the emotional trauma and pain suffered entailed extensive spiritual support, professional counseling, and prayers from many others for a successful restoration; and spiritual recovery.

On one Sunday morning, the time would come after several years when Jacob and Paris decided to close the church. They had a plan to announce this decision to close the church on that same morning, ironically on a day when Paul and Stella were late for church service. Paris would later learn that Paul and Stella were late because they were reluctant to come back to church at all, and had also decided that they were going to leave the church as well on that same day. The fact was that this same Sunday was to be their last Sunday attending no matter what. Sadly enough, for Paul and Stella, after considering their overall emotional trauma and experience from Jacob, abuse—that they had enough! Paris would only later learn that the only reason they stayed as long as they had or would come to church on any Sunday morning was in support of her.

When Jacob and Paris announced that Sunday morning to closed the church, Paris felt relieved even though her heart still loved the work and call of the ministry. On that day, when Jacob and Paris returned home, Paris began thinking: "what now?" After a small break in ministry, Jacob and Paris grew deeper in financial distress, and there was a threat to lose their home and automobile. Reluctantly, they decided to place their house on the market. During this time, Paris learned later that Jacob had turned down an opportunity to move to Dallas, Texas to be part of the ministry there. Not knowing about the opportunity in Dallas, they began exploring the opportunity in moving to southern, Florida. Paris decided to try coordinating a travel work position process to use as a vehicle to move them there. Subsequently, the ideal worked out for Paris at that time; and her employer-assisted in relocating them to Florida. Once all of the travel position was confirmed, Jacob and Paris packed up part of their belongings and placed a "For Sale" sign on their front yard and headed to Florida. Eventually, their home sold within that year, and they had a mindset that they would live out their lives in beautiful southern Florida.

The move to southern Florida became a bittersweet experience. As fate would have it, Jacob and Paris would live in Florida for eight years, which became the core root of a productive ministry. Their level of intense sufferings would prove to be the "trial of their faith," and a patch of life-event that will never be forgotten. Initially, Jacob and Paris felt blessed and believed they were in the perfect will of God. Their housing was paid through Paris' employment in a beautiful elite housing complex setting in beauty southern Florida. Even perhaps, like a paradise!

Before Paris left New York, she asked Paul, her son-in-law and Stella her daughter to move to southern Florida with them. Paul and Stella strongly considered moving there; however, decided not to move there due to their experience with Jacob. During this time-frame, they both worked full-time, earned their bachelor's of science in business administration, and continued to earn their master of science in business administration—MBA at a prominent university in New York. Additionally, during that time-frame they had two homes built and began to prosper and re-build their lives together. Paris continued working full-time as a traveling employee in southern Florida, and she and Jacob began to settle in the beautiful community and enjoyed the change in the cultural atmosphere.

Jacob and Paris began to visit various churches to determine where they would hold their membership. This brief happiness wouldn't last for long! To Jacob's and Paris' devastation shortly after they moved to southern Florida the pastors from the church were, Jacob ministered in the crusade and where Paul had formally attended publicly announced over the church pulpit—addressing the congregation to: "Stay away from" Jacob. When Jacob and Paris learned about this slander, Jacob became angry, and Paris was deeply wounded. Over their next eight years that they were in southern Florida, the action by Paul's former pastor would be detrimental, a severe battle, and would become a solidified stronghold in their local church communities. Looking back on this situation, Jacob and Paris would suffer intensely for eight years in southern Florida as a result of this statement of smear and slander. When Paris began to analyzed Jacob's behavioral patterns, abusive behaviors, and unpredictability—somehow deep down she understood why this local pastor elected to take this stance. This life event proved to be grave and difficult for Paris. However, overtime Paris released slowly, let go, and eventually forgave this local pastor for the serious damage.

Once this devastating event occurred, Paris decided to commit more to her theological studies in seminary by correspondence, and continue to work the night shift at her travel position in the community. Jacob continued his commitment to intense telephone calls across the country (predominately women) and proclaimed that he had Bible studies at night in their apartment when Paris was at work. For a time, Jacob and Paris began steadily to attend one of the churches in the community that would accept them regardless of the slander. The pastor of this church offered Jacob the opportunity to preach at this church one Sunday morning. After that, arrangements were set-up to rent one of the pastor's properties for Jacob to start a church. The area that they began to rented was a huge chapel located on a naval base, and they proceeded to build a new pastoral ministry. Jacob and Paris felt that they were given a second chance and felt so blessed to have this opportunity, and worked hard to build the church membership. Unfortunately, the ministry at the chapel did not last long, and the membership never grew. The pastor sporadically came to one of the services on Sunday morning and what Paris described as a gross "interception" of their ministry. The "interception" was their last service at the chapel; as this pastor abruptly ended their occupation and rental of the chapel. The only thing that Jacob and Paris could do is returned to their home stunned and in shock thinking: "What just happened!"

Alongside this time, when Paris was at work, she experienced a severe back injury and was diagnosed with a bulge in her disc located at $L_3 L_4$. As a result, Paris had to undergo medical treatment and prolonged physical therapy. After the events of losing a second church and suffering an injury to her back, Paris devoted most of her time and life to studying the "Word of God," and managed to earn two degrees all at once during her recovery. Paris graduated with honors, summa cum laude, distinguished graduate status, and was the valedictorian of her class. During the commencement ceremony, Jacob and Paris met another couple who was planning to begin pastoring, and they began to fellowship with them. Not long after this, the four of them brainstormed together on Jacob's and Paris' patio and decided to begin a theological university. This couple wanted to become part of the administrative board and teach at the school as they had a call to pastor a church. Having a school was one of the long-term dreams that Jacob and Paris had, thus; it appeared that things were coming together for them. Finally, it seemed for Jacob and Paris that they had entered into a ministry that God prepared and called them to do.

Over three weeks Jacob and Paris worked diligently to bring this new vision to past, and they established their first class renting a classroom on one of the state's campuses to launch the school. They both worked steadfastly in southern Florida in doing the work of Christian education ministry. They further established this university to become a state nonprofit 501 (c)(3) religious organization with a state and federal status. This school became a state-approved institution—offering various degree programs. Within a year, God gave Paris the wisdom and knowledge to work steadfastly to bring the university to establish its full accreditation credentials, and the university became registered with the state of Florida. The student enrollment began to grow, and Jacob and Paris remained steadfast and committed to this ministry. They both loved this work of the ministry and invested most of their time and resources to assist in furthering a mission of Christian education.

Paris began to organize the leadership and staff for this Christian educational ministry. Paris began serving as the co-founder, co-president, executive administrative director, provost, associated adjunct professor in theological studies, and dean of colleges and indeed loved the Christian education ministry. Additionally, Paris had the opportunity to design and write numerous books to enhance student studies, thesis, dissertations, established numerous university courses and designed curriculum for the colleges from associate to doctorate degrees, educational books, and materials to enhance the educational programs.

After the university was up and running smoothly through God's direction, another vision was born. God gave Paris a vision to establish another nonprofit 501 (c)(3) religious corporation with state and federal status, that encompassed Christian services and outreach entities. Paris became the founder, president, CEO, and Chief Executive Director of this Religious Corporations. During this time, Paris had an amazing opportunity in coordinating and assisting several pastors within the community in organizing and establishing outreach ministries for several local churches.

After about two years, Paris had recovered from her back injury and became physically stable. Paris returned to work in the community to help with their personal needs and support the educational ministry. During this time, the university continued to grow, and their life seemed to be going well. However, shortly after this period the previous slanderous statement by many local pastors began to "take a wind" in the community, and this nightmare had re-surfaced in their life again. The enrollment in the university began to drop, and other pastors became leery in allowing their parishioners to attend the university.

Again, Jacob and Paris were experiencing another devastation in their lives, and tension began to grow in their marriage. Awkwardly enough, as a result of this tension, Paris experienced occasional physical abuse from Jacob during this time, and their marriage seemed to be on the rocks. Shortly after this second devastating experience of slander, Paris was traveling to work one morning, and as Paris exited the freeway another automobile T-boned her automobile on the driver's side. Paris' knees were thrust forward into the dashboard, and she suffered several soft tissue injuries. As a result of this motor vehicle accident, Paris suffered bilateral knee, right shoulder, soft tissues neck injuries—with exacerbation and aggravation of previous symptoms causing increased severity of pain and stiffness to her back. Also, the X-rays of her knee and back revealed: arthritic changes of her left knee and further degenerative disc disease of her entire vertebra. This motor vehicle accident resulted in long-term medical treatment and the third course of physical therapy. By this time, Paris had developed mild hypertension secondary to the related injury, stress, increased weight gain, physical pain, and her condition was not improving. Paris' physician recommended her to have an MRI scan of her left knee. This scan showed severe meniscus tears medial and lateral, moderate effusion, arthritic changes. Then, another MRI scan of her right knee was conducted which showed a moderately extensive degenerative change of the medial compartment involving both the medial femoral condyle, medial tibial plateau, and the meniscus. A discrete meniscal tear was not evident; however, there was a moderate extensive chondromalacia of the medial compartment with both increased signal and subtle irregularity of the surface of the cartilage, or otherwise known as severe osteoarthritis.

Sometimes the pain and suffering in Paris' back and knees would seem to overtake her. However, Paris always had a will to conquer every challenge that she faced, she knew that God was with her; and that He would fight her battle. Even though Paris' health and condition were not improving, she never gave up hope in her faith and the divine healing process. Paris' chief concern at that time was how would the university carried on and how would she and Jacob maintain their home.

The slander incident and motor vehicle accident would begin one of the most devastating living conditions of Paris' life and created much pain and suffering for them both. Due to Paris' condition, she was unable to work, and the university seemed to be folding. As a result, Paris lost her automobile, and they eventually lost their home in Florida. Jacob and Paris were forced to place all their belonging in storage and began experiencing the world of homelessness. For nearly nine months Jacob and Paris resorted to living in Jacob's

1989 automobile, living in hotels, and living with others, sometimes with individuals they didn't know—between various cities in southern Florida. During this time, Paris remained in severe back and knee pains; and needed to walk with two canes to get around.

After living in a hotel for about one week, Jacob arranged for them to live with one of the students from the university. By this time Paris was nearly bed-ridden and living with severe daily pain from the past injury and motor vehicle accident. This living arrangement lasted for about three months until one evening Jacob verbally insulted the student. One next morning after Jacob had verbally insulted this student; there was a knock at their bedroom door. When Jacob opened the door, there was a gun pointing at him by a law enforcement officer, and they were abruptly asked to leave the home. From there, Jacob and Paris returned to a nearby hotel for about a week to regroup. The incident occurred during the fall just before the holidays, making this incident even more daunting for Paris.

Subsequentially, Jacob made another arrangement for them to move in with some church members that they didn't even know for about three months. While living with these church members, Paris felt vulnerable, weak, remained in severe pain, and eventually, she became extremely depressed. Paris began crying every day with worsening vulnerable, hopeless, and helpless. Sadly enough, Paris began suffering more frequent verbal and physical abuse from Jacob while they were living with these members they barely knew. For Paris, the burden was difficult to hold as she was emotionally suffering and susceptible to further abuse—as Jacobs behavior was unpredictable. Paris reluctantly shared this abuse with the church members in reaching out for help in desperation. When this happened, the members telephone their pastor, who later came to the home and confronted Jacob about his behavior. This episode would be the last times that he physically abused Paris for a while. However, the abuse was not the end. Jacob was asked to leave their him, and Paris was permitted to stay. After a few days, the members permitted Jacob to return to the home with forgiveness. This event would never die for Paris, as after the event periodically Jacob would never allow Paris to forget it. By the holidays season, Jacob and Paris were asked to leave their home and ended up living in a hotel for about one week. Jacob eventually found a minister friend leaving in southern Florida who was willing to allow them to come and stay. On Christmas Eve Jacob and Paris moved into the minister's apartment and lived there for about three months. Jacob got into multiple confrontations with this minister; however, he continued to allow them to stay.

Oddly enough, through the entire trauma, deep down Jacob and Paris never gave up on the university or Christian education ministry, and struggled to keep the school going around their homelessness. By the winter season, Jacob and Paris received notice from the church members they were previously living with, that another pastor in the nearby area was seeking help to enhance their school and gain their accreditation. Jacob and Paris made contact with this pastor and arranged a meeting at this church. A new door had opened up for them, and somehow Paris physically rose up from her bed of affliction, but barely walking—and with occasional canes. Paris began diligently working on an educational proposal, and in planning for this meeting with a pastor in another city. Paris created a relevant business plan, proposal, PowerPointÓ Presentation, and contract documents, etc., and conducted a professional presentation for this pastor and the administrative staff.

After the meeting, Jacob and Paris agreed to work together to enhance their school to become accredited. On a consultant bases, Jacob and Paris initially relocated to this city and stayed in a nearby hotel for a while. Paris began working diligently to enhance the church's school, and they became members of this congregation. For Paris, she was looking for a much-needed place of stability and desired a sense of belonging within a church community. Paris wanted to do everything she could to maintain this position as coordinator in the enhancement of the church's school. The Christian education ministry was Paris' passion, and she felt honored to do so, as well as becoming a faithful member of this church.

After working diligently on this project that spring, God blessed Jacob and Paris to have a new home. Through the work and consultation services that Jacob and Paris provided, they eventually were able to stabilize again; and moved out of the minister's home. Shortly afterward, Jacob and Paris were able to move into a beautiful home near a golf course and were able to move their belonging out of storage, and Paris established herself enough to purchase a new automobile. Jacob and Paris became faithful members of this new church, and the school that they were working to help rebuild at this church became a university and fully accredited.

As the school continued to grow, and students completed their requirements for graduation; it became time for the first commencement exercise for this school in this city. The planning, rehearsal, and commencement were beautiful. The graduation experience brought so much joy and happiness to the students and their families. After the commencement, Jacob was called to the pastor's office early the next week. Until this day, Paris does not know what completely happened on that day between Jacob and the pastor. However, Paris knew that the outcome was not favorable. When Jacob came home from the meeting, he stated that: "the pastor threw my back up against the wall, and punched me in my chest!" Initially, Paris was speechless and didn't know what to say. Jacob and Paris never attended this church again, and they were about to embark upon another phase of instability.

By this time, Stella, Paris' daughter had become an executive for her employer and was traveling the country. She had a business travel assignment to Florida and, from where she took a flight to visit Paris for the first time in years. Paris never looked at her condition the way Stella would come to view her status at that time she came to visit. Later on, Stella would come to describe her mother's condition as deplorable and devastating to her. What Stella saw, was her mother Paris had been confined to an air mattress bed, she was barely mobile with two canes, and was experiencing intense severe pain. Stella, unsettled by arriving into town and assessing her mother's bleak physical condition; decided to try and relaxed and grab a snack. She opened the refrigerator door to find absolutely no food, only two bottles of water. Stella was literally heart-broken! Although Jacob and

Paris lived in a beautiful home surrounded by a paradise in southern Florida off a golf course, it was apparent that her mother was in an extremely unhealthy situation from many different perspectives. After collecting herself that evening, Stella took Jacob and Paris out to dinner at a beautiful restaurant on a famous route in Florida; and later she took them to the grocery store to buy food. Putting her pain aside, Stella mustered up the strength to take them out for a night on the town. Paris felt so loved and alive when Stella was there; it was like "old times" when they were so close. Paris was not fully aware or cognizant how much Stella was aching and heart-broken on the inside due to her mother's condition. Stella hated to leave her in that level of state and suffering to travel back home. She knew that the situation was out of her control, and all she could do was pray.

After Stella's visit, Paris tried desperately to revamp their university and pick up the pieces to start again. Despite Paris' pain and suffering from her back and knees and emotional trauma over the past seven years, she began looking for another job. However, Paris was unsuccessful in finding employment, and she knew her condition would limit her performance. Earnestly, Paris wasn't sure how she could physically endure working due to her degree of back and knee pains. During this time, Paris' local physician ordered additional diagnostic testing, and she underwent another MRI scan of her back and knees to determine if there were any pathological changes. Late fall an MRI of Paris' Lumbar-spine and bilateral knees showed no change from the MRI conducted previously. However, Paris' Lumbar-spine films showed severe stenosis or further narrowing at L_3-L_5 and multiple protrusions throughout her vertebrae. The MRI of her knees showed severe arthritis with atrophy, chronic tear, and effusion. Paris' physician suggested that she undergo orthoscopy surgery to "clean out around her knees," and recommended a knee replacement, or continue with steroid injections.

Soon after Stella returned to New York, she pleaded for Jacob and Paris to return home to New York. However, Jacob would not hear of it; and was adamant that he wasn't moving back to their hometown. Additionally, at this time Stella informed Paris that she was pregnant with her first grandchild. The time and condition would come when Jacob and Paris were forced and had no other choice in the matter, but to return to New York. They could no longer maintain the beautiful home that they had grown to enjoy, and Paris' health was failing. From this point, it became expedient that Jacob and Paris could only gather their resources, pack, and head back to New York.

Ironically, on the same month and day Jacob and Paris left New York to relocate to Florida; would be the same month and day that they packed up all their belongings in Florida returning to New York. Jacob and Paris shipped their belongings back to New York and traveled separately in individual automobiles heading northeast. After eight years, in shock, they traveled the route back home to New York. During the long travel back, Jacob's behavior, mood, and demeanor was nothing but angry. Most of Jacob's anger was targeted toward Paris as they traveled back. Anytime Paris would unintentionally speed ahead of him on the Interstate highway; Jacob would become furious. At times, he would telephone her on his mobile device crying in rage and fury—demanding that she not drive ahead of him on the highway.

The travel back to New York was pivotal—and life-changing! When they left Florida, Jacob would never be the same again from the day forward, even until the end of their union. Circumstance would come to past, that Paris would physically, mentally, and emotionally pay for their return home. When Jacob and Paris crossed the New York state line, Jacob's unpredictable behavior, his abusive behavior toward Paris and her family would be augmented. Paul and Stella had just built their second new home in the country and were prospering well. Their unconditionally love toward Jacob and Paris were unwavering, and they allowed them both to come and stay with them without any obligations. Yet, Jacob never appreciated their generosity and love. They ended up staying with Paul and Stella for nearly two years; to no prevail in the change of Jacob's abusive behavior or angry character toward them.

Shortly, after returning home, Paris strengthened to get back on her feet and was blessed to find full-time employment. Paris developed a financial plan to stay with her daughter, and son-in-law until they got back on their feet. Things seemed to be going well for Paris until one winter she fell on ice in a parking lot and suffered a neck, shoulder, and back injury—which further exacerbated her past chronic condition and pain level. As a result of these injuries, Paris was off work for an extended period, which created a delay in getting back on her feet, and created a financial setback. Jacob became adamant to leave Paul and Stella's home, however; at that time the plan to get their own home was not an option.

Jacob and Paris stayed with Stella and Paul for 24 months which would prove to be a "hell on earth." Jacob continued to insist that Paris, and he moved out their home despite her physical condition and their financial status at that time. Jacob was extremely defiant and uncomfortable living in the home with Stella's daughter and son-in-law. What's more, his behavior remained bizarre during this time, and he engaged in inappropriate and controlling relationships.

During the time Jacob and Paris lived at her son-in-law's and daughter's home Jacob befriended one of their neighbors. This neighbor was 20 years old male who was recovering from polysubstance abuse and was searching for answers, and positive leadership. The opportunity could have become a wonderful time for Jacob to embrace spiritually, demonstrate God's Agape love, share the "Word of God," and become a positive witness. Instead, over some time, this relationship would become abusive, damaging, critically threatening, and daunting for this young person. The neighbor was devastated at what he'd witnessed of Jacob— "a bishop and minister." The neighbor was a dear friend of Paul and Stella—who would never recover from the poor character witness demonstrated by Jacob.

Jacob's emotional insecurity created tension between the two of them, which lead to Jacob threatening to harm Paris physically. Stella (5 foot 2 inches) was in her last trimester of pregnancy at this time and stood toe-to-toe in front of Jacob (6 foot 8 inches and 285 pounds) to block him from physically attacking Paris. The circumstance would be the first time that Stella made a step intervening to protect her mother from Jacob. The thought of someone intervening was essentially one of the things that Jacob always dreaded—and he feared that someone would do. As a result of this incident, Jacob would repeatedly falsely accuse Stella of attaching him; and Jacob never allowed her to forget the incident. Jacob somehow had convinced himself that this was "truth." What would usually play out time-and-time again—that "Stella attached him." Before this time, Stella would always hold back from intervening in any way; thus, preventing any repercussions for her mother. After this incident, Jacob became enraged and never recovered from Stella intervening. Therefore, Jacob insisted that they move out of their home immediately. Within months, Jacob found a new home for them to move to about 30 miles away from Paul and Stella's home. One winter, and two years from when Jacob and Paris had returned to their hometown they moved in a beautiful new home and began to start a new—so it seemed.

Shortly, after they moved into the beautiful new home, there was a death of a friend that Paris grows up with from the first church that she attended from birth. Jacob and Paris attended the wake and funeral services, and during the wake, one of their dear friends came up to greet Jacob and Paris. During this time, Paris could barely walk on her knees and was experiencing excruciating pain in her back. At the wake service, Jacob displayed a manner of arrogance and was viewed as being inattentive toward Paris, in the likes of not being "a gentleman" or "helping her along to walk."

The dear acquaintance later telephoned Paris the next day, and expressed their serious concerned regarding Jacob's behavior, and stressed how uncaring that he seemed to be. The acquaintance was deeply disturbed by Jacob's actions, and the conversation progressed to be a major 'milestone' of Paris' LIFE. At this juncture, Paris' eyes would begin to finally open, and she would gradually see: "A WAY TO ESCAPE." Then, the acquaintance made a startling statement that forever changed Paris' LIFE. The friend stated: "I will never forget what Jacob told me and so many others years ago, and boasting how he put Stella—your daughter out of your home!" Paris knew beyond a shadow of a doubt that this friend was not in the hurting business, was not lying, and was a caring person. Paris knew that this friend was not attempting to hurt her or split them up. However, what this friend had shared with Paris was like: "scales falling off her eyes."

In essences, for the first time, Paris saw Jacob for what he was. On that same day, Paris unconsciously withdraws from Jacob and became bitter toward him. As the author of this writing in telling Paris' story of "tell-all," I must be candid here! The "spirit of bitterness" is not a healthy spirit to possess, and this dark spirit can be extremely damaging to relationships. The "spirit of bitterness," can be linked to additional spirits presented in demonic spirits or groupings. For instance, adding to the "spirit of bitterness," could result in the spirit of (e.g., resentment, rejection, rebellion, or distrust, etc.), and these various spirits can consist of an array of emotions that can be seriously destructive. For Paris, after this conversation with this long-term friend began to withdraw from Jacob, and there was a serious disconnect in the relationship due to her feelings of bitterness toward him.

Regardless of this incident, Paris began thinking deeply about "their" future stability and decided to prepare more concretely for what was happening to her physically. Paris became concerned if she would be able to continue to work due to her physical suffering. Therefore, Paris decided to earn another degree in her field to enable her to take care of herself, thus; creating a more stable source of income stability for herself. Consequently, Paris began working part-time and pursue higher education full-time. During this time, Jacob and Paris grew further apart. Jacob invested most of his time conversing on the telephone particularly with females, and between these conversations would adventure to find odds and ends bazaar projects to earn monies to 'support himself.'

Over that next two years, Jacob's behavior continued to change; and he became more aggressive toward Paris. Looking back during this time, Paris suffered abuse on every level. Jacob exhibited intensive domestic violence, and abuse manifested in the clusters of (neglect, physical, sexual, and emotional) affecting Paris resulting in an array of emotions such as fear, anxiety, depression; and including her feeling threatened. Occasionally, Jacob would demonstrate fixed delusional thoughts chiefly directed toward Paris and her family. As a result, Paris continued to distance herself from Jacob. At this same time, Jacob continued to engage in conversations throughout the day predominately with females over the following years; and engaged in bizarre social media postings.

Over these years, Paris remained diligent and focused on earning an additional degree. By spring, Paris began working a new part-time position in supervision and administration and continued school full-time. As far as her marriage, it continued to deteriorate gradually. Paris developed a mixed array of ambivalent emotions, e.g., of guilt for not recognizing the past cruel treatment of her daughter at hand and actions of Jacob. These emotions would eventually instill immense heartache and disappointment in the context of her marriage as a whole; and her ministry. Heretofore, Paris would intensely struggle with these emotions for the next five years and grew grievously depressed.

Paris' health continued to decline and caused her to miss an extensive amount of work. Keeping up with her job, home, and other financial commitments became challenging for her. Jacob was unwilling to help financially and showed gross neglect. Paris' back condition worsened, and she could barely walk on her knees. From this point, on their relationship became a rocky road ahead relating to Paris' health and marriage. Paris began to experience an increased stress level on her job due to the dynamics of her marriage and physical infirmity. As a result of Paris' stress level, she developed chest pain while she was at work and was forced to go to the emergency room. In early December Paris was admitted to the hospital for chest pain to rule out a "heart attack" or myocardial infarction—MI. Paris was in the hospital for several days, and many diagnostic tests were conducted showing an abnormal EKG and abnormal stress test. The test result indicated that Paris needed to undergo an emergency cardiac catheterization on a Sunday morning. When Paris was on her way to the catheterization lab, she cried, prayed, and asked God to heal her—as she knew that she was facing a critical medical issue. Somehow, Paris believed that God was with her and that He would "submit the final divine report." As things turn out, Praise God Paris' cardiac catheterization test showed "no blockage," and she was later discharged that same Sunday. After her hospitalization, Paris returns to work for a short period after this incident; however, the situation with her marriage continued to decline seriously.

That summer Paris' condition progressed that she needed to have a total right knee arthroplasty/replacement with aggressive physical therapy postoperative. When Paris return home after her surgery, the relationship with Jacob during her recovery was turbulent, and she found that she was mostly caring for herself after major surgery. Paris knew that after undergoing major orthopedic surgery that she would need heavy assistance, would need to rely upon family members for help; and community home healthcare for support during recovery.

During this time-frame, Jacob would leave Paris home alone for extended intervals of time. Jacob forbid Paris to have Paul and Stella come to assist her with care. On one incident early postoperative, Paris became weak and nearly passed out while in the shower. Paris yelled out to Jacob for help and knew he could hear her, but he never came to help. Paris then cried out to God to help her and managed to make it out of the shower without fainting or injury. Once Paris was able to ask Jacob the question: "Did you hear me calling for help?" His response was: "What did you want me to do about it?" Additionally, for some reason, Stella rarely came to her home to help out with post-operative care, even though Paris never mentioned to Stella that Jacob had forbidden her to ask her daughter and son-in-law to come to assist her with care.

Unfortunately, Stella and Paris would later learn that Jacob detoured her from coming to their home while she was recovering. Instead, Jacob informed her that he had everything under control regarding Paris' care and that she didn't want her to come because she needed to rest. Needless to say, when Stella and Paris learned of what was transpiring, they were both stunned and upset. As a result of this stunted, diminutive, and lack of care—Paris' overall recovery was prolonged and more painful. What is more, Paris' suffering became compounded due to learning that she had severe allergies and side effects to narcotics or "painkillers" postoperative. As a result of lack of pain control, Paris suffered through grievous pain with little hands-on care by her family. Despite all obstacles, Paris' surgery was a success, and there was an initial medical plan for her to have her left knee replaced six weeks later. However, Paris postponed this surgery reluctantly since she was extremely concerned about the level of care that she would need postoperative while experiencing a strained relationship in her marriage.

After a total knee replacement normally, it takes 18 months to heal completely from this type of surgery fully. Partially recovered postoperative Paris was financially forced to return to work to save her home before her complete healing. Over the next year, she continued to heal from her knee surgery, the demand for employment increased, and marital problems continued to worsen. Eventually, over the next year, it became necessary for her to return to work part-time, and Paris sought out different employment.

By January Paris began working two days per week, while in school full-time. During this time her home environment became increasingly toxic, chaotic, tumultuous, and unsafe. Jacob continues to be verbally threatening toward her, would taunt her, bully her, and would posture himself in positions while Paris was lying down in bed suffering in pain and suffering from sleep deprivation in attempts to intimidate her. Wow, was this familiar! The very same aggression that Stella had experienced at the beginning of their marriage; Paris was now facing the same behavior and actions from Jacob. There was one particular night that Paris would always remember and that eventually became a nightmare for her. Paris was up one particular night late completing an assignment for school and had only three hours of sleep before she needed to go to work that morning. Jacob became verbally aggressive toward her when she attempted to sleep those 3 hours. He began speaking word curses over her head, began to taunt her seriously; and relentlessly. Jacob vowed to Paris that she "would not get any sleep" that night, and he kept his promise. To note, when individuals speak negative words over you this can be destructive and damaging:

> "Death and life are in the power of the tongue, and those who love it will eat its fruit" (Proverbs 18:21).

That morning when Paris went to work this episode significantly affected her job performance, as she essentially had no sleep. The burden of needing to professionally perform her job, meet all her school requirements timely, mixed with a troubled marriage was not a healthy combination. This particular day would prove to be one of the worse days of Paris's professional career and one that she would never forget. Paris worked in an atmosphere requiring keys and locked facility; ironically only to returned to her home locked up, and imprisoned in her bedroom months for her safety. Sleep deprived Paris would inadvertently misplace her work keys that day generating a panic by her employer and her being reprimanded.

When Paris went home that evening from work, she made a drastic decision that she would always regret, and further augmented the issues at hand. Paris made a stance that they must have separate rooms, and this became the beginning of an unyielding separation. In a sheer rage, Jacob moved upstairs within their home. When Paris made this conscious decision to request separate rooms; Jacob's behavior escalated completely out-of-control. Jacob began chanting, yelling, screaming, pounding his feet on the floor above her, began speaking "word curses" upon her life over the banister upstairs, and developed a serious "unclean spirit." Paris felt threatened and feared for her safety and elected to lock and barricade herself in her bedroom.

Early in January, Paris developed major depression and was contemplating divorce. The problem that Paris was facing was that she truly still loved Jacob and always wanted her marriage to work. Although Jacob and Paris had moved away from Paul and Stella's home, Jacob continued to contact the 20-years-old male neighbor who was recovering from polysubstance abuse, a heroin addict, who was searching for answers, and positive leadership. In one of their subsequent encounters, this neighbor witnessed Jacob engaging in an appropriate conversation with another woman on the telephone. The conversation became extremely upsetting for the young neighbor to the point that he was compelled to share the contents of the conversation with Paris' son-in-law who was his friend. Eventually, Paris learned fragments of this conversation, however; never revealed to Jacob that she was aware of his association with this neighbor or about the upsetting conversation he experienced. Instead, Paris relayed to Jacob that she felt he was engaging in infidelity; and asked him if he wanted to seek counseling. Jacob became angry, verbally aggressive, haughty, and arrogant. Due to Jacob's grandiosity, he was not receptive to counseling and stated to Paris that he wasn't going to any counseling. Instead, he stated: "Our pastor needs to come to me!" Paul and Stella elected not to tell Paris about this encounter with Jacob and their neighbor. Paris did not learn the degree of this incident and all the facts surrounding their young neighbor's daunting experience with Jacob until several years after. However, Jacob later returned to the neighbor's home and became verbally threatening toward the young man and his mother with a gun. Jacob warned the neighbor if he spoke anything else about his conversations that he would kill him. After this incident and over time, this young neighbor who was vulnerable, had an opioid addiction, he would eventually overdose; and passed away. Before this young man's demise, Jacob, "the bishop" had a wonderful opportunity to help, witness, share salvation, and encourage Christian discipleship with this individual. Instead, he offered him no beacon of hope, help, or healing. This incident critical damaged this young man and his family—that would never be forgotten.

In looking back on Paris' state of mind, during this period the issue of codependency was apparent; and had manifested by staying in an environment of sheer toxicity. From this time forward Paris became a prisoner in her own home and stayed locked up in her room for 18 months at risk for her safety, suffering from depression, helplessness, hopelessness, worthlessness, and a sense of betrayal—all the while Paris continued to work and attend school.

During this time, Jacob and Paris were living their lives separately, and Paris would only come out of her bedroom when necessary. Over the months, there was an escalation of telephone calls between him and others; and again, particularly with females. One particular day Paris came out of her room to obtain something from her office when she over hard Jacob talking loudly. Paris usually didn't listen to Jacob's conversations and became numb to them. However, this particular time was different, and this conversation caught her ear. This particular conversation draws her to hone in on what Jacob was saying, as it sounded familiar, and sounded like the days when they were courting over the telephone. Paris heard Jacob fostering a relationship and telling another woman that he loved her. Paris' knees buckled, and she almost clasped in the hallway outside her room. She quickly needed to collect herself and maintain control of her emotions since she was in one of the last few classes that were needed to complete her studies and degree. The demand to complete the necessary mandatory weekly assignment that day was at hand, and there was no negotiation in "falling apart." Paris returned to her room and cried, and pulled herself together to do her complex assignment. Within a few days, Jacob began pounding on her bedroom door saying: "free me, free me, and set me free!" Jacob began asking her for a divorce, and Paris felt compelled to give him what he wanted.

Feelings: Entrapped in a room of bondage in despair with a broken heart

By spring, Paris found herself at a lawyer's office filing for divorce. During this time, Jacob's abusive actions, verbal aggression, and delusional thoughts persisted. Within days of Jacob was served with the filing documents for divorce, he began to convey his relationship with another female openly. Jacob continuously talked on the phone, loudly, and openly regarding these relationships. Jacob's outbursts became quite painful to listen to, and Paris' days of bondage grow incredibly difficult to cope.

After several weeks of Jacob beings served the filing documents, Paris began to suffer from the pain, depth, and seriousness of the divorce process, and develop second thoughts. Jacob seemed to have calmed down some from his anger, and they had a brief, cordial conversation about their marriage. The cordial conversations didn't last long! For Jacob, he expressed that he didn't want to be married to Paris anymore. The context of their discussions drastically changed and became quite painful for Paris to hear. Somehow, she needed to find a way to accept where he was with his thoughts and emotions.

In the summer shortly after these bizarre conversations, Jacob traveled internationally to Australia for about one month for a preaching engagement. When Jacob informed Paris of his travel plans to Australia, she pointed out to him the financial consequences. Additionally, Paris cautioned Jacob that if he moved forward with this choice, that there would be no recourse; as it related to the expensive of the trip. At the end of this discussion Jacob understood that if he elected not to assist with the obligation of the home, the consequences would be that their home would foreclose. Jacob replied that he understood this risk, however, in actuality, he didn't care.

While Jacob was in Australia, Paris had time to think and regroup some in her life. When he returned to New York, he exhibited a demonic demeanor and activity while staying in his room nearly a week. During this time, Jacob placed his mobile bill for $25,000,00 on the kitchen counter with a sticky note to Paris saying: "You said you would pay this!" Wow, what boldness and how unnerving. As Paris reviewed the bill consisting of numerous international and roaming charges, Paris was in "total shock and all." What would eventually become more shocking, by the end of their marriage there would be *additional* cellular expenses of nearly $16,000.00 and totaling $41,000.00. Jacob expected Paris to pay for his international mobile expense; insisting that she pay. How does this even happen?

Several weeks after Jacob's returned to New York, he traveled to another preaching engagement in Dallas, Texas. During his travels to Texas, Paris had time to peacefully fast, pray, and seek God about her life, and God healed her of the bitterness that she had toward Jacob. At this time, Paris could not afford a lawyer anymore. Thus she proceeded at that time as pro se—and she filed the necessary document for "motion to dismiss." As a result, the divorce proceedings were canceled, and the appointed judge granted this request to dismiss. By this time, Jacob had hired a lawyer and filed a legal motion to continue with the divorce proceedings. The divorce process would continue, the crisis-event became so painful for Paris. However, eventually, the 'looking back' on the divorce was the best thing that could have happened for her in such grim circumstances.

By fall, Jacob returned to Australia for over a month. When Jacob returned to New York, he demonstrated a sheer picture of cold, hostile, demonic, arrogant, demonstrated grandiose behavior that became brutal verbal abusive. Jacob walked into the home stating: "they call me LORD over there… and think that I am handsome!" In choice words, Jacob spoke condescending toward Paris and conveyed that Paris was worthless to him. Jacob continued to foster a relationship with a female openly by talking loudly over the telephone while still living upstairs. The dwelling became a house of terror! Paris retreated to her room that now had become a storage place with walking room only, and a medium for injury—and nowhere to turn. The reason for this was that Paris needed to supply her room with water, nutritional supplement meals, non-perishables, and stored all her valuables/belongings to prevent Jacob from confiscated them. Paris' feelings of low self-esteem, worthlessness, hopelessness, helplessness, depression, and thoughts of "why am I here?" were prevalent. Paris felt suicidal and wanted to die. Deep down, Paris believed that she could never take her own life. However, she regretfully asked the 'Almighty God' to take her.

As the author of this writing, allow me to insert a provocative thought and perspective: Perhaps, unknowingly the notion of suicide would cause great pain for her family, but also be deemed a selfish act on her part—resulting in cheating her family by ending her life. Also, allow me to be lucid, life is so precious— and we must thank God daily for the breath that we breathe. We must not take life for granted, as life is not promised on a day-to-day basis, and many 'fall asleep,' and pass away in the mid-night hour who genuinely want to live. The truth is—depression and suicide thoughts are temporal and will eventually pass; however, the acts of suicide are permanent and will not ever pass. That said, the issue of suicide or suicidal ideations *must* be taken seriously!

The trauma and toxicity grew in their home. Strategically Jacob created devious traps and scenarios that would give him the opportunity to call the local police department by creating events in an attempt to have Paris arrested. Jacob would create domestic incidents with an intent to have her incarcerated, and decided to call the police department on Paris numerous occasions. Heretofore, the local police department coming to their home almost became a common event.

One of the most devastating situations occurred when Paris mistakenly picked up the home line not knowing that Jacob was on the other line talking internationally to another woman. Paris began to listen toward the end of the conversation. While she was listening, she could not believe what she was hearing. Still married, essentially Jacob was having a graphic inappropriate 'phone sexual' conversation. At the end of the conversation, Paris informed them both that she was on the phone listening. Immediately, after Paris had spoken there was silence, and soon two hang-ups. What was Paris looking for here? A possible: "I'm sorry that you had to hear that!" or perhaps, "I'm sorry I hurt you in this way?" That would be asking a little much! Instead, Jacob and Paris didn't see each other for over a week living in the same home.

On that day, one week later, Paris received and reviewed the rebuttal from Jacob's lawyer by mail. The document indicated that Jacob was litigating Paris for alimony, half of her belongings, and the court was ordering her to pay all of his monthly bills—up until and even after the divorce. The reason for this was Jacob had reported a false calculated annual income to his lawyer who presented false earnings to the county court. Receiving this document became more than Paris could endure. Paris had a panic attack and exploded by yelling at Jacob while he was upstairs, by asking him to move out of the home. Instead of an apology, within minutes there was a gun pointing at her with his right hand and his cellular phone in his left hand with a #911 operator on the phone as he came down the stairs. Jacob aforetime planned to call #911 to have her arrested. The irony of it all, Paris was asked by the police officers to leave the home overnight for peace' sake. Jacob seized the opportunity to share with the police officers about all of his chronic illnesses to gain their sympathy and support from them. Due to Paris' fury over the court demands and the yelling episode, while #911was listening, one of them had to leave the home overnight. Thus, Paris elected to leave home and stayed at a hotel that night and sheer shock!

When Paris returned home, the next morning Jacob had broken the lock and handle off Paris' bedroom door to prevent her from gaining re-entry. The broken door handle became a strenuous task to pry open for her. On that morning, Paris was feeling pressed to work on her school assignments and refocus after the incident. Once Paris opened the door, she instantly realized how much physical damage it had caused her. Paris knew immediately that she had pushed the limits of her back condition and diseased left knee too far. Not making excuses here, Paris realized that her learning of Jacob's devilish actions, suspect infidelity, the contents of Jacob's international conversation, and court demands upon her—precipitated her outrage. She knew that the reaction by Jacob's to call the police on her was a desire to "pay-back!" Jacob's behavior and plan of action were created in advance, and with an expected outcome to have her arrested.

There is a *paradox* here. Paris would leave her locked toxic room, to go work at a locked facility. Paris would effectively work with the sickest mentally ill population in her community—still; Paris was unable to manage the conditions in her home. Although for years her philosophy was never to allow her problems to be carried over into her workplace or job—this scenario is difficult to envision. For Paris, in this circumstance there was no balance in her life; and her ability to cope was limited. In actuality, Paris was in a life-crisis. Crisis—is an event or a turning point of which one's normal coping mechanisms are no longer helping, and 'outside' professional intervention is indicated. Paris' life became similar to mixing water with oil. However, this chemistry would never work.

Fortunately, unexpected help came her way! Paris needed to undergo required training on her job, however; was unable to perform due to her physical condition effectively. As a result, Paris' employer mandated that she seek medical attention and counseling with the employee assistance problem—EAP due to a decline in her overall work performance and in keeping up with the required employment competencies. Overall, Paris could not physically perform the demands and training required for her job due to the damage to her back and left knee. There became a serious exacerbation from the episode related to her regaining entry after the breaking of the lock and handle off her bedroom door. Therefore, Paris was encouraged to seek medical treatment, was placed on medical leave; and underwent counseling. EAP became a benefit that would prove to be a "God-Sent" and another pivotal turning point for Paris' future and escape.

Before this time, Paris had sought counseling on various levels. First, Paris sought out counseling with a local church, and quite frankly the counselor was perplexed and baffled in how to help her. One Sunday morning while Paris was at worship service, she realized that her "heart was broken," and she began crying while sitting on the pew during church services; and desiring help. Toward the end of service, the pastor offered discipleship or prayer to any parishioner that desired. Paris got up from her seat, walked forward to seek prayer or counsel during this pulpit altar call. Shockingly, even the seasoned elders/ministers of the church stood petrified, became muted, and walked away without saying a word unable to help her. For Paris, this cold perplexing encounter of inadequate counsel 'from the church,' became a premise of emotional setback. Her initial thoughts were: "How, could season ministers not be equipped to offer me counsel in a crisis?" Then she thought, "how is it that these clergymen or faith-based helpers who are called to the ministry have *not* equipped themselves for effective crisis counseling?"

Fortunately, Paris was able to take part in secular counseling through EAP, and with a counselor who happened to be a believer. After several counseling sessions with this secular counselor, one of the most helpful things this counselor offered to Paris after the assessment was, she was a "natural caregiver." Also, the counselor stated that Paris had a compulsion to "care or serve others" stemming from her childhood, evolved in codependency. This counselor determined that this was why Paris corresponded well with the multiple roles as a nurturing person. Still, the most vital fact of reality shared by this counselor was that she revealed Paris had "given all that she could give to Jacob." The counselor concurred that Paris was in a toxic situation and that she couldn't give anymore. Over time, through the counseling process, the counselor perceived that Jacob had a borderline personality disorder. However, the counselor had a *primary* concern for providing a foundation for Paris' behavioral responses. Interesting enough, most of Paris' counseling sessions were related to her relationship with her father and the impact of the relationship upon her life—as "a child of an alcoholic father." The counselor's *secondary* concern was focused on her current relationship with her husband, Jacob.

After a series of counseling sessions that winter, Paris' psychologist shared the general impression and conclusion of the overall sessions that included: a.) her past relationship with her father involving elements of codependency, and b.) her current relationship with her husband involving domestic violence or intimate partner violence and the manifestation of Post-traumatic Stress Disorder—PTSD.

First, Paris learned through her counseling sessions that: Adult Child of an Alcoholic/(Home/Parent)—ACOA is a "Personality trait of a child related to an alcoholic personality of a parent/home." Next, she learned that: Codependency—is an exaggerated dependent pattern of learned behaviors, beliefs, and feelings that make life painful. It is a dependence on people and things outside of self, along with neglect of the self to the point of having little self-identity. Codependency is "A serious psychosocial problem, psychological condition, or a relationship addiction in which a person is controlled or manipulated by another. Codependency is a learned behavior which can be passed down from one generation to another. This issue becomes an emotional and behavioral condition that affects an individual's ability to have a healthy and mutually satisfying relationship." In addition to this, she learned that the codependency is "associated with a dysfunctional family in which member(s) suffer from fear, anger, pain, or shame that is ignored or denied" (Mental Health America, 2014, p. 1).

Second, Paris learned that: "domestic violence is an act within a family unit that has threatening or violent aspects; that result in injury, whether physical or emotional; that have a lack of consent on the part of the victim; and that are excessive or inappropriate to the situation" (Benner, D. G.& Hill, P.C. (1999, pp. 363). Additionally, she learned that domestic violence actions are not normal. She learned that: *acquiring* an acceptance that she is "indeed" a victim of abuse and domestic violence—awareness and acknowledgment is the first step; *acquiring* knowledge regarding the issue of abuse and domestic violence—education through resources, references, and helping agencies is the second step; and *acquiring* preventative measures against any abuse and domestic violence—through coping skill-sets demonstrating safe self-help actions and exercising or using survival interventions separating the victim(s) from any abuse and domestic violence circumstance was the next step. *Last*, Paris learned that: Post-traumatic Stress Disorder—PTSD is a condition stemming from torture, or trauma, etc., PTSD, is a debilitating psychiatric condition that is the result of a terrifying event. A stress disorder that can occur with anyone who has survived a severe and unusual physical or mental event. First, this condition is associated with war veterans or "shell shock." However, PTSD, also results in an overwhelming assault on the mind and emotions.

When Paris initially learned of the counselor's impression and conclusion she was offended. Perhaps, it was the "shock and all" and reality! However, over time and when she processed the facts; and accepted all that had taken place in her life—after the counseling sessions ended, she felt liberated! Soon after, she believed that gaining the "self-awareness" generated clear understanding, divine healing, and supernatural HOPE!

In the end, Paris could immensely relate to all the was revealed due to her genuine honesty and "self-evaluation" of recognized behavior. First and foremost, Paris slowly progressed to realize that she needed to take control of the current threat and intimate violence partner crisis in her life. She knew that as a 'victim' this could only be achieved by stopping any further abuse and domestic violence; and that she must employ the following three basic steps for survival: ongoing awareness; education and prevention.

As Paris began to heal, recover, and grow from this life experience she asserted that the most vital point to first understand is that parenting, environmental factors, major psychosocial stressors that individuals face; e.g., (marriage, divorce, death of a loved one, losses such as jobs, and the more), etc. can have a significant psychological impact on persons in a variety of perspectives. While self-awareness is essential, Paris refused to be paralyzed by what she had learned about herself and becoming a victim of abuse and domestic violence. She grew to realize that: "Sometimes the physician must heal himself or herself" during the recovery process. For instance, in St. Luke 4:23 Jesus ministered by illustration to the believers present in the synagogue or "church" by making a profound statement for survival:

> "And he said unto them, Ye will surely say unto me this proverb, Physician, heal thyself: whatsoever we have heard done in Capernaum, do also here in thy country."

As the author of this writing, it is important to point out here that individuals must take heed to what is learned, observed, comprehended in any situation or environment. On the way 'To escape' —circumstance(s), the symbolic process of a life event reacts as a type of catalyst that constitutes a learned behavior, that can produce substance of, (e.g., success, triumph, opportunities, and power—S.T.O.P.); to facilitate positive change, empowerment through endurance, and momentous experience. "Experience" comes from taking heed, paying attention to, or taking notice to what "your circumstance has taught you!" In other words, "healer: heal yourself!" Then the significance of the learned behavior through the "escape process" becomes not the "why we suffered," but; becomes: "what was the suffering for? ~ or ~ what has the suffering taught?"

Jesus made this statement (in St. Luke 4:23) after He was abused and rejected at Nazareth. This place was where he was brought up or His past environment. Capernaum is a city of Nahum, located on the western coast on the "Sea of Galilee," and is symbolic (St. Matthew 4:13; 9:1; St. Mark 1:33; St. John 6:24). This city is associated with the life, evangelism, and teaching of the Lord Jesus Christ. This "city" was the residence of Jesus and His apostles; and the scene of many miracles and treatise. For instance, it was a place that Jesus healed the man afflicted with an unclean demon (St. Mark 1:32; St. Luke 4:33). In this Scriptural passage, Jesus went into the synagogue and read St. Luke 4:18-19:

> "The Spirit of the Lord is upon me, because he hath anointed me to preach the gospel to the poor; he hath sent me to heal the brokenhearted, to preach deliverance to the captives, and recovering of sight to the blind, to set at liberty them that are bruised, to preach the acceptable year of the Lord."

Jesus then closed the book, and He gave it again to the minister and sat down. He later proclaimed his earthly ministry, "And he began to say unto them, This day is the scripture fulfilled in your ears" (St. Luke 4:21). The listeners began to question if this was Joseph's son or not. The point here is that Jesus' experience of abuse and rejection by his hometown geared and guided Him toward 'a process of purpose' and destiny!

Sometimes the cost of suffering and experiences yields purpose and healing through the power of God. The power of God defeats the negative odds of life—even circumstances, e.g., like abuse, domestic violence, depression, and suicide ideations! Jesus gives the purpose of His Spirit-anointed ministry and firmly establishes himself. Thus, the "physician heals himself or herself" by learning, observing and comprehending what Jesus did and beam from His leadership example. The power of God or the anointing power comes to heal those who are bruised and oppressed, and this healing involves the total person (mind, body, spirit). In other words, once the truth comes to light—an individual can be healed mentally, physically, and spiritually. The "Word of God," can open the spiritual eyes of those blinded by their circumstances, world, and what Satan's domain will bring, e.g., sin, fear, and guilt, etc. (St. John 8:3; Acts 26:18). In "healing yourself," through awareness and yielding to the "Spirit of God" individuals can gain a deep realization of the suffering needs and misery of the human race. Some examples that have resulted from this are parenting, environmental situations, sin, the power of Satan, enslavement of evil, and physical abuse or distress—that can reverse, e.g., afflictions, adversity, and generational curses, etc. When Jesus says: "Physician, heal thyself," He is suggesting for believers to reflect on the healing and miracles He wrought but places the power back in the believer's hands to help himself or herself.

Continuing Paris' story: After the huge life-changing counseling sessions and a significant turning point in Paris' life; in the early spring she decided to attend a women's conference to hear from God, seek further divine guidance; and hopes to gain spiritual inspiration. Paris traveled to the conference alone and planned that time to pray and hear from God. The conference ended on Saturday afternoon after a banquet and was spiritually uplifting. After the final banquet and upon Paris' departure back home another mutual friend of both Jacob and her who attended the conference decided to travel back with her to their home city. The conversation during their route home was quite interesting. As the mutual friend proceeded to converse with Paris driving back, she stated to Paris: "You must be happy about getting a divorce." Paris' response was: "No. Getting a divorce is quite painful!" At that time, Jacob and Paris were still married and undoing the divorce process. Despite all, Paris was still questioning if she had made the right decision to divorce. Therefore, the question of divorce remained a very sensitive one. The friend continued to say that Jacob had recently telephoned her to meet with him at a local restaurant for dinner. During that dinner meeting, Jacob shared multiple wedding ceremonial pictures of him embracing a woman he had married while in Australia. Paris of course, while driving toward home, was in shock as the friend preceded describing this dinner meeting. Although Paris maintained her composure, she felt like a dagger had just pierced her heart.

Once they reached the home destination and went their separate ways. Paris pulled herself aside and parked her automobile. She began to cry profusely while she called her daughter for help. Stella immediately met her mother at the location where she was pulled over and followed her home. Paris was in shock, feeling utterly betrayed, and devastated to the point that she couldn't move or get out of the automobile once she arrived home! As a result, Stella came to the driver side, pivoted her mother's legs out of the car, assisted her to 'the locked bedroom of bondage' and tucked her in bed. Stella knew that she could not stay in the home with her as it would escalate the demonic activity in the house. Therefore, she began praying and ministering to her mother; begged her to come home with her. However, Paris would not yield and encouraged Stella to return home. In minutes shortly afterward Jacob began yelling, screaming, and stumping his feet on the upstairs floor over their heads. Paris looked at Stella and urged her to go home, as she knew the environment was too toxic for her to stay.

Reluctantly, Stella left the home in emotional distress and again heart-broken. As Stella, backed out of the driveway and looked up at the upstairs window. At that moment, Stella saw Jacob's dark demonic-appearing shadow as he stood to stare/gazing out the upstairs window at her as she backed out of the driveway. Stella had confirmed in her spirit that evening as she drove home, that she could see and sense a demonic atmosphere as she pulled out the driveway. The next day, Stella later told Paris what had happened when she left the house the evening before. Stella told her mother when she arrived home, she felt sick, vomited, fell on her knees, cried out to God, and began reading the Bible to regain spiritual focus. Leaving her mother's home, she could feel and witness the demonic forces, which made her ill. Stella strongly believed what she had experienced was grossly pathetic and was a scene of sheer diabolical activity and quite disturbing.

The next day was Sunday, and regardless of the pain and dampened feelings of betrayal Paris pressed her way to church services that morning. After church service, Paris managed to seek counsel from her pastor which was quite unusual to do after a Sunday morning service. Paris received wise pastoral counsel who also informed her that her marital situation had become "a legal matter." Later that week Paris had enough courage to confront Jacob regarding this bigamy matter without releasing her source. Of course, he denied that he had married another woman and became outraged. In looking back, it was only God that sustained Paris for nearly three months after this incident. She continued to barricade herself in her bedroom for her safety and suppressed these circumstances until divorce court.

Gavel of Justice Verses Gavel of Truth: Now June, the day of divorce court would arrive. Important to note, taking the steps of divorce can be quite frightening as it is a legal matter ending a marriage; and permanent. While this permanent separation appears to be a clear departure from God's intention for human marriage as discussed in Chapter One of this writing; in some circumstances, divorce is warranted. Sometimes, allowances for these particular situations are presented in the Holy Scriptures. For instance, it is mentioned in St. Matthew 5:31-32, and 19:3-9; in which Jesus says that a man is not to divorce his wife unless the wife is guilty of fornication. This scenario also can relate to a single instance of extramarital intercourse or affair and habitual sexual immorality. The depth of Biblical perspectives will not be discussed in this writing, however; some other reference includes: (Genesis 2:24; Deuteronomy 24:1-4; Jeremiah 3:1; Malachi 2:16, 8; St. Mark 10:2-12; St. Luke 16:18; Romans 7:2; I Corinthians 7:10-17, 39). Nevertheless, divorce is a negative

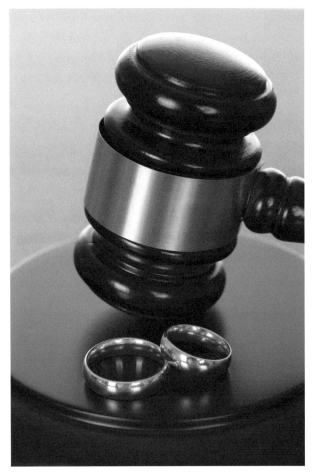

phenomenon in society and remains a global concern. While divorce is a way 'to escape,' within the process of divorce, it is impossible to escape emotional damage or wounds for all individual involved (e.g., adults, children, and family members). The end result of divorce should never become minimized.

The matter and consideration of divorce when morally permissible in any particular situation should be based on the biblical guidelines that we have been given. Last, we all should remember the Christian character attributes of love, forgiveness, and empathy when dealing with those who are going through martial transitions.

Jacob appeared to court with his lawyer having an arrogant attribute and behavior. Paris presented without legal representation, and only had God to help her. The judge decided that Jacob's lawyer (the defendant) would state their case *first*. Once the defense presented their evidence, Paris crossed examined Jacob under oath. Surprisingly, Jacob rarely said any truths; and denied marrying another woman while he was in Australia. When the subject matter of his travels to Australia was brought up, he began to brag about how they all honored him there and regarding all of his leadership accomplishments. Jacob would frequently respond by stating his answers boldly into the courtroom microphone before the judge, would often laugh after each answer he gave while gazing back at Stella and Paris sitting to the right of him in the courtroom. Jacob was chucking as he knew that he wasn't telling the truth, and began looking back at us to gauge and await their reaction to his dishonesties and deceitfulness. Then Paris (who was the plaintiff) presented her case with "the help of God." She spoke from the heart, and with complete truths! When the gavel sounded to end "their day in court," it was uncertain how the judge would rule. Paris and Jacob both left the courtroom driving in separate directions; only to return to the same toxic environment and destination—'the house of terror.'

Within days, Paris took a flight to a national convocation and again sought out hearing the "Word of God." When Paris returned to New York the final certified divorce decree was in the mail waiting for her. She trembled as she opened the court envelope, not knowing what to expect. The final court decision ruled: The divorce was finally granted to Paris on the grounds written within the decree in capital letters stating: "GROSS NEGLECT AND EXTREME MENTAL CRUELTY." Contain within the document in capital letters also indicated: "MINISTER." The judge denied Jacob alimony and rights to Paris' personal belongings. Without a fight, Paris released any material items granted to Jacob by the court. Paris also, released everything about their past shared ministry which was the most challenging piece, as she had diligently worked so hard to build, along with the enjoyment of serving others; and loving the Lord with her whole heart while doing. What got her through this challenging piece was knowing that she could always begin a new—and God had given her a "way To escape, that ye may be able to bear it" (I Corinthians 10:13).given her a "way To escape, that ye may be able to bear it" (I Corinthians 10:13).

A Stony Heart

Have you ever met a person with a heart of stone? The Bible speaks of a "stony heart," about the analogy of an uncircumcised heart (Romans 2: 25-29). The "stony heart" is also boldly referenced in the "Book of the Prophet Ezekiel," (Ezekiel 11:19; 36:26) Ezekiel—baring the name of the biblical prophet meaning "God is strong." Ezekiel's messages are dated between the years 593-571 B.C. and were given to his fellow exiles in their Babylonian captivity. In Ezekiel, the 11th chapter this prophet sends a message which references the HOPE for the remnant of Israel (Ezekiel 11:13-25) during their captivity (entrapment or bondage) to assemble out of the countries where they had been scattered due to their disobedience, idolatry, sin, and abominations. God sent a message through His prophet or "mouth-piece" therefore saying: "Thus saith the Lord God; I will even gather you from the people, and assemble you out of the countries where ye have been scattered, and I will give you the land of Israel" (Ezekiel 11:17). God desired to clean up Israel and give them a heart of flesh. In Ezekiel 11:19-20 it says:

> "And they shall come thither, and they shall take away all the detestable things thereof and all the abominations thereof from thence. And I will give them one heart, and I will put a new spirit within you; and I will take the stony heart out of their flesh, and will give them an heart of flesh; That they may walk in my statutes, and keep mine ordinances, and do them: and they shall be my people, and I will be their God. But as for them whose heart walketh after the heart of their detestable things and their abominations, I will recompense their way upon their own heads, saith the Lord God."

In this passage of Scripture God sent a message through a "vision by the spirit of God" (Ezekiel 11:22-25) to convey a word of promise that He would be willing to live in the heart of the believer—taking away the "stony heart" of corruption and evil.

The "stony heart" is made mentioned here, as toward the end of Paris' marital journey and after her brutal divorce proceedings, she described Jacob's state of mind and behavior as callus, cold, cunning and calculated. His heart was hard as a stone of corrosion! Initially, after the divorce, Paris felt as though she had been freed from a relationship of difficulties, damage and destruction; and knowing that recovery from the last 30 years would be an intense process. However, during this time Paris never realized that the difficulties, damage, and destruction was not over. This timeframe became a turning point of no return and would prove to create even deeper scars and suffering. Looking backing in the road leading up to this, she realized after the fact these vital key points: never stay in an abusive relationship— remove yourself from the environment immediately; abusive behavior *equals* damage; abusive behavior

equals grace is not there; abusive behavior *equals* emotional or potential physical pain is guaranteed to come.

Assuredly, Paris' thoughts were that Jacob would move out of the home after the final divorced process. Time would prove how wrong she was! After their divorce, Jacob communicated to Paris that he had a preaching engagement in Dallas, Texas, and afterward he would come back to New York to move out his belongings. Strangely enough, Paris believed him. Jacob's point in mentioning this was that he was making sure that Paris would let him back in the home when he returned. When Jacob left for Dallas, Paris changed the locks on the doors, garage, and codes of the security monitor.

Meanwhile, Paris arranged to have her second major knee surgery. A few days after Jacob left for Dallas, Paris underwent a total left knee replacement, and she was scheduled to have aggressive physical therapy postoperatively. Paul, Stella, and now two grandchildren made arrangements to come live with Paris and care for her during her recovery. After the successful surgery, Stella brought her mother home from the hospital, and for some reason, the garage door would not go up. Therefore, Stella went to the front door to unlock it, however; before she could ultimately open the door, Jacob opened the door from the inside—as if he had been waiting in anticipation. Stella swiftly walked back to the automobile where Paris was waiting to inform her that Jacob had returned and was inside the home. While Paris was in the hospital, Jacob had broken into the home, destroyed the remote garage door, demolished the house alarm system, and had smashed in several windows. Jacob was camped out in the living room and demanded that he would not leave the home. Paris immediately telephoned #911 to call the local law enforcement for help, and within minutes the police arrived at the residence. As fate would have it, even though they were divorced, the police would not force Jacob to leave the home since his name was also on the deed.

Paris began making her way into the home using a walker at 72-hours fresh post-operative from major surgery; she reengaged with Jacob enraged to find that he had confiscated many of her items and belongings awarded to her by the divorce court. Stella moved forward in an extremely venomous and potentially lethal environment to care for her mother that evening and 'nightmare.' Paris was instructed to faithfully to apply ice packs to her left knee around-the-clock to reduce inflammation and swelling. Thus, Stella was following the hospital instructions to maintain ice packs on her mother's left knee after surgery and knew that it is imperative postoperative to do so.

The next morning Jacob had a moving company come to the home and remove the refrigerator out of the house, along with some of his belongings only to place these items in storage. Abruptly out of nowhere, Paris was unable to have ice for the therapeutic medical treatment or a place to store food that needed refrigerating. Stella was four weeks postpartum from having her second child and lactating, but; realized that she needed to intervene as soon as possible. Therefore, Stella and Paul purchased a small refrigerator and placed it in her mother's bedroom that evening. Stella needed to carry the small fridge into the house (four weeks postpartum), as Jacob hated Paul and forbidden him to come into the home.

The plan fell through for Paris' family to come and live with her while she recovered from the second knee replacement, and the environment grew increasingly hostile. Therefore, Paris insisted that her daughter return home to care for her grandchildren and since she was still nursing a newborn at that time. Undoubtedly, this was not a medium for peaceful healing. This circumstance left Paris recovering on her own without someone physically being there to help her and barricaded in her room with a locked door. Over those next few months of the recovering process, Paris would suffer immensely from isolation, was nutritionally deprived, and needing to be locked up in her room for safety. After a week of care for herself, Paris becomes dehydrated, had inadequate nutritional intake, and was in serious poor pain control since she had allergies to analgesics or couldn't take: "painkillers, but only acetaminophen— Tylenol for pain. Paris's affliction and recovery were prolonged due to the extraordinary circumstance, noxious, and harmful environment.

Howbeit though Paris was alone, in a negative situation, things turned positive when God began to deal and speak to her spirit about the vision "to tell all" and to help someone in cases of abuse and domestic violence after her HOPE and way "to escape" was fulfilled. During this period, Paris knew that she was still in bondage but had the faith that she would someday soon experience complete freedom!

Over the next nine months following their divorce, Paris would live in a worsening demonic atmosphere and near-deadly condition recovering from major surgery. This 'test and trial' period would prove to be the cruelest psychological attacks coupled with severe emotional suffering—more than Paris ever experienced in her life. Jacob continued to refuse to leave home after their divorce and insisting that Paris take care of him. Jacob's behavior became progressively bizarre, and the daily encounters became extremely "frightening" for her. Oddly enough, over four months of these nine months, Jacob began sleeping and living inside his closet in one of the upstairs bedrooms, and began exhibiting an "unclean spirit."

Life would not be easy suffering and recovering alone postoperatively under dark demonic forces. Paris was in bed so long that she began to develop 'pressure sores' or small decubitus ulcers on the heel of her feet. Paris, CRIED OUT to God for help! This experience was like a *Job Experience* of great suffering (Job 2:7-10). Job, whose name means: "*He that weeps*," wanted God to let him die; however, through faith, he knew God promises deliverance (Job 5:17-27). Likewise, God Almighty began to help raise Paris from her bed of affliction with a plan for her healing and divine purpose. Somehow, Paris always knew "that all things were working together for her good," and she never gave up or lacked faith according to the "Word of God." The Apostle Paul encourages the believer in the book of Romans where he says:

> "And we know that all things work together for good to them that love God, to them who are the called according to his purpose" (Roman 8:28).

The fact of knowing as a believer that everything will concurrently come together in God's perfect timing for those who love God is awe-inspiring and humbling. Paris genuinely loved God with all her heart and soul, and she was a witness that He would honor His Word and any cry in the midst of a storm—creating the 'good' out of adverse conditions! God began orchestrating Paris' emotional healing over the next several months unveiling a vision of serving humanity especially when she was fully recovered. What is more, God opened up the door for her to begin journaling her vision and inspirational thoughts on paper.

Shortly after this, Paris began helping the local community and church as she continued to heal and recover. Howbeit, *initially* challenging for her still recovering physically, while piloting community projects—it became the premise for keeping her focused on things above (St. Matthew 6:33). These activities detoured Paris from the turbulent terrain conditions in her home and *initiated* a long road to emotional healing. To note here, Jesus instructs and empowers the believer when He says:

> "But seek ye first the kingdom of God, and his righteousness; and all these things shall be added unto you" (St. Matthew 6:33).

This uplift experience wouldn't be with a fight or battle for Paris. By the fall of that year, Paris' stress level began to escalate further. The milestone of her physical recovery from major surgery, rehabilitation, submerging herself in multiple projects, and attempting to cope with an ailing home environment became problematic. Paris would experience a major disappoints at this time in her prolonged recovery in losing her job, and had no income. Unfortunately, Paris missed the required time-frame in recovering physically in time to return to work. Paris considered herself to be a relatively strong individual and usually coped with high stress effectively, and recover from stressful events quickly. However, during these series of events this period was different, and in essence, Paris had suffered far too many losses. As Paris began to build herself up spiritual, her past trauma and stress began to take its toll on her.

As the author of this writing, it becomes vital to note the ramification of stress and trauma here. When humans face dangerous situations, especially when under chronic 'stress,' there are physiological ramifications on the body. Research has proven that stress over time can superimpose human's physical problems to the point of causing an alteration in health status. 'Stress' is a commonality, and everyone feels stressed from time to time. What is more, it is vital to know your stress limits to avoid more serious health effects. According to the U.S. Department of Health and Human Services National Institutes of Health and the National Institute of Mental Health (2014), and says that:

> "Stress can be defined as the brain's response to any demand. Many things can trigger this response, including change. Changes can be positive or negative, as well as real or perceived. They may be recurring, short-term, or long-term and may include things like commuting to and from school or work every day, traveling for a yearly vacation, or moving to another home. Changes can be mild and relatively harmless, such as winning a race, watching a scary movie, or riding a rollercoaster. Some changes are major, such as marriage or divorce, serious illness, or a car accident. Other changes are extreme, such as exposure to violence, and can lead to traumatic stress reactions" (U.S. Department of Health and Human Services National Institutes of Health & National Institute of Mental Health, 2014 pp. 1-2).

In general, stress not only affects the body and your overall health. Some other physical signs of stress may include: (a) immune system disorders, (b) sleep disturbances and fatigue, (c) visual disturbances, (d) muscle twitching and tremors, (e) chills or sweating, (f) aches, pains, and headaches, (g) problems with gastrointestinal system. Also, "when you face a dangerous situation, your pulse quickens, you breathe faster, your muscles tense, your brain uses more oxygen and increases activity—all functions aimed at survival." There are three types of stress: routine, acute or "sudden negative change," and traumatic stress. The difference in chronic stress is that when problems go on too long, this represents a great risk to your physical and mental overall health. While the response to all stress is relatively similar, humans may feel stress in various ways. Regardless of the different types of stress, they all can lead to serious health problems such as heart disease, hypertension, diabetes mellitus, depression, anxiety disorders, and an array of other illnesses. The major solution to stress is learning how to cope with stress by "taking practical steps to maintain your health and outlook" which can "reduce or prevent these effects:" by seeking, e.g., counseling, health care, emotional support, awareness of stress, priorities in your life, acknowledge your daily accomplishments, guidance (faith-based or professional mental health entities), physical fitness or exercise daily, relaxation on a daily basis, and coping programs (U.S. Department of Health and Human Services National Institutes of Health & National Institute of Mental Health, 2014 pp. 1-2).

Unfortunately, Paris experienced all three types of stress during this fall year and the experience became a wake-up call for her. In late November Paris was admitted to the hospital for chest pain, hypertension, and (neck, left shoulder, and arm) pains. Numerous diagnostic tests were conducted such as X-rays, chest scan, stress test, left neck, shoulder, and left arm films. Fortunately, her cardiac workup and assessment deemed to be negative. However, her doctor came into her hospital room to share that the diagnostic testing indicated significant osteoarthritis of her left shoulder, extensive degenerative disc disease, hypertension, e.g., the blood pressure reading of 154/117. The chest scan showed a left lower lobe nodule. Paris *initially* became overwhelmed with the results, but; soon after realized that the stress played a significant part in her medical finding. She was discharged a few days later from the hospital, and it was determined that she needed to make changes in her life to lower her stress level.

The circumstances dictated that Paris could no longer keep her home due to life's trauma and losses. Thus, it became the turning point of her escape. This juncture became the time to pack up and prepare herself to move out of her home; and distress. During this time, Paris made numerous attempts to find the right job for her that would not be so stressful, and that would accommodate her physical limitations. This process became emotionally challenging and devastating. Jacob continued to live upstairs and days would go by, and they would never see one other—living in the same home. Emotionally it was evident that Paris was going through the stages of grief based on her many losses. In actuality, Paris was experiencing the same five stages of grief or loss cycle that Paris had once shared with Jacob on that particular day when they met on the church parking lot in the spring nearly 30-years prior: (denial, anger, bargaining, depression, and acceptance). In looking back, Paris was suffering from an emotional heartache. Her heart was indeed broken from disappointment, grief, and a failed marriage.

Toward the end of the final nine months, there would be times that Jacob and Paris would briefly talk in passing by each other within the home. Paris' limited conversations with Jacob continued to be strange, and his dialogue was bizarre and inappropriate. Jacob's conversations were hypersexual, or he had a sexual preoccupation. One day in December, Paris' last discussion and encounter with Jacob in the home would prove to be costly, which resulted in a sexual and physical assault. Paris thought that Jacob could be once cordial, turned and abruptly assaulted her without warning. As a result, she suffers from a left parascapular strain/ or rotator cuff (RC) strain/tear from this violent attack. Paris would later continue to suffer from the injury for years after; and ongoing memory of those last nine months of vulnerability, terroir, and fear of Jacob's unpredictable behavior.

Feeling completely violated and somewhat contaminated Paris began to put the pieces together learning from this last costly encounter in this co-dependency relationships was destructive. This emotional and behavioral condition grossly affected Paris long after in the ability to have a healthy and mutually satisfying relationship. This "relationship addiction," (Mental Health America, 2014, p. 1) caused her to maintain a relationship that was mostly one-sided, emotionally destructive, and abusive on every level. Paris' relationship with Jacob affected her overall interpersonal relationship with others and was leading her down the road of agony, despair, defeat, and death. After this assault, Paris' low-self-esteem features re-surfaced stemming from her childhood and the encounter took her to a "pit of hell," state of mind if you will—of suffering through human bondage.

Moreover, Paris also learned that nothing could indeed make her feel better about life or help her go on to heal in life—was only God Almighty and His Word. While her intentions were sound, real, genuine, and seemed godly, for staying with Jacob for thirty years in attempting to remain in the marriage, desiring to be a useful 'help met," and unusually the person taking care of him—would prove to be to no avail. Instead, the union and caretaking became extensively traumatizing, compulsively ineffective; and self-defeating.

The fact is, codependency "often takes on a martyr's role and the person become a benefactor to an individual in need" Mental Health America (2014). Paris had given until she in actuality could not give anymore! Reflecting, Paris believed that she only existed as a benefactor to Jacob, and he had no regard to her emotional feelings. Existing as Jacob's wife throughout the thirty years of marriage she covered, made excuses, "pull some strings," due to Jacob's behavior, and sometimes keeping him from suffering the consequences for his unpredictable actions. This ongoing problem became critical for her because the repeated rescue attempts allowed for this needy individual to continue on a destructive course for thirty years. As a result of this unwarranted permission, Paris became more dependent on the unhealthy caretaking of the benefactor—Jacob. Over the years, as this reliance augmented, "how be it strange" as Paris the codependent person, developed a sense of reward and satisfaction from being needed. The nurturing process and being needed was a level of serving humanity was something Paris enjoyed doing. However, this satisfaction caused Paris to experience being compulsive, choiceless, helpless, hopeless, and worthless in the relationship with Jacob. The frightening piece is that Paris became unable to break away from the cycle of behavior that caused it. Therefore, she was feeling contained within a *box* of "bondage, entrapment, imprisonment, and entanglement."

Whether Paris was willing to admit it, or not, she was in an evil vice of manipulation with underlying power and control; and adverse behaviors by the perpetrator or intimate partner of violence—IPV. Some could say, howbeit that Paris called 'a victim' in this matter, but the fact of the matter is, that she was attracted to the weakness based on the substance of her background. Think about this, perhaps Paris had the tendency to: (a) have an exaggerated sense of responsibility for the actions of Jacob, (b) confuse her godly love for pity for Jacob's background, (c) do more than her share all the time, (d) become hurt when Jacob didn't recognize her efforts, and (e) had an unhealthy dependence on their relationship. Sadly, to say, Paris' codependency was rooted and engrafted during her childhood as a result of her parental experience.

For Paris, overcoming this problem would need to come from the exploration into her childhood issues and her relationship to the destructive behavior patterns that she experienced with Jacob. Heretofore, she needed to accept this fact! Then, move forward to educate herself, rediscover herself, establish new healthy relationships, and identify healthy behavioral patterns. Additionally, Paris needed to regain touch with her feelings that had been suppressed during childhood and reconstruct what happened within her family dynamics. The ability for Paris to experience the full range of emotions would heighten awareness to the fact that she was facing a negative issue of codependency, and needed to 'break the chain' of bondage and dependency.

As the author—a final point of this matter is that any caretaking behavior that allows or enables any level of abuse or intimate partner violence (IPV) to continue in any relationship is unacceptable; these negative behaviors need to be acknowledged and ceased. Once the condition of codependency becomes recognized by an individual, he or she must embrace their feelings and needs, and strive to resolve the problem. In other words, this may include learning to say "no" to others when deemed necessary, staying spiritual strong through the struggle, and establishing self-reliance. As a result, individuals who have suffered from codependency may again be able to experience "liberty, freedom, safety, equality, survival, love with trust, and a healthy lifestyle."

Finally, the end would come! On one early spring day, Paris decided to 'let go and let God' help her '*To escape*.' For her to begin her freedom, she decided to give up her home that she attempted so long to keep. The day would come on that spring day when Jacob and Paris went separate ways. In so doing, Paris went to live with Paul and Stella, and now three grandchildren; and with a plan to get back on her feet. The transitioning period would become a difficult adjustment in Paris' life, and she fell into the realm of lamenting, sackcloth (a token of grief), and of the ashes. For Paris, this phase of life seemed her mind, body, and the spirit was clothed with mourning and penitence. At times even, guilt and remorse! Thinking how could this all happen? She felt a sense of hopelessness that was beyond despair and she wanted to die. At the time, Paris could not see her way clear and appeared like there was not an end to any tunnel.

For nearly three months or more the feelings of ambivalence travailed from relief and new freedom—to anger, unhappiness, anguish, desolation, gloom, depression, and loss *hope*. Paris became entrapped with the notion that there was no way to pull herself up from this state of mind and condition. Also, there were many times she would impulsively sleep in her automobile to get away, regenerate, or think. Confronting the disappointment, created a spirit of guilt, shame, and despair after the long-term earthquake, the aftermath—or *the paradoxical union.*

KNOW, God will always send help in a time of need! Even in the grimmest circumstances the "Word of God," will pull you through. In a time of opposition: "God is our refuge and strength, a very present help in trouble" (Psalms 46:1). The turning point would come for Paris when she would meet two elders and godly friends who continued to touch bases with her off and on. Out of nowhere, a devout couple who had been married for 35 years were elders of the church were Paris attended, faithfully began calling, praying, intervening, counseling and ministering to Paris from afar who had recently moved from New York to Miami for retirement. These elders demonstrated God's Agape love and compassion that became a sheer turning-point in Paris' recovery process. True advocates of faith, the irony with this period was these elder friends had moved out of state, however; they still had 30 days before the sale of their home. At that time, their home was not being used, and they offered their place 'for recovery' until their closing. Paris had expressed to these elder friends that she needed time away to regenerate and think—and believed this opportunity was God sent!

The elders immediately booked a flight to New York on the next day to open up their home for Paris and gave her the keys. On that same day, Paris began staying at their home; which became a haven. From this act of kindness, was where her life started to turn around for her healing. Paris loved the water and beach, and the sound of 'the waters' always relaxed and calmed her. When she sat and gazed looking out the patio window of her elder friend's home, she noted a beautiful blue and peaceful lake of water. Daily for long hours Paris sat and watched the water spring up from the lake. One day she asked God two questions: "How?" and "How, does one bounce back from so many losses and suffering?" God's response was "write!" He instructed Paris to 'journal,' and she began to write down what she had lost during the thirty years of marriage to Jacob. Upon writing these losses and devastating events, Paris realized that each loss had co-occurred. After Paris examined the list of losses, she counted numerous different painful, pressures, and sufferings. These vital losses expressed were both permanent and temporary; some were vital, and some were not. These losses included: her husband, companionship, marriage, health, employment, livelihood, healthcare/insurance, home, community, positive self-esteem due to abuse, domestic violence and codependency, family/a disconnect causing isolation, close relationship and fellowship, church membership and support, church position, personal possessions, self-respect, self-confidence, peace of mind—suffering from post-traumatic stress disorder/ depression/guilt, personal integrity, honor replace by shame and embarrassment, satisfactions replaced by disappointment and setbacks, financial creditability, stability, life balance, control, love/affection/approval, the effectiveness of ministerial witness, the effectiveness of professional creditability, and businesses. One of the most important things that she learned from this 'journaling' was that: "only what I do for Jesus Christ will last," and not one of these things are more important than her relationship with God and the salvation he afforded her to partake.

Experiencing the freedom and peace at this residence became priceless. Paris used this time to regroup, pray, meditate on the "Word of God," and concretely hear from God. At this peaceful place, was where God spoke and reminded Paris of the vision, He gave her when she was once entrapped: *the tell-all* message. God softly and sweetly instructed her to heal, and to begin ministering to His hurting people; and that her pain and experience was not in vain. God's communication, direction, guidance, and answers became vividly clear to her during those 30-days; and the vision was birthed within her spirit. During this time Paris developed the unction to 'journal' which helped her to gain strength and peace. Over the month God gave Paris precise details of His premise for serving others spiritually. Paris began renewing and cultivating her Christian faith and walk and regain strength to rise in boldness. This act of love and kindness, by her two elder friends, was critical and profoundly pivotal in her life. Paris expressed deep appreciation for their kindness, as she picked up the pieces in her life to start—*a new*. Paris felt revived on the 30th day of her shut-in and from hearing so distinctly from God. Over time, Paris grew to cherish and value the relationship with her two friends and counting them as her family. She was forever grateful to these two yielding vessels, and marvel at the love and kindness that they showed her in time of need.

That mid-summer the end of stay and the closing of her friend's home would take place. Paris returned to Paul and Stella's house to further re-define herself. She began following the instructions that God had given her during those priceless 30-days of consecrations and spiritual shut-in. Over the next four months, Paris began to move forward in her life, was motivated by her call, purpose, and destiny in life. Paris was slowly starting to feel further renewed to revisit how important her call and ministry was. Overall, Paris desired to fulfill this call and to devote her life entirely to God. As well, she began exploring employment opportunities to regain financial stability and to supporting herself.

By the early winter, Paris accepted a position that required ongoing travel. This new position was along the lines of what she was doing before—in helping and serving other hurting people. While working in this consultation field, Paris begins experiencing what would be called the "cries of vulnerability" as expressed in her 'personal journaling.' Paris could relate to the people that she was helping and came to realize that: "Sometimes when you've been through the *valley* you see things differently, and your awareness, discernment, gifts, will sharpen. Through the human press experience, your ministry will be enhanced and refined by living for God, and the advancement and upbuilding of God's Kingdom." The fact was, as she looked around her work surrounding, the atmosphere, and the world—her life seemed and felt different after this *valley* experience. This traveling position "experience" reaffirmed the call bestowed upon her life in the summer of when God called her to the healing ministry, and when God placed into her spirit-man to begin ministering to the hurting, sick and afflicted.

By the New Year, toward the end of one of her consultation travels she felt that life was moving forward in the realm of independence, autonomy, productivity, and financial stability once again. At this point in her life, Paris was fully recovered from both knee surgeries and was progressing toward recovery from grief and losses. By February, Paris would experience an unexpected challenge; and this new-found freedom would take a severe detour back to the *valley*, and a place Paris never had accounted. While enjoying the tropical surroundings, palm trees, and warm weather Paris received a call from Stella that was shattering. At the time, Stella did not realize the effect this information would have upon her mother and made a decision to tell her. Stella informed Paris that Jacob' infidelity was fact; and affirmed that Jacob indeed had married another woman while they were still married—during his last travel to Australia. One would likely to image or wonder: "Why should this news or revelation devastate Paris?" or "Why would Paris feel such pain?" On the flip side or in contrast: Paris would ask: "What type of person does this?" or "Is there any regard to human feelings or respect as it relates to a marital union?" Although Jacob's and Paris' marital relationship was deteriorating, headed toward divorce, and going their separate ways was inevitable—her thoughts were: "Who does this type of thing before the eyes of God?"

For Paris' caring heart and spirit, this was staggering and demonstrated the ultimate act of betrayal by Jacob. Paris' further response and further questions were: "When you've given your all-in-all to someone, and live under the same roof with someone for thirty years, how can that person disregard the pain that such action could cause to another?" In actuality, this was the 'dagger in the heart' and the 'stab in the back' for Paris. The pain was too high for her to endure when the truth was confirmed, even though she had been already informed about the act of bigamy toward the end of their marriage. There was still a part of Paris, that *hoped* this devious action wasn't real at all. Nevertheless, the act of Bigamy was a severe crime, and against the law of domestic relations. The willful contracting of a second marriage when the contracting party knows that the *first* union is still subsisting; or it is the state of a man who has two wives, or of a woman who has two husbands living at the same time.

After learning of this evil, for about a week, Paris attempted to push through the surmountable pain. However, the pain was too much to bear. Thus, by mid-February she returned home from her travels to New York with the feeling like a "scab had been pulled off an old deep wound." Her grief process took a significant set-back! Grief began all over again, and she wanted to give up. Paris asked God again, to "take her" because the pain was too deep to carry. The feelings of lamenting, sackcloth, and of the ashes returned. For nearly eight weeks Paris stayed in a dark room with the resurfaced feelings severe major depression. Paris prayed and cried out to God to help her, all while knowing that He again was the only one who could. Finally, Paris heard a still soft voice say: "WRITE!" Paris held on to the fact, knowledge, and prior experience that she served an Almighty God, He would pull her through, and that He is:

- Omnipotent: God is all-powerful (invincible, supreme)
- Omnipresent: God is in all places (equally present at the same time, ubiquitous, all-pervading, and universal)
- Omniscient: God knows all things (all-knowing, knows everything)
- Eternal: God is timeless

God's voice again raised her up! Paris began to move forward in writing and 'journaling' that indeed became therapeutic, and a blessing from God that empowered her. Paris would evolve from this state and completely recovered from her grief related to Jacob in itself. Paris STOPPED, looking to Jacob *or* man in what he could *or* could never do. Instead, Paris moved FORWARD, listening and seeking God, experiencing joy unspeakable that is full of glory as expressed in I Peter 1:7-9:

> "That the trial of your faith, being much more precious than of gold that perisheth, though it be tried with fire, might be found unto praise and honour and glory at the appearing of Jesus Christ: Whom having not seen, ye love; in whom, though now ye see him not, yet believing, ye rejoice with joy unspeakable and full of glory: Receiving the end of your faith, even the salvation of your souls."

The Life Lesson for PARIS HOPE: Always remember that through any human *valley or press*, there is a cost for the anointing power, and there is a process for the divine purpose in life. When you emerge from the *valley or press*, you can rise to the *top*, and nothing will *stop* anyone from success, triumph, opportunities, and power that God has destined for your life. NEVER give up. Faulty emotions such, as, e.g., suicide ideations, helplessness, hopelessness, and worthlessness, etc., are all temporary and will pass away. However, permanent self-harm, successful suicides, or destroying another is permanent. Always hold out, and hold on to God's unchanging hands. After this, Paris never stopped writing and 'journaling' for God! She would go on to continue to serve and help hurting people. Daily she strived to give God His glory and in experiencing His love, joy, and peace that He brings in to her life.

TABOO: *"But, I must tell all!"*–There are many instances and subject matters that church folk will not talk about or will struggle to keep issues to themselves, and eventually acquiring various disease processes superimposed by the elements of distress. But this story must be told for Paris to be set entirely free to help some**ONE** '*to escape*' out of entrapped anguish!

The term "taboo" must be analyzed. Taboo, is a noun that depicts "a social or religious custom prohibiting or forbidding discussion of a particular practice or forbidding association with a particular person, place, or thing." In the church, "being taboo" may constitute behaviors of prohibition, proscription, veto, interdiction, and so much more—to keep things undercover. Some elements of being taboo, usually meaning "offensive or unmentionable," can be prohibited or restricted by social custom and traditional religious societies that can paralyze oneself for life! Subject matters such as sex, abuse, adultery, infidelity, domestic violence, etc. are taboo topics that are kept hushed sometimes to maintain status and entitlements. However, in the end, if these matters are placed under prohibition—the actions will eventually cause destruction. Heretofore, sometimes the *truth* must be expressed for survival! The *truth* must be divulged for deliverance! The *truth* must be said for healing, and HOPE!

Heretofore, there must be a reiteration here of the purpose of this writing. This message is for those who are experiencing or who have experienced the depth of abuse, domestic violence, intimate partner violence, marital bondages or interrelationship strongholds, betrayal, and infidelity when seemly contradictory. This book of a "must tell all," has been written as a deliverance and healing aid for individuals with a distinct need to find answers or a godly *"way to escape*, that ye may be able to bear it"* (I Corinthians 10:13, KJV); in the context of marital ungodly entanglement—but whereby will receive assistance with reversing pain and disappointment to gain hope, strength, encouragement, liberty, freedom, safety, equality, survival, and joy— relevant to taboo topic matters.

The events that Paris shared regarding her life were only the 'tip of the iceberg' in her realm of sufferings and became virtually impossible to express her entire story of grief. What Paris shared regarding her life, she prays some**ONE** will be blessing or some**ONE** will find a way *'to escape'* devices of entanglement.

The telling of the story may be perceived as "too neat, I know!" Allow me to be candid, during the human ***valley and press*** process regarding Paris' second marriage she had "thoughts" of wanting to die; and experienced suicide ideations and homicide ideations. Through it all Paris experienced what it felt like to have a sense of betrayal, hopelessness, helplessness, and worthlessness, wanting to die and not live, and to feel how the Apostle Paul felt when he stated in Scripture: *"pressed above measure that I despaired even life."* Struggling with depression and thoughts of suicide is a serious mental health issue and should never be taken lightly.

Nevertheless, due to her godly nature, Paris could *NEVER* do such a thing. She felt that when you're down in life or feeling depressed the enemy will bring anything, and everything, including the kitchen-sink to destroy you. In growing up in Christianity, Paris knew the way of walking holy in Christ Jesus. She could not commit these acts because of the "Word of God" within her heart. The Holy Commandments or "Law of God" that was present during the times of abuse and domestic violence experience, was still written: within her heart, her mind, her spirit, thus, she was able to fulfill all righteousness and reframe from committing such sin. In all, Paris knew that she could not kill anyone; steal from anyone, etc., because the law of love would not allow! These biblical principles become important to note here enforcing that, the "Word of God," will lead and guide the believer into *all* truth, justice, and righteousness regardless of the circumstance. Life is all about choices!

Paris' desires to help some**ONE**! She knew that it was God and her faith that brought her through the negative state of mind, and the only way that she overcame this painful condition was through:

- Staying rooted and grounded in the "Word of God."
- Maintaining a robust or stable prayer life and relationship with God.
- Trusting and depending on God for every need.
- Understanding and realizing that the feelings of depression and suicide ideations are always temporary, however acting upon these feelings and successfully committing suicide is permanent.
- Realizing that she was a survivor and delivered by the grace of God.

For Paris, there was never an intent or plan to commit such an act of self-harm, because of her faith and relationship with God. In her experience, Paris became a broken vessel. She became the clay in God's hand, and He has made—and continues to make her over again. Additionally, Paris did not want to be selfish in placing such a burden upon her family and friends in ending her life. Instead, she sincerely thanked God for keeping her through all heartache, pain, and sufferings. In the end, she believed that she had so much to look forward to in the future and, and remained focused on being a vessel of God fit for the master's use. Paris decided to stay genuinely committed to helping those who have these same feelings by caring for others hurting, experiencing depression, or suicide ideations, etc. have a distinct understanding, compassion, and empathy in abusive situations.

PARIS HOPE is a symbol and fictitious character in this novel. The symbol represents the 'victim' of a serious societal issue of the endemic matter of abuse, domestic violence is otherwise known as intimate violence partner (IVP)—presented in a pathetic sense. Some problematic relationships resemble toxic environments that are like a poisonous venom medium or pus formation. In using an analogy and in medical terms, for instance— problematic infectious wounds or abscesses filled with pus. The condition will eventually come to a head. In this case, the medical decision and intervention may be to perform, a procedure called "incision and drain" or "I & D" to facilitate a healing process—coupled with antibiotic therapy to cure the infection. Likewise, when there is a poisonous, toxin, malice relationship, or grown negative circumstances—a problem that may need to be a "cut to heal." There may need to be a draining or purging process due to ongoing evil, hatred, or bitterness in the relationship, etc. Thus, curing the relationship affliction. Paris eventually decided to "cut and heal," stand and proclaimed that being in an emotionally destructive relationship can become a life-crisis event of no return. Thus, concluding that staying in a relationship too long is critical when there is nothing produced but endless destruction. Also, it becomes vital to note, that one does not always know what God is keeping you from or how He is supernaturally protecting. Therefore, it becomes crucial to listen to the voice of God, and be guided by His word.

In Paris' case and after the divorce—over time she learned many unexpected outcomes and involvements regarding Jacob that were difficult to accept. Parish struggled, and eventually, she needed to accept that Jacob committed a crime of bigamy. Also, that Jacob's was beginning to displayed delusional thought processes of grandiosity, e.g., (verbalizing that he was divine and developed strange followings). He established an inner circle, demonstrating features similar to a cult leader, and con artist.

Another vital point after the divorce—with time Paris learned many demonstrated patterns by "church folks" or specific people who call themselves Christian may view the divorcee differently or with ill-treat those who have undergone a divorce process. Therefore, for Paris, the feelings of rejection from the church also created a devasting impact on her view of the church as a whole; and causing bitterness. None the less, she eventually worked through the feelings of rejection, bitterness, and pain toward the church, as she knew this was eating away at her; and was unhealthy. By her strong faith, she knew this also would pass, and that God would assist her through these feeling moving toward victory.

In looking back, Parish realizes that divorcing and dissociating herself from this near fatal situation was the best decision that she ever made. However, she also realized *the paradoxical union* was not without repercussions for staying in an adverse relationship too long. As a result, Paris remained a 'work in progress' needing ongoing counseling, prayer, and spiritual connection with God to rebuild her life over again. After the divorce, she continued to suffer from Post-Traumatic Stress Disorder–PTSD and continued to experience frequent nightmares and flashbacks.

After the sexual assault by Jacob due to her vulnerable and unsafe condition, Paris often struggled to push past the long-term traumatic event out of her mind. The experience vastly affected her to the point when she would take a shower; she was plagued with never feeling clean—just remembering the sexual assault and physical effect. For the most part, Paris would wash over and over sometimes 2-3 times in the shower process; wanting to feel clean and rid herself of that feeling of assault. She felt that all of these scenarios could be compared and contrasted to a "bad scar" that won't heal. However, Paris continued to look to God for her complete healing, health, wholeness, wellness, and deliverance all in all.

Overtime for Paris, and in looking back on her traumatic sexual attack in a setting saturated in her vulnerability—she would grow to understand the evolving national social movements against sexual harassment and sexual assault. After her sexual assault encounter, she took a stance with and joined in with this movement to support survivors and end sexual violence. Paris was able to gain additional strength in her healing process and realized that she was not alone. Paris would go on to show great knowledge or erudite these types of movements: Parish made a stance to "tell all" about her experience believing that sharing the experience one day would help someone in such circumstance.

No matter what transpired in Paris' relationship with Jacob—she fully understood his enter chambers of unresolved pains, brokenness, woundedness from "parental acceptance-rejection" and events throughout his life. Paris began to assert in action and her mind, that she will always love and cherish the years that she experienced in doing the work of the ministry, especially as once the "Elect Lady," the God-given role that she so enjoyed. Paris reconciled herself to the fact and belief that when God used them to do "greater works" over the 30 years that it was not in vain or ineffective. Paris knew that she did all in serving others as unto the LORD!

JACOB is a symbol and fictitious character in this novel. The symbol represents the *'perpetrator'* of a serious societal issue of the endemic matter of abuse, domestic violence is otherwise known as intimate violence partner (IVP)—also presented in a pathetic sense. The hope would be that the *offender* will find help, effective intervention, *hope*, restoration for the soul. Also, noting a special prayer for all 'JACOBs of the world' would experience health and wholeness (mind, body, spirit) as well in Jesus' Name!

"Against All Odds"

"There hath no temptation taken you but such as is common to man: but God
is faithful, who will not suffer you to be tempted above that ye are able; but will
with the temptation also make a way *to escape*, that ye may be able to bear it."
(I Corinthians 10:13)

Sometimes when a person is going through a physical, emotional, or spiritual battle, he or she may feel alone, and the depth of the suffering seems surmountable. However, when he or she learns that it is a common issue or an event that has already happened to another who survived—ideally that uncomfortable experienced seems bearable and endurable.

In the first letter to the Corinthians, was written by Apostle Paul during the three-year ministry at Ephesus (Acts 20:31) on his third missionary journey (Acts 18:23—21:16) to Corinth, an ancient city in Greece, and a most prominent Greek metropolis of Paul's time. He is teaching the believer or church about problems and solutions as he penned this epistle. The purpose of this writing was to reprove and correct the severe problems in the Corinthian church which had reported to him. These problems were serious issues and disorders including sin. Another purpose of this message was to provide counsel and instructions on a variety of questions including doctrinal matters, personal and corporate conduct, and purity. In this passage of Scripture, I Corinthians 10: 13, and core verse for this book The Paradoxical Union the Apostle Paul is providing a profound precept that *'God is Faithful.'* Here he is stating that a professing believer may not justify his or her infirmity, circumstances, problems, issues or perhaps sins by merely being human or not perfect. At the same time, Paul assures the believer or Corinthians in this text that no true believer need fall from grace and mercy of God. Instead, Paul affirms with them that God provides His children with sufficient grace, mercy, to overcome every temptation along with resisting sin as well.

As the author of this short story and to further interject here, this key Scripture presented in this novel (I Corinthians 10:13) can be compared to one favorite song written by Thomas O. Chisholm & William M. Runyan entitled: "*Great is Thy Faithfulness,*" which represents a special message of God's Faithful Expression as (a.) no test will come to a believer's path, that has not already been corporately experienced by humanity or which the almighty God will not be committed to bringing you through, (b.) God will not allow a believer to undergo or become tested beyond any level that he or she can handle, or have been created to withstand, and (c.) but, while in the test or trial, additionally will force, cause, or create a route, method, pathway *TO* break away from or flee. As a result of the supernatural escapism or exodus the believer, he or she; will be able to withstand. To assert, God or the Holy Spirit will not allow us to be tempted above that which we can bear. Instead, God will with every temptation provide a way by which we can endure the temptation, and overcome any problem, or issue including sin.

Also, I will provide a message of "*Faith & Prayer*" to comfort you during a dark or darkest hour, or moment of pain, pressure, suffering, and distress (See Appendix B).

In combination, with the grace, mercy, and Agape love of God produces sufficient power for the believer's well-being through (a.) the blood of Jesus Christ, (b.) the "Word of God," (c.) the indwelling power of the Holy Ghost/Spirit, (d.) the divine intercession of Jesus Christ—that creates spiritual empowerment for the believer's health and wholeness. This spiritual empowerment helps sustain the believer against adverse conditions, diabolical devices, chicanery, warfare, spiritual forces of wickedness, or perpetrator that comes against the believer or church. God's "divine power hath given unto us all things that pertain unto life and godliness" (II Peter 1:3, KJV). Through the deliverance and salvation process provided by the power of God and His faithfulness:

> "That ye might walk worthy of the Lord unto all pleasing, being fruitful in every good work, and increasing in the knowledge of God; Strengthened with all might, according to is glorious power, unto all patience and longsuffering with joyfulness; Giving thanks unto the Father, which hath made us meet to be partakers of the inheritance of the saith in light: Who hath delivered us from the power of darkness, and hath translated us into the kingdom of his dear son: In whom we have redemption through his blood, even the forgiveness of sins:" (Colossians 1:10-14, KJV).

We are also empowered to conquer temptation in the wilderness, bondage, entrapment, imprisonment, etc., just as Jesus did when He was led up to the Spirit into the wilderness to be tempted of the devil according to

St. Matthew 4:1. We can also "*bear*" every temptation and "*escape*" if we sincerely desire to and depend upon the faithfulness and power of God.

Therefore, without controversy, God brings good tidings of salvation and deliverance to the godly. Through faith, at the end of your pain, pressures, sufferings, and distresses God will: restore your joy, clothe you with the "garments of salvation," and cover you with the "robe of righteousness" that He might be glorified, and rich praises spring forth.

In this narrative, the character PARIS HOPE did not need to look far to understand that others may be suffering far more than what she had in her life. She did not minimize another individual's level of pain or distress. However, she had endured intense levels of pain, pressures, sufferings, and distresses throughout her life that had been the premise and "sealed picture frame," that thrust her to recognize her call, purpose, and destiny to serve humanity. Paris did not make any excuses that she was simply human, imperfect, or that she was a "born-again" believer continuing in her dilemma, sin circumstance in word, thought, and deed. Instead, Paris counted these various levels of struggles as gifts from God that encompassed who she became. She learned and realized that the beauty of her salvation and deliverance were divinely constructed from ashes. In essence, Paris had come to know that the 'spawned oil of joy' comes from the cusps of any life or human press and was the direct result of her mourning. In the end, the garment of praise sprung forth from her spirit of heaviness, and her branches of righteousness were cultivated from her godliness.

Ashes have symbolic meaning as it related to the Holy Scriptures. The term ashes in the Greek translation is *SPODOS* and is associated with sackcloth, as a token of grief, of the ashes resulting from animal sacrifices, or metaphorically of someone who describes himself or herself as dust and ashes (Genesis 18:27). Historically, the ashes on the altar of burnt offering were removed each morning by a priest. The priest accomplished this by wearing his official garment and was carried by him attired in his unofficial dress. The priest carried the ashes to a clean place outside the camp according to Leviticus 6:10-11. One example of the use of ashes was with the red heifer sacrifice that illustrates a ceremonial picture of purification (Hebrews 9:13). Other expressions for ashes were destruction (Ezekiel 27:30; 28:18; II Peter 2:6); symbolic of grief and mourning (Esther 4:1; 3; Job 2:8; 42:6; Isaiah 58:5; 61:3; Jeremiah 6:26; Jonah 3:6; St. Matthew 11:21 & St. Luke 10:13); and for the righteous, the wicked are said to be "ashes under the soles of your feet," (Malachi 4:3). For Paris, "*The Paradoxical Union*," became that product of ashes resulting from ruins, remains, residue or ash from an intense fire, yet, the beauty is that the spiritual empowerment was built upon its elements. In the biblical times, this ceremonial tradition was the rationale for the sacred priest offering by the process of carrying the aches to a "*clean place*" to cultivate its beauty and for purification.

In the end, PARIS HOPE was able to rise solely with the divine help of God. She found the strength to succumb and give way to the will of God. She made a stance not to look back on her past ashes, nor did she want to exchange the beauty for what she had experienced in correlation with her renewed relationship with

God Almighty. In essence, her life was now built on burned ashes of deliverance and the anointing power in leadership. The experience of her life relationships had been symbolic as in 'a death, and funeral of burnt sacrifice, that was turned into aches of grief and mourning.' The fire from Zion (heaven) was taken away by the "High Priest" or heaven "shall take away the ashes" (Exodus 27:3; Numbers 4:13). Heretofore, she was now on a spiritual mission to fulfill her call, purpose, destiny in serving others—and to do the perfect will of God in life. After her divine escape, Paris moved on in life to exclaim her call:

> "THE SPIRIT of the Lord God is upon me; because the LORD hath anointed me to preach good tidings unto the meek; he hath sent me to bind up the brokenhearted, to proclaim liberty to the captives, and the opening of the prison to them that are bound; To proclaim the acceptable year of the LORD, and the day of vengeance (Jesus' second coming) of our God; to comfort all that mourn; To appoint unto them that mourn in Zion, to give unto them beauty for ashes, the oil of joy for mourning, the garment of praise for the spirit of heaviness; that they might be called trees of righteousness, the planting of the LORD that he might be glorified" (Isaiah 61:1-3).

In this Scriptural passage Isaiah 61:1-11 resides a precise prophetic vision of a glorious future for Zion's prosperity and peace spoken by the author Isaiah. When Jesus began His earthly ministry, he quoted these verses and applied them to Himself in St. Luke 4:18-19 demonstrating fulfillment of His ministry. Jesus was anointed by the Holy Spirit to preach, heal, break the bonds of evil, open the spiritual eyes of the lost, etc. Paris realized as the 'elect lady' and for her 'namesake' that the same expectation of fulfillment was still placed upon her as a type of the "church" or the "true church" or even those who sincerely answer to the call of ministry. Paris did not allow *the paradoxical union* to prevent her from responding to that call, purpose, and destiny.

PARIS HOPE concluded that there *is* a price for the anointing power, and there *is* a process for the divine purpose to get there. Still, through Paris' life experience she was fully aware that the 'Spirit of God' was upon her, and the anointing rests upon her life that was built upon sackcloth and ashes (repentance and humility before God), orchestrated through her sufferings process to fulfill the higher call to ministry. In retrospect, Paris asserted that in her sufferings spiritually she: (a.) exercised faith throughout *the escape process*, and relied upon the "Word of God." She learned since she was rooted and grounded in God's word, she was able to withstand. (b.) determined that without prior spiritual stability, could have led to heightened negative adversity, lead to faltering faith, in sinning; and even her death. (c.) sought to sound genuine Biblical counsel during *the escape process* and difficult periods, (d.) sought to eradicate faulty thinking in exchange for positive thought processes, and (e.) stay reminded that ultimately that only "God" and "time" could ultimately complete the healing process after experiencing *the escape process*. Through *the escape process*, she learned that healing comes from the "inside-out" and from "the heart" which is manifested by physical demeanor (e.g., expressions of joy, peace, happiness, etc.). Paris eventually learned how to *smile* again, by asking God to heal her facial nerves and neurological components that generate a beautiful smile and joy. Finally, in the end, God helped her to redefine who she was again, to learn what true happiness was, to learn what true love was; and how to reset her life goals after *the escape process.*

Though God's help and healing process, Paris learned to push through her past pain and sad memories while growing up and to cherish meaningful relationships in the future. What is more, she learned how to enjoy the family components, and what God intended family to be. After her divorce, Paris' daughter Stella contributed greatly in her healing process and breaking the chains of bondage, the generational curses, and nuisance of her memories of alcoholism associated with holidays. Stella fully celebrated most holidays, consistently teaching and instilling moral principles in her grandchildren's lives. Stella was vastly creative, gifted, and had a unique talent during holidays that brought Paris much joy and happiness to their family as a unit. Each year Stella began to decorate numerous Christmas trees having unique and pleasurable themes for her family placing them throughout their home, and created Christmas trees to give to the less fortunate to enjoy (e.g., nursing homes and the elderly). Holiday celebrations became one of the ways that Stella moved on in serving humanity and community. Due to this ongoing mindset and demonstration of love by Stella, created a way for Paris to gain a paradigm shift in her thinking. This act of love and kindness facilitated a move for Paris to heal and immensely experience memorable holidays with her family.

Paris began reflecting and realized that she and Lamont, (Stella's biological father) were successful in their parenting with Stella. Paris was at awe and amazement about who Stella had become, and her ability to also survived such intense adversity. Paris firmly believed that she did something powerful in raising Stella, and she made her so proud. *Against all the odds*, Stella moves on to become a beautiful, intellectual, talented, creative, gifted, and successful woman of God reflecting great parenting; despite any past turmoil or paradoxical union. Stella would rise to be the leading lady in her life story. She went on fulfilling multiple roles as a daughter, wife, mother of three children, family member, friend, and public figure that made her family proud. Stella went on to college to earn a bachelor's, master's, and Ph.D. from a prominent university in New York. She became gifted in journalism and broadcasting becoming a prominent news anchorwoman for a cable network. Also, Stella went on to become a politician, received individual political honors in Washington DC, was a community icon, and an astute public figure in leadership. Eventually, Stella also went on to become a renowned public speaker, model, singer, minister, and entrepreneur. Through her platform as a politician she develops a fantastic and distinct foundational mission in enriching young women promoting educational scholarships, elegance, and success; and became an advocate for women suffering from domestic violence or intimate partner violence (IPV).

For Paris, the sharing in Stella's accomplishments, mission, and platform became such a joy to witness.

Both Paris and Stella grow on to believe that all they'd been through was not in vain, but; worth it all! What is more, Stella's overall accomplishments helped caused Paris to heal, watching her only daughter grow and develop as a woman. Paris moved on to enjoy watching Stella discover her gifts, talents, creativity, dreams and grow into her ministry/spiritual calling. Afterward, Paris often thought about if something would have seriously happened to Stella or if she had perished when Jacob deliberately locked in the basement for such an extended time—how costly this would have been. Paris realized that she could have been denied the chance of watching Stella grow up to be such a beautiful and classy lady she'd become. Instead, the light that's continues to shine since her birth remained very much alive! Paris richly honored her daughter Stella and growing closer together again as mother and daughter. Paris was so proud of her daughter's life, moral/ethical principles, strong positive outlook on life, serving others, possessing an intriguing platform, and thanking God daily for creating within Stella the ability to withstand the past evil.

Paris professed, after her escape experiences that she had the duty to pray for all leadership. Also, she was charged by God to always intercede in prayer for every nation leader including but not limited to the president, political leaders, and especially Christian leaders. God placed within Paris this burden and charged to daily uphold these leaders in prayer in HOPES that each will lead by positive influence, and "do the right thing!" within the context of their leadership. What a high call and responsibility upon Paris!

The call to leadership is critical and serious occupation, especially a call to Christian leadership or a bishop—which should never include abuse to anyone. The Christian Leadership/of a Bishop is most critical. According to Holy Scripture the office of a bishop employs "good work, workmanship of souls, servanthood of Jesus Christ and so much more according to (I Timothy 3:1-7; I Timothy 5:18-20; I Peter 2:25; Philippians 1:1; Titus 1:5-7 KJV; Acts 20:28). To expound on this matter can be sharply described in I Timothy 3:1:7 where it says:

> "This is a true saying, If a man desire the office of a bishop, he desireth a good work. A *bishop* then must be blameless, the husband of one wife, vigilant, sober, of good behaviour, given to hospitality, apt to teach; Not given to wine, no striker, not greedy of filthy lucre, but patient, not a brawler, not covetous; One that ruleth well his own house, having his children in subjection with all gravity; For if a man know not how to rule his own house, how shall he take care of the church of God? Not a novice, lest being lifted up with pride he fall into the condemnation of the devil. Moreover he must have a good report of them which are without; lest he fall into reproach and the snare of the devil."

What a contrast to this short story, especially in regards to this symbol PARIS HOPE, the elect lady, and type of church who was treated in the complete opposite. In fact, somewhat contradictory and paradoxical in comparison. Paris, the elect lady, and church symbol was abused, neglected, and brutally wounded through cruel and ruthless behavior coupled with a severe issue of domestic violence.

As author of this writing, the vital point that I wish to convey in this novel is that regardless of Paris' experience, despite what the enemy attempted to do, and intent in the diabolic assignment created by the devil—after her divine escape she went on in her life to reap glorious benefits after *the escape process*. Paris humbly embraced the experience as a lesson learned by worshiping and thanking God for the *valley experience* of her life; and allowing the CRUSHING to create her betterment. For instance, the crushing of the olive produces oil, which is symbolic of the "anointing" spiritually. The 'anointing always requires a crushing' and what is produced is the oil of divine works! Thus, through this process of suffering it becomes a privilege to suffer for the sake of the gospel of Christ and salvation (Philippians 1:27-30). Today, God is CRUSHING His people to walk in the fullness of life and to live life more abundantly. The CRUSHING of the olive from the *press* is what produces the precious pure oil [anointing power], herbs [healing of brokenness], and riches of divine fragrance and sacrifices [honor, praise, worship, and sweet smelling savor/savour] before the Lord according to the 'Word of God (e. g., Genesis 8:21; Exodus 29:18, 25, 41; Leviticus 1:9; Numbers 15:3, Ezra 6:10; Song of Solomon 1:3; Ezekiel 16:19; II Corinthians 2:14-16; and Ephesians 5:2).

One Biblical example was Epaphroditus (Philippians 2:25). He demonstrated godly character in his dedication to serving as brethren of high appreciation, as a companion in the 'labour' of the gospel or "fellow worker," "fellow soldier," and as a messenger of the church of Philippi. He ministers to the Apostle Paul during his imprisonment at Rome, and he was entrusted with their contributions for Paul's support. While Epaphroditus was in Rome, he contracted a dangerous illness brought on by his ministering to the apostle (2:27-30). The Apostle Paul says:

> "But I have all, and abound: I am full, having received of Epaphroditus the things which were sent from you, an odour of a sweet smell, a sacrifice acceptable, wellpleasing to God. But my God shall supply all your need according to his riches in glory by Christ Jesus" (Philippians 4:18-19).

Apostle Paul knew the source of his blessing during his *valley* situations, and understood the high calling of God in leadership upon him (Philippians 3:12-16), and realized the importance in glorifying God.

> "Brethren, I count not myself to have apprehended: *but this one thing I do*, forgetting those things which are behind, and reaching forth unto those things which are before, I **PRESS** toward the mark for the prize of the high calling of God in Christ Jesus. Let us therefore, as many as be perfect, be thus minded: and if in any thing ye be otherwise minded, God shall

reveal even this unto you. Nevertheless, whereto we have already attained, let us walk by the same rule, let us mind the same thing" (Philippians 3:13-15).

"But this one thing I do,"—Paris saw herself as a runner in a spiritual race according to Hebrews 12:1, exerting all her strength and pressing on with intense concentration, not to fall short of the goal that Jesus Christ has set for her life—regardless of the negative things she experienced. Paris knew her relationship with Christ, the salvation He affords, and His resurrection from the dead ensures victory. She was cognizant of God's grace and mercy and centered her life around the determination to **press** on in life, and one day will get to heaven to see Jesus Christ face-to-face (II Timothy 4:8; Revelation 2:10, 22:4). This mindset became the ultimate rationale for Paris to move forward in life after her ***divine escape***.

Possessing such a determination is essential for all of us! Adversity is inevitable, and throughout our lives, there are all kinds of distractions, temptations, and sufferings (e.g., worldly cares, wealth, and evil desires, etc.), that daily threatening to "choke-off" our eternal blessing and our commitment to the Lord Jesus Christ. Instead, in contrast, the need to becomes a release, let go, and forgive, by "forgetting those things which are behind," and run the race set before us associated with our ordained call, purpose, and destiny.

Always remember at the end of *the escape process…* God will raise you to the **T.O.P.** and nothing can **S.T.O.P.** him or her to experience (success, triumph, opportunities, power)! In other words, God will open doors that—no man can close and will close doors that— no man can open! After *the escape process*, Paris became eternally grateful to God that He empowered her to 'journal' which became therapy and her story.

In the end, Paris was profoundly honored and humble before God in counting her worthy to serve Him in the capacity of a "tell all story" with a vision of helping others to be free. Paris learned that it takes integrity, morality, and discipline to fulfill a dream and vision. She made a stance never to allow her circumstances to interfere with the HOPES and vision that God had placed in her heart. She sincerely believed that what God told her about the future would come to pass. Indeed, the vision and her dreams came to past:

> "For the vision is yet for an appointed time, but at the end it shall speak, and not lie: though it tarry, wait for it; because it will surely come, it will not tarry. Behold, his soul which is lifted up is not upright in him: but the just shall live by his faith" (Habakkuk 2:3-4).

Journaling and telling her story became a dream that demanded patience, integrity, and leadership. Most of all, Paris prayed that telling her story would help someone to cope, heal, recover, or become delivered from the pain and memories caused by abuse, domestic violence or intimate partner violence—IPV. What empowered her was the vision and mission in helping others or humanity with their dreams as well:

"Knowing that whatsoever good thing any man doeth, the same shall he receive of the LORD, whether he be bond or free" (Ephesians 6:8).

Most important, God replaced beauty for ashes, created restoration, and happiness in Paris' life that only He could give and maintain. Paris' message to you the reader, "Make your life and story count!"

"No Box"

As the author of this book, it becomes essential to establish enhanced clarification and to provide heightened awareness regarding this subject matter in bringing an S.T.O.P. to the severe issue of abuse, domestic violence, or intimate partner violence—IPV. To accomplish this objective, I will use the analogy of a '***BOX***' to explain further.

Pages 147-152 will provide *six* illustrations associated with this critical message as follows:

- Figure 1.   The box
- Figure 2.   Outer or surrounding the box
- Figure 3.   Outside the box
- Figure 4.   Inside the box
- Figure 5.   No box
- Figure 6.   The Model: Abuse & Domestic Violence Summary

Everyone commonly uses the term 'box' (a noun and verb) and everywhere that depicts describes containment or to control the contains. The general definition of the word 'box' is a container with a flat base and sides that are typically square or rectangular having a lid. A box is an area or limited space that is to be filled in or set off by a border. The box eventually becomes a separate section or enclosed area within (e.g., closet, room, living corridors, pit, prison, etc.), that can be reserved for various groups (e.g., person, people, a victim(s), etc.). The action of a 'box' is vast as it could include a protective or guarded casing (e.g., a surrounding, exterior or interior), like a vice, or a mechanism that can resemble a shell or covering. In other words, a place to "put in or provide with a boxing" of encapsulation.

As it relates to the subject matter or abuse and domestic violence the encapsulation could represent repression, suppression, power, control, restraint (voluntary or involuntary), inhibition of another's will or willpower. The encapsulation process becomes an action of enclosing something or someone in or as if in a capsule. The "encapsulation of contaminants can be within a solid glass-like matrix," or can become a living hell or medium of toxicity, injury or harm.

Figuratively, the term 'box' is complex. As the writer of this self-help and self-awareness novel, I view this serious global issue symbolic of a "box." For instance, 'box' can symbolize a fight, battle, defense, adversary or to be packed, and contained within:

FIGURE DESCRIPTIONS

Figure 1: Demonstrates "the box," that symbolizing → the place, space, location or medium of the abuse and domestic violence action. To further expound, the following four illustrations will further demonstrate my view during an active abusive and domestic violence process.

Figure 2: Demonstrates the "outer or surrounding the box," that symbolizes → the perpetrator, abuser, or intimate partner of violence.

Figure 3: Demonstrates the "outside the box," that symbolizes → the bondage, entrapment, imprisonment, and entanglement.

Figure 4: Demonstrates "inside the box" both constituting the identical meaning as Figure 3, symbolizing → bondage, entrapment, imprisonment, and entanglement. The reason for this is that even if a victim is situated "outside the box," or "inside the box" of abusive or domestic violence he or she remains out of the "ark of safety," or lacks the status of safe refuge. Why? Because, in remaining outside the box, he or she can be subject to <or> he or she can potentially go back into the box of—encapsulation continuing with the toxicity, injury, and harm.

Figure 5: Demonstrates the contrast concepts based upon the approach to acquired awareness, education, preventative measures facilitating "No Box," symbolizing → Liberty, Freedom, Safety, Equality, and Survival.

Figure 6, Demonstrates overall "*The Model: Abuse & Domestic Violence Summary.*" First, consider "The Box" itself as the medium where the abuse, domestic violence or intimate partner of violence reside:

ILLUSTRATION

Figure 1.

'THE BOX'
| Fight, Battleground, Adversary, Pack, Container |

The 'box' becomes the place, space, location or medium of the abuse and domestic violence.
~ View the following illustrations that further explains— "The Box" ~

I of VI

ILLUSTRATION

Figure 2.

Abuse & Domestic Violence Model
Outer & Surrounding the Box Symbolizes | Perpetrator, Intimate Partner Violence (IPV) |

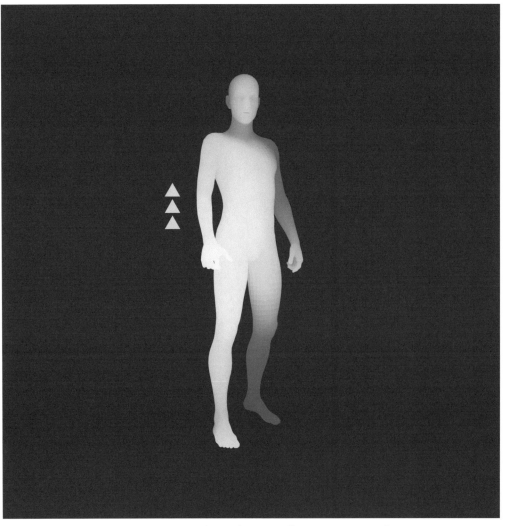

Outer & Surrounding the Box Illustration: II of VI

ILLUSTRATION

Figure 3.

Abuse & Domestic Violence Model
Outside the Box Symbolizes| Bondage, Entrapment, Imprisonment, Entanglement |

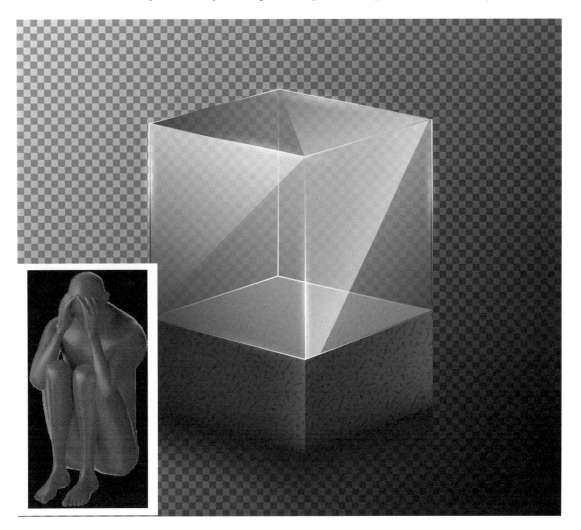

Outside the Box Illustration: III of VI

ILLUSTRATION

Figure 4.

Abuse & Domestic Violence Model
Inside the Box Symbolizes| Bondage, Entrapment, Imprisonment, Entanglement |

Inside the Box Illustration: IV of VI

ILLUSTRATION

Figure 5.

Abuse & Domestic Violence Model
"Don't think outside the box, think like there is *NO* box"

NO **Box Symbolizes** | Liberty, Freedom, Safety, Equality, Survival |

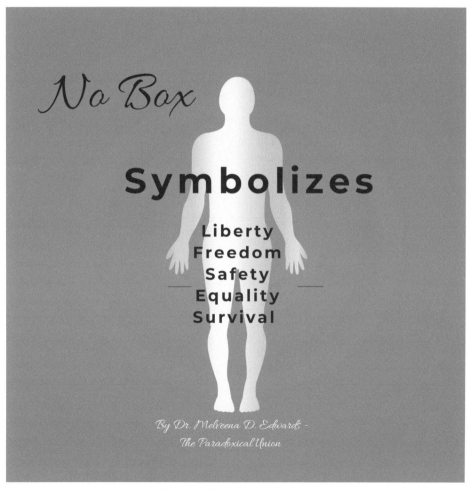

NO **Box Illustration: V of VI**

ILLUSTRATION

Figure 6.

The Model

Abuse &
Domestic Violence
Summary

**The Box
Inside or Outside:**

Bondage
Entrapment
Imprisonment
Entanglement

LEFT

Fear

Abuse:
Physical,
Psychological,
Emotional, Sexual,
Economic, Neglect

FRONT

Intimidation

Domestic Violence:
Aggression, Assault,
Endangerment,
Threats, Stalking,
Injury, Harm, Pain,
Trauma

BACK

Rejection

Helpless
Hopeless
Worthless
Suicide ideation
Homicide ideation

Sides of the Box

They represent the
perpetrator or
intimate partner

TOP

Word Cursing

Verbal threats,
Humiliating or
Degrading remarks,
Plaguing.

No Box

Liberty
Freedom
Safety
Equality
Survival

BOTTOM

Power & Control

Adverse
Behaviors
by Perpetrator (IPV).

RIGHT

Lack of Awareness

Confusion

The premise and pathway to "*NO BOX*," symbolizing → Liberty, Freedom, Safety, Equality, Survival or the goal: "Don't think outside the box, think like there is *NO* box" is accomplished through three-fold main components:

- *Acquiring* an acceptance that he or she is "indeed" a victim of abuse and domestic violence—awareness and acknowledgment is the first step;
- *Acquiring* knowledge regarding the issue of abuse and domestic violence—education through resources, references, and helping agencies;
- *Acquiring* preventative measures against any abuse and domestic violence—through coping skill-sets demonstrating safe self-help actions and exercising or using survival interventions separating the victim(s) from any abuse and domestic violence circumstance.

To simplify, the **HOW TO** in stopping any abuse and domestic violence is that the victim(s) must embrace and employ the following *three steps* for survival:

- ✓ Awareness
- ✓ Education
- ✓ Prevention

Below are several resources, references, self-help, and survival entities to assist anyone regarding abuse and domestic violence:

Domestic Violence Resources and References

- Abused Women's Aid in Crisis—AWAIC: (24-Hours Crisis and Hotline) Website: http://www.awaic.org/about-abuse/the-facts
- The Centers for Disease and Control and Prevention—CDC: (24-Hours Internet) Website: https://www.cdc.gov/features/intimatepartnerviolence/index.html
- The Me Too. Movement—#MeToo: (24-Hours Internet) Website: https://metoomvmt.org/
- The National Domestic Violence Hotline—NDVH: (24-Hours Crisis and Hotline) Website: http://www.thehotline.org/resources/statistics/

Domestic Violence Self-Help & Survival Interventions

- **Faith**: Exercise any existing level of faith even if it's the size of a mustard seed
- **Pray**: Steadfast prayer coupled with your belief opens of the door *TO* escape
- **Scripture**: Use of the Holy Scriptures can provide spiritual support and guidance throughout your escape process (Reference **Table 3** on pages 156-159).
- **Tools**: Domestic Violence 24-Hours Crisis and Hotline Resources and References (Reference *some* Resources and References examples listed on page 153).
- **Alleviation**: When any form of abuse or violence is observed or identified, it must be reported, dealt with, and addressed. In cases of brutal forms of violence, the involvement of law enforcement or incarceration could result. Otherwise, in lesser circumstances counseling, anger management, education, and training may be implemented. Sometimes this may involve needing to be removed from the situation or 'the box' to finding shelters for battered women, foster homes for children, adult protective services, and some unique homes for seniors are available to remove the victim(s) from the problem or environment.
- **Prevention Measures**: Within the community are various resources who genuinely want to assist in this public health issue. These measures may include, but are not limited to churches, educational agencies with a vision and mission that focuses on prevention of abuse and domestic violence; and with efforts to increase awareness or empower victims with skill-sets. These preventative measures can be the premise for establishing a healthy and safe living that is fostered through awareness.
- **Step to Growth and Favorable Outcome**: One approach to growth can be to reaching out to someone or victim(s) that have experienced and successfully come through an abusive or domestic violence situation. The reference to those who have come from abusive families, have dealt with and addressed this problem is priceless—as they understand the process, the pain, and realize how much it hurts. In other words, this experienced victim can better empathize with your situation. Next, there are numerous books and well as the contains included in this novel: The Paradoxical Union that reference inner healing, help, and HOPE to restore wholeness and peace. These inspiration readings can catapult oneself or victim(s) to identify elements through dysfunctional pasts, backgrounds, codependency or unfavorable relationships, toward growth, maturity, and positive outcome.

One fact that becomes critical to note in dealing with this serious public health issue, and becomes even deeper if acknowledged by anyone involved, is regarding the spirit of "guilt" and "shame" that could rest on both the victim(s) and perpetrator. These feelings must be dealt with and addressed for complete deliverance. Interesting enough, the victims may readily push through to a whole healing process. However, the perpetrator or abuser can become stagnated or trapped for life with these feelings of guilt or shame due to denial, lack of self-awareness, lack of coping skills to adjust, or avoiding truths is a typical scenario after abuse and violence. Note, if the acts of abuse and domestic violence continue by the perpetrator or abuser—it is virtually impossible to recover from guilt or shame. Therefore, for the perpetrator or abuser, the state of denial, lack of awareness and skill, and avoiding truths can make healing challenging to experience complete or long-term growth.

Additionally, as Christ-Centered lay or professional counselors, or therapists your attitude, self-aware, and stance regarding this severe public health subject matter of abuse and domestic violence must be considered of which will inevitably affect your approach, effectiveness, and success as interveners. As the author of this book and from my experience, I know God will guide you—in guiding others needing godly counsel and intervention. Hence, remember that in your consecration to God, commitment to service, the appropriation, and application of Biblical Scripture, godly principles, and your psychological knowledge base— can enable you to counsel those who seek our help in HOPE

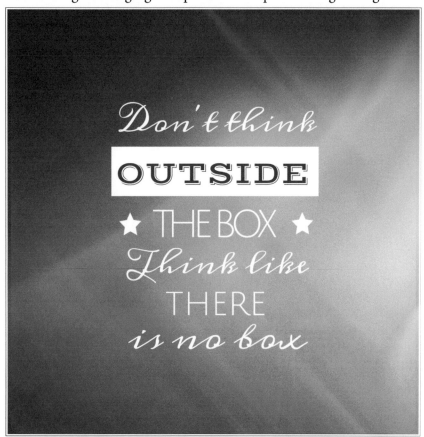

effectively! Then, in the case of any counseling that you are unable to compartmentalize this component in positive effect; it would be best to refer the counselee to another counselor who can effectively do so.

Last, in this section entitled: "No Box," the removing of the top, sides, and bottom of the box must be figurative, literally and supernatural removed through the victim's (his or her) faith, Scripture, and willingness to move forward in freeing oneself from the entrapment.

To do so, reference **Table 3** Entitled: *"No Box Supporting Scriptures"* on pages 156-159 that illustrates inspirational and divine elements of delivery through the use of Holy Scriptures. Each Scripture correlates with the top, sides, and bottom of "the box." Note, that there are certainly multiple other Scriptures in the Bible applicable to every part and symbol line relevant to "the box." However, these are *some* example Scriptures to reference each scenario depicted in 'the box' illustrations to aid, help, strengthen, and comfort any victim(s) undergoing abuse and domestic violence.

Table 3.

"NO Box" Supporting Scriptures Relevant to *Deliverance* & *Survival*

Parts of Box	Symbol	Counter Holy Scripture
Sides or surrounding of Box	Represents the perpetrator or intimate partner—IPV	"Beloved, let us love one another: for love is God; and every one that loveth is born of God, and knoweth God. He that loveth not knoweth not God; for God is love" (I John 4:7-8); "Let all bitterness, and wrath, and anger, and clamour, and evil speaking, be put away from you, with all malice. And be ye kind one to another, tenderhearted, forgiving one another, even as God for Christ's sake hath forgiven you" (Ephesians 4:31-21). Also, reference: I Corinthians 13:1-8a, 13; I John 15:9-10; St. John 14:21; St. John 15:12-14, 17; Romans 8:38-39; St. John 8:32, 36; Joshua 24:15; Psalm 101:2; I Peter 3:8-11; Proverbs 3:5-6; Proverbs 10:12; I Peter 1:22.

Top: Word Cursing	Verbal threats, Humiliating or Degrading remarks, Plaguing	"But ye are a chosen generation, a royal priesthood, an holy nation, a peculiar people; that ye should show forth the praises of him who hath called you out of darkness into his marvelous light: Which in time past were not a people, but are now the people of God: which had not obtained mercy, but now have obtained mercy" (I Peter 2:9-10); "I Can do all things through Christ which strengtheneth me" (Philippians 4:13); "So that we may boldly say, The Lord is my helper, and I will not fear what man shall do unto me" (Hebrews 13:6); "But none of these things move me, neither count I my life dear unto myself, so that I might finish my course with joy, and the ministry, which I have received of the Lord Jesus, to testify the gospel of the grace of God" (Acts 20:24). Also, reference: Philippians 1:6; Habakkuk 3:19; Romans 8:37.
Bottom: Power and Control	Adverse Behaviors by the perpetrator or intimate partner violence—IPV	"Behold, I give unto you power to tread on serpents and scorpions, and over all the power of the enemy: and nothing shall by and means hurt you" (St. Luke 10:19); And ye shall know the truth, and the truth shall make you free. If the Son therefore shall make you free, ye shall be free indeed" (St. John 8:32, 36). Also, reference: Isaiah 9:4.

Side 1: Fear	Abuse: Physical, Psychological, Emotional, Sexual, Economic, Neglect	"For God hath not given us the spirit of fear; but of power, and of love, and of a sound mind" (II Timothy 1:7); "For ye have not received the spirit of bondage again to fear; but ye have received the Spirit of adoption, whereby we cry, Abba, Father" (Romans 8:15). Also, reference: I John 4:18; Psalm 91:1, 4-7, 10-11; Psalm 91:10-11; Proverbs 3:25-26; Isaiah 54:14; Psalm 56:11; Psalm 23:4-5; Romans 8:29, 31, 35-39; Psalm 31:24; St. John 14:27; Psalm 27:1, 3; Hebrews 13:6.
Side 2: Intimidation	Domestic Violence: Aggression, Assault, Endangerment, Threats, Stalking, Injury, Harm, Pain, Trauma	"When though passest through the waters, I will be with thee; and through the rivers, they shall not overflow thee: when thou walkest through the fire, thou shalt not be burned; neither shall the flame kindle upon thee" (Isaiah 43:2). Also, reference: Ephesians 3:12; Isaiah 40:31.
Side 3: Rejection	Helpless, Hopeless, Worthless Suicidal Ideation Homicidal Ideation	"For the Lord thy God is a merciful God; he will not forsake thee, neither destroy thee, nor forget the covenant of thy fathers which he sware unto them" (Deuteronomy 4:31); "And they that know thy name will put their trust in thee: for thou, Lord, has not forsaken them that seek thee" (Psalm 9:10). Also, reference: Psalm 94:14; Psalm 27:10; St. Matthew 28:20; Isaiah 62:4; II Corinthians 4:9; I Peter 5:7; Psalm 37:25; Isaiah 41:17; Psalm 91:14-15; Isaiah 49:15-16; Psalm 43:5; Deuteronomy 31:6; I Samuel 12:22.

Side 4: Lack of Awareness	Confusion	"For God is not the author of confusion, but of peace, as in all churches of the saints" (I Corinthians 14:33); For where envying and strife is, there is confusion and every evil work. But the wisdom that is from above is first pure, then peaceable, gentle, and easy to be entreated, full of mercy and good fruits, without partiality, and without hypocrisy. And the fruit of righteousness is sown in peace of them that make peace" (James 3:16-18); "Beloved, think it not strange concerning the fiery trial which is to try you, as though some strange thing happened unto you: But rejoice, inasmuch as ye are partakers of Christ's sufferings; that, when his glory shall be revealed, ye may be glad also with exceeding joy" (I Peter 4:12-13).
		Also, reference: Isaiah 50:7; James 1:5; Proverbs 3:5-6; Psalm 32:8; Psalm 119:165; Psalm 55:22; Isaiah 43:2; Isaiah 40:29; Isaiah 30:21; Philippians 4:6-7.

CHAPTER FIVE

Epilogue

In conclusion, there is no such thing as a perfect marriage. It can be perceived that being married to a minister would be ideal and made perfect from heaven. This fact can be true! However, the reality is that this type of marriage should be viewed as two individual that have been united to be holy, acceptable unto God which is a reasonable service (Hebrews 12:1, KJV), and have been joined together with a higher call to serve humanity. In marriages encompassing ministry the attributes and behavior must stay humble, prayerful, and maintaining the intense need to remain committed to God is mandatory. The divine union should be centered around a reverent fear of God and compassion for those in need.

In contrast, when a marriage partner in ministry decides to fall, does not remain humble, prayerful, and committed to God it can be detrimental for both resulting in destruction. This type of scenario could result in the unimaginable! This scenario could create an image or representation of — a man or woman preacher in his or her cloak looking into a mirror, however; reflecting the devil 'clothed in red with horns and pointed-tail' or the personification of an adversary itself. This union would then seem contradictory to the norm, inconsistent, or paradoxically inconsistent with methodical thinking— that this could happen! Or even described as The Paradoxical Union.

Against all the odds, there is always a way out! Know that the situations and outcome ascribed in this novel do not indicate defeat. Instead, God can make a way '*to escape,*' that ye (he or she) may be able to bear it……... (I Corinthians 10:13, KJV).

PARIS HOPE, her story of survival continues…

—*Dr. Melveena D. Edwards, Survivor*
Against all Odds!

Marriage—A Divine Union

Paris vowed to devote her life entirely to God by becoming goal-directed with a vision and mission to help the hurting globally~

Finale questions: After reading this story regarding the symbol PARIS HOPE, how would you vow now? Has your vow changed?

"A way to escape!"

Your Vow Notes~

About the Author

BIOGRAPHY

Dr. Melveena D. Edwards is the author of ^{The} $_{Paradoxical}$ U_{nion} — a Christian-center novel. She is a loving and compassionate individual who is highly passionate about serving others, her ministry, and her leadership that is committed to helping individuals who are hurting and recovering from a traumatic relationship.

Website: http://www.mdemllc.org/

Melveena D. Edwards
R.N., B.S.N.,
B.A., Th.M., M.C.E.-C.C., D.D., Ph.D.,
D.C.E., D.C.C., D.Min., Ph.D., R.A.
N.C.C.A.-L.C.C.C. and L.C.P.C.-A.C.,
A.A.C.C.-I.B.C.C.-B.C.P.C.C.
Psychiatric/Mental Health Nurse
Parish Nurse (PN)/Faith Community Nurse (FCN)

Melveena D. Edwards is a humble servant of Jesus Christ with a call and passion for serving others in, education, counseling, nursing, and with a belief in caring for people Gods way. Dr. Edwards is an advocatory leader and affirms in the philosophy of effective leadership exhibiting positive influence and commitment. Melveena has been a nurse for 42 years with a vast background in the nursing practice. She is an ordained clergywoman (overseer/chaplain) who loves the "Word of God." She has been used in evangelism, pastor/pastoral care, teaching, and preaching the Gospel of Jesus Christ. Melveena's ministry is primarily geared toward hurting people, the healing and deliverance ministry, the wholistic approach to health and wellness (mind/body/soul) or the Faith Community Nursing (FCN) practice, and equipping other clergies for successful ministries. Melveena holds 11 earned degrees (two in the science in nursing and nine in seminary/theological studies) Bachelor of Science in Nursing Degree (BSN) from the University of Phoenix. She has 17 years of seminary and religious studies. Her highest degree(s) earned Ph.D. in Administration and Organization from the Apostolic University of Grace and Truth of Richmond, IN; 2nd Ph.D. in Clinical Christian Psychology from the Cornerstone University in Lake Charles, LA.

Credentials: Sarasota Academy of Christian Counseling (SACC)-Certified Pastoral Member, SACC-APS-Certified Therapist/Pastoral Counselor, Board Certified Temperament Counselor/Therapist, National Christian Counselors Association (NCCA)-Board Certified Professional Clinical/Pastoral Member, Board Certified Death and Grief Therapist, Licensed Clinical Christian Counselor-Advanced Certified/Licensed Clinical Pastoral Counselor-Advanced Certified, SACC- International Representative/Certified Academic Institution (CAI) for the College of Christian Counseling (providing academic training for certification and licensing in Christian counseling), American Association of Christian Counselors (AACC) Membership/Presidential Membership-Silver, AACC Certificate in Biblical Counseling, AACC Grief Crisis and Disaster Divisional Membership-GCD, AACC-International Board of Christian Counselors-Board Certified Professional Christian Counselor (IBCC-BCPCC): Good standing as a Christian counselor who serves as a state licensed mental health professional. Among the vanguard of professional Christian Counselors who exemplify the standards of ethical excellence in practice (July 2007). Melveena established her own clinical Christian/pastoral counseling practice and is the founder, president, and CEO of two nonprofit Religious Organizations (2000, 2001) with a state and federal 501 (c)(3), which encompass a vision/mission for Christian counseling, education, ministry, and community outreach. In seminary Melveena was an honor student, earned honors of Summa Cum Laude, distinguished graduate, and valedictorian. Melveena was inducted into the Honor Society of Nursing: The Omicron Delta Chapter Sigma Theta Tau International (STTI) in 2012, and now she is a member with the rewarding connection. STTI is designed for professional, academic achievements/success, and personal commitment/dedication to nursing excellence. STTI is one of the largest and most prestigious nursing organizations in the world.

Acknowledgments & Awards:
(2018) Who's Who In Black Columbus-Fifteenth Edition
"Celebrating African-American Achievement in Columbus, Ohio."

Inducted and featured in 2018 Who's Who In Black Columbus Fifteenth Edition and among many other distinguished leaders. The event: "The Who's Who In Black Columbus 15th Anniversary Awards and Unveiling Ceremony" was held at The Ohio State University-OSU Student Union, Archie Griffin Ballroom on Wednesday, March 7, 2018.

Awards & Honor:
(2012) Inducted into the Honor Society of Nursing: the Omicron Delta Chapter-Sigma Theta Tau International (STTI), and now she is a member with the rewarding connection. STTI is designed for professional, academic achievements/success, and personal commitment/dedication to nursing excellence. STTI is one of the largest and most prestigious nursing organizations in the world.

Acknowledgments:
(2007-2008) Recognized as an honored member and in the registry of accomplished individual/professional mark of achievement with Cambridge Publishing, Inc. - Who's Who, Uniondale, N.Y., among executives, and professionals in Nursing/health care.

First Scholarship Award:
(1980) Honored by the Black Organization of Registered Nurses (BORN) with a scholarship and the first recipient to receive this scholarship for nurses from this organization originated in Columbus, Ohio.

General background experience:
Melveena has served as an executive administrative director of the theological university, university provost, associate adjunct professor in religious studies, dean of the college(s). She loves to teach on a college level, has designed, and written numerous books, thesis/dissertations, established multiple college courses and curriculum for eight colleges from associate to doctorate degrees. She has developed numerous educational publications, materials, and noted as a Global Authors Registry/Registered Author (RA), is a Consultant for Christian Education Programs (CCEP), and has ACI teaching certification. Dr. Edwards developed and organized accreditations for several theological universities with an accrediting commission international: namely in 2001, 2005, and 2017, and established one of the university's registry with the State of California as a Religious Exempt Institution by the Bureau for Private and Postsecondary and Vocational Education of

Sacramento, California (BPPVE). She is a (former) American Red Cross (ARC) certified instructor November 1998 (trained to teach Basic and African-American HIV/AIDS classes). Through God's divine direction Melveena is the founder, president, CEO, and Chief Executive Officer of the Lighthouse Christian Counseling and Outreached Center, Inc. (LCCOC)—California & Ohio and Consultants for Christian Education Programs (CCEP) founded February 1, 2001 (A religious nonprofit 501 (c)(3) corporation (state and federal status) that encompasses Christian counseling, Christian education, various ministries, and outreach entities. Website: http://www.lighthousechristiancounseling.org. She is the Founder, Manager, and Chancellor of the Capstone Excelsior University, LLC (C.E.U.)—California and Ohio. Website: http://www.CapstoneEU.org. She is the Founder and Manager of "Melveena D. Edwards Ministries, LLC—T.O.P. THE olive PRESS (MDEM)" (Melveena D. Edwards Ministries LLC, 2019). Melveena has been instrumental in coordinating and assisting several churches in organizing and establishing a Health Ministry (HM)/congregational health or Faith Community Nursing (FCN) programs.

Registered Nurse/nursing background experience:
Dr. Edwards has practiced in numerous areas of nursing some of which include tertiary and quaternary hospitals and community health settings-Medical, Surgical, Pediatrics, Obstetrical, Rehabilitation, Community Health/Public Health Nursing- PHN (public health case management, communicable disease/immunizations, community, and clinic nursing), cancer care- hospice care/oncology/hematology/chemotherapy certification/infusion nursing, occupational health, congregational health/parish nursing/minister of health and wellness or Faith Community Nursing- FCN (completed a Parish Nursing Course at Otterbein College of Westerville, Ohio, August 1998), specialized training by the Ohio Department of Health in obstetrical nursing and childbirth education/educator, and travel nursing. Nursing Specialty: Psychiatric/Mental Health Nursing-PMHN encompassing forensic milieus, immediate supervisor for psychiatric hospital, correctional juvenile nursing, inpatient psychiatric units/milieu, psychiatric emergency room-Psych ED, psychiatric/mental health administration: clinical nurse manager, house nursing supervisor, clinical program director of acute care services - for child, adolescent/residential training center, and adult-geriatric of a psychiatric hospital, Director of Nursing-DON for adolescent psychiatric hospital. Most recent position: healthcare organization specializing in Utilization Review, Managed Care, Medical Claims Review Nurse, Care Review Clinician II Inpatient Behavioral Health - (CRC II). Educational Goals and seeking certifications: N.C.C.A. Diplomat Clinical Supervisor; and certification in Crisis and Abuse Therapy.

Most of all Melveena loves the Lord, her primary ministry and mission are to win souls for Christ, and to be used in the advancement/upbuilding of God's Kingdom:

"Beloved, I wish above all things that thou mayest prosper and be in health, even as thy soul prospereth."
(III John 2, KJV)

~ Overseer of Organizations ~

Lighthouse Christian Counseling and Outreach Center, Inc. • LCCOC
(Consultants for Christian Education Programs • CCEP)

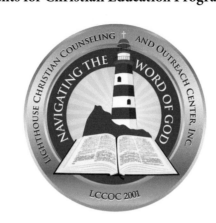

Capstone Excelsior University, LLC (CA) • CEU

Melveena D. Edwards Ministries, LLC • MDEM, LLC Movement: T.O.P. THE olive PRESS Ministries

SUCCESS • TRIUMPH • OPPORTUNITY • POWER

For more information about author visit:

Business:
Lighthouse Christian Counseling and Outreach Center, Inc.—(L.C.C.O.C.) http://www.lighthousechristiancounseling.org
Capstone Excelsior University, LLC—(C.E.U.)
http://www.CapstoneEU.org
Melveena D. Edwards Ministries, LLC—(M.D.E.M.)
http://www.MDEMLLC.org
E-mails:
Personal- mdedwards.phd@att.net
Business- drmdedwards@MDEMLLC.org
Facebook Timeline:
https://www.facebook.com/MelveenaDEdwardsLLCTHEolivePress/
https://www.facebook.com/groups/1768538943417888/
http://www.facebook.com/mdedwards.phd
https://www.facebook.com/LighthouseChristianCounseling/
https://www.facebook.com/CapstoneEU/

Bibliography & References

The Holy Bible (KJV unless stated otherwise).

American Association for Marriage and Family Therapy. (2018). Domestic Violence. Alexandria, VA: American Association for Marriage and Family Therapy. Retrieved on July 15, 2018, from website https://aamft.org/

Arno, R. G. & Arno, P. J. (1993, pp. 1-5, 8-9, 243). *Creation Therapy – A Biblically Based Model for Christian Counseling*. Sarasota, FL: Sarasota Academy of Christian Counseling—SACC.

Benner, D. G.& Hill, P.C. (1999, pp. 359, 363-364). *Baker Encyclopedia of Psychology & Counseling—Second Edition*. Grand Rapids, MI: Baker Books. USA.

Bible History Online (2019). *Divorce* Vancouver, WA: Retrieved on December 29, 2018 from https://www.bible-history.com/ and https://www.bible-history.com/jesus/jesusuntitled00000478.htm.

Centers for Disease Control and Prevention. (2018). *Violence Prevention*. Atlanta, GA: CDC. USA. Retrieved July 15, 2018, from https://www.cdc.gov and https://www.cdc.gov/ViolencePrevention/intimatepartnerviolence/

Clinton, T., Hart, A., & Ohlschlager, G. (2005). *Caring for People God's Way*. Nashville, TN: Thomas Nelson, Inc.

Hosier, D. (2014). *Childhood Trauma Recovery—The Long-Term Effects of Parental Rejection*. WordPress. Retrieved on June 11, 2014, from www.childhoodtramarecovery.com and http://childhoodtraumarecovery.com/2014/01/07/the-long-term-effects-of-parental-rejection/

Kelleher, K., Gardner, W., Coben, J., Barth, R., Edleson, J., & Hazen, A. (March, 2006). *Co-Occurring Intimate Partner Violence and Child Maltreatment: Local Policies/Practices and Relationships to Child Placement, Family Services and Residence.* Retrieved from website on July 30, 2018, at https://www.ncjrs.gov/pdffiles1/nij/grants/213503.pdf

Khaleque, A., & Rohner, R. P. (2002). *Perceived parental acceptance-rejection and psychological adjustment*: A meta-analysis of cross cultural and intracultural studies. *Journal of Marriage and the Family, 64,* 54-64. doi:10.1111/j.1741-3737.2002.00054.x.

Melveena D. Edwards Ministries, LLC. (2019). *Authorship ‖ Public* Speaking. Galena, Ohio: Powered by Net Ministry Technology Corporation. Retrieved on January 1, 2019, from website http://www.MDEMLLC.org .

Mental Health America. (2014). *Co-Dependency.* Alexandria, VA: National Mental Health Association. Received from website on August 8, 2014, at http://www.mentalhealthamerica.net/co-dependency

Miethe, T. L. (1998). *The Compact Dictionary of Doctrinal Words.* Minneapolis, Minnesota: Bethany House Publishers.

National Institute of Mental Health. (2014, pp. 1-2). *Facts on Stress.* Bethesda, MD: U.S. Department of Health and Human Services NIMH. Retrieved August 27, 2014, from website http://www.nimh.nih.gov/health/publications/stress/index.shtml

Nelson, T. (1995, pp. 2093). *The Woman's Study Bible Opening the Word of God To Women the New King James Version.* Nashville, TN: Thomas Nelson Publishers, Inc. USA.

Pedersen, D. D. (2005). *Psych Notes Clinical Pocket Guide.* Philadelphia, PA: F.A. Davis Company. USA. www.fadavis.com . Retrieved September 27, 2014, from website http://www.scribd.com/doc/21025719/PsychNotes-Clinical-Pocket-Guide-Scanned

Psychology Dictionary. (2014). *What is Parental Rejection? Definition of Rejection (Psychology Dictionary).* Retrieved June 11, 2014 from website http://psychologydictionary.org/parental-rejection/

Rohner, R. P., & Khaleque, A. (2002). Parental Acceptance-Rejection and Life-Span Development: A Universalist Perspective. *Online Readings in Psychology and Culture, 6*. Received June 11, 2014, from website http://dx.doi.org/10.9707/2307-0919.1055

Stoop, D. (2005, pp. 241-255). Caring for People God's Way-Challenging Issues In Biblical Counseling—*Family Systems: Breaking Unhealthy Patterns*. Forest, VA: American Association of Christian Counselors—AACC. USA.

The Me Too. Movement. (2018). You are not alone. The Me Too. Website Retrieved September 30, 2018, from website https://metoomvmt.org/ and https://metoomvmt.org/resources

The National Domestic Violence Hotline. (2018). *Get the Facts & Figures*. Austin, Texas: The National Domestic Violence Hotline Website. Retrieved July 15, 2018 from website http://www.thehotline.org/

United States Department of Justice. (2016). *Resources for Domestic Violence Victims*. Portland, Oregon: The United States Attorney's General Office, District of Oregon. USA.gov. Retrieved July 29, 2018, from website https://www.justice.gov/usao-or/psn_dv

Vine, W. E. (1981). *Vine's Expository Dictionary of Old and New Testament Words*. Tarrytown, NY: Fleming H. Revell Company.

Vine, W. E., Unger, M. F., & White, Jr., W. (1996). *Vine's Complete Expository Dictionary with Topical Index*. Nashville, TN: Thomas Nelson Publishers.

Zondervan Publishing House. (1992). *The Full Life Study Bible—King James Version*. Grand Rapids, MI: Life Publishers International. USA.

Appendices

APPENDIX A: Helpful Tools for Marriages

The main two areas that create problems in marriages are *communication* and *financial* issues. Below are helpful tools to consider in marriages.

TEN FACTORS THAT INFLUENCE MARRIAGES | What frustrates communication in marriage?

- Workaholics
- Excessive Television and Electronics (social media)
- Fixation on sports
- Fixation on hobbies
- The Church— "Too much time spent on committees, etc."
- Marriage "Staff Meetings"
- Scheduled time together (around children, extracurricular activities, etc.)
- Prioritize the time
- Protect the time
- What to discuss—Calendar coordination, family goals, listening time, productive criticism appreciation.

As the author, I wish to pray for *all* marriages—especially those marriages under attack by the enemy; and plagued by the circumstance of abuse, and domestic violence. I further decree and declare peace upon each relationship or marriage union. I ongoingly speak a special pray for positive marital outcomes encompassing:

- conflict resolutions
- healing and wholeness
- life focus or re-focusing
- effective couple communication
- family union and restoration
- peace, joy, and HOPE from God!

Remember "**GOD IS LOVE!**" Exercise God's love in your marriage and problems. Love is not abuse, and love is not domestic violence. Always attempt to resolve marital issues before it results in abuse or violence. Unfortunately, some marriages do end in divorce for various reasons as discussed in this novel. If divorce is decided, remember that the divorce process can be excruciating and brutal. Seek God for spiritual guidance as you journey the process of divorce, and as you build and reestablish yourself.

APPENDIX B: Faith & Prayer

By
Melveena D. Edwards, Ph.D.

Faith:

Now faith is the substance of things HOPED for, the evidence of things not seen (Hebrews 11:1, KJV).

Prayer:

Dear Lord, I pray today that the "Now faith" will manifest upon the reader in agreement with this prayer. I decree and declare the breaking of any chains of bondage, entrapment, imprisonment, or entanglement governed by diabolical forces become eradicated by your divine power extending to the core root of its existence. As we agree, we proclaim liberty, freedom, safety, equality, survival, and complete healing, health, and holistic deliverance. In Jesus' Name. Amen!

APPENDIX C: T.P.U. The Paradoxical Union

Appendix C – Part II Summary

The Paradoxical **U**nion

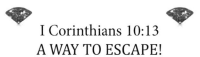

I Corinthians 10:13
A WAY TO ESCAPE!

Have you ever experienced domestic violence or intimate partner violence (IPV)?
Have you ever experienced an abusive relationship?
Have you ever experienced marital bondage?
Have you ever experienced betrayal?
Have you ever experienced infidelity?
Have you ever experienced a broken heart?

Herein this book: The Paradoxical **U**nion — Paris Hope presents as the main character in this novel who embodies *survival*. Paris is fully aware that she is not the only person who has experienced a broken heart—built upon deception, delusions, untruths, and ultimately betrayal at its worse. Paris determines that "it's time to tell all" …and she is convinced that the world is in a desperate need of a voice that will declare truths about domestic violence or abuse!

Surviving damaged emotions from a destructive and damaging relationship requires help from God, especially when it seems illogical and contradictory. In this story, Paris is an advocate for true love and healthy marital relationships. She believes that marriage is a privilege. However, learns over time that when you're in a problematic relationship, embedded in a toxic environment that resembles a poisonous venom medium—there needs to be a way out. At the end of her journey, she proclaims that emotionally destructive relationships and intimate partner violence can become a life-crisis-event. Thus, discovers staying in a relationship too long is critical when there is nothing produced but destruction.

How can you escape from a marital union of sheer bondage, entrapment, imprisonment, and entanglement when there seems like "there is no HOPE or a way out;" and remaining in God's perfect will? This book will delve into how God will make a way TO escape that ye may be able to bear it according to I Corinthians 10:13, and how God can reverse your pain and disappointment into restored HOPE, strength, encouragement, liberty, freedom, safety, equality, joy and wholeness—after the escape.

Dr. Melveena D. Edwards, Author of this novel, affirms, that upon reading this book, you can be empowered by the shared life lessons surrounding the main character Paris Hope. Dr. Edwards asserts that the life lessons contained within this short story will demonstrate and encourage individuals how: *to* stand up with spiritual boldness, *to* become empowered, *to* be strengthened through endurance, and *to* survive violence and abusive circumstances as she…

- Depicts the commonality of these domestic issues providing easy to understand solutions
- Gives an account of God's daily renewal of faithfulness upon the victim, suffering person or believer
- Outlines Biblical principles for the way *to* escape and survive diabolical assignments, demonic forces, and temptations that have come to bind, entrap, imprison, and destroy individuals.

The main character **PARIS HOPE** shares her story of brutal heart-break progressing to triumph, providing details of her way *to* escape, and remaining in God's perfect will. In the story Paris' chief role is elect lady that spirals into a world of domestic violence, abuse, anguish, torment, and nuisance. This narrative will share how Paris emerges serving humanity in multiple roles surrounding the field of health care, education, ministry, spiritually coaching others in fulfilling her call, purpose and destiny. Along her life's journey, she evolves into a profound visionary and leader. After her experience and deliverance from domestic violence and abuse, she vows and devotes her life fully to God, that becomes goal-directed with a vision and mission to help the hurting globally.

APPENDIX D: Abuse & Domestic Violence Model

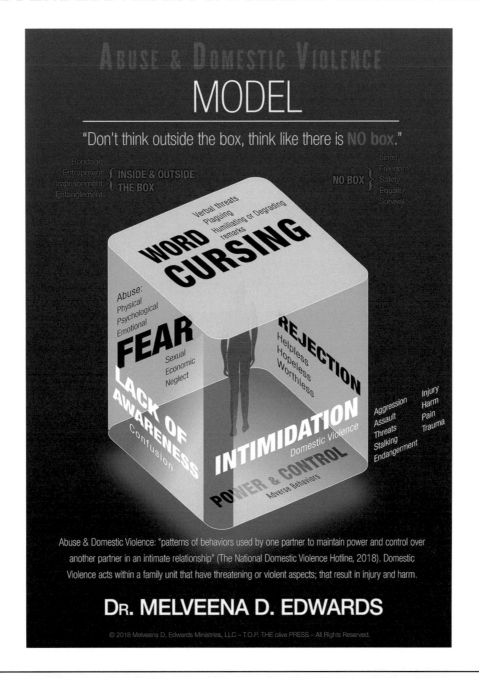

APPENDIX E: The Model: Abuse & Domestic Violence Summary

The Model

Abuse & Domestic Violence Summary

The Box Inside or Outside:

Bondage
Entrapment
Imprisonment
Entanglement

Fear LEFT

Abuse:
Physical, Psychological, Emotional, Sexual, Economic, Neglect

Sides of the Box

They represent the perpetrator or intimate partner

Intimidation FRONT

Domestic Violence:
Aggression, Assault, Endangerment, Threats, Stalking, Injury, Harm, Pain, Trauma

Word Cursing TOP

Verbal threats, Humiliating or Degrading remarks, Plaguing.

Rejection BACK

Helpless
Hopeless
Worthless
Suicide ideation
Homicide ideation

No Box

Liberty
Freedom
Safety
Equality
Survival

Power & Control BOTTOM

Adverse Behaviors by Perpetrator (IPV).

Lack of Awareness RIGHT

Confusion

Dr. Melveena D. Edwards
© 2018 Melveena D. Edwards Ministries. LLC – T.O.P. THE olive PRESS – All Rights Reserved.

APPENDIX F: The Virtuous Woman

"Her Price is Far Above Rubies"

Proverbs 31:10-31

10:	Who can find a virtuous woman? for her price is far above rubies.
11:	The heart of her husband doth safely trust in her, so that he shall have no need of spoil.
13:	She seeketh wool, and flax, and worketh willingly with her hands.
14:	She is like the merchants' ships; she bringeth her food from afar.
15:	She riseth also while it is yet night, and giveth meat to her household, and a portion to her maidens.
16:	She considereth a field, and buyeth it: with the fruit of her hands she planteth a vineyard.
17:	She girdeth her loins with strength, and strengtheneth her arms.
18:	She perceiveth that her merchandise *is* good: her candle goeth not out by night.
19:	She layeth her hands to the spindle, and her hands hold the distaff.
20:	She stretcheth out her hand to the poor; yea, she reacheth forth her hands to the needy.
21:	She is not afraid of the snow for her household: for all her household *are* clothed with scarlet.
22:	She maketh herself coverings of tapestry; her clothing is silk and purple.
23:	Her husband is known in the gates, when he sitteth among the elders of the land.
24:	She maketh fine linen, and selleth *it*: and delivereth girdles unto the merchant.
25:	Strength and honour *are* her clothing; and she shall rejoice in time to come.
26:	She openeth her mouth with wisdom; and in her tongue is the law of kindness.
27:	She looketh well to the ways of her household, and eateth not the bread of idleness.
28:	Her children arise up, and call her blessed; her husband *also*, and he praiseth her.
29:	Many daughters have done virtuously, but thou excellest them all.
30:	Favour *is* deceitful, and beauty is vain: *but* a woman that feareth the LORD, she shall be praised.
31:	Give her of the fruit of her hands; and let her own works praise her in the gates.

*~A whole life centered around a reverent fear of **GOD** and compassion for those in need~*

APPENDIX G: There is a Way Out

I Corinthians 10:13, KJV
"A Way *TO*, No Box"

APPENDIX H: HOPE: "October Domestic Violence Month"

"October is Domestic Violence Awareness Month. Numerous ways exist to enhance prevention efforts in your community. A key strategy in preventing domestic violence, often called intimate partner violence, is promoting respectful, nonviolent relationships."

(CDC, 2018, retrieved on August 25, 2018, from the website: https://www.cdc.gov/features/intimatepartnerviolence/index.html).

APPENDIX I: Glossary

Domestic Violence – A public health problem, that "Acts with a family unit that have threatening or violent aspects; that result in injury, whether physical or emotional; that have a lack of consent on the part of the victim(s); and that are excessive or inappropriate to the situation"—toward, an intimate partner, spouse (wife, a husband), children or elderly. "Abound and focus on everything from the nature of the act itself to the physical and psychological impact and the community standards regarding appropriate conduct" (Benner & Hill, 1999, pp. 359, 363-364).

Divorce – "The legal ending of a marriage." The "cutting," or "separating." "A legal separation between husband and wife utilizing a formal process of some sort. Biblical Perspective: As the ordinances respecting marriage have in view the hallowing of that relationship, so also was the Mosaic regulation in respect of divorce" (Deuteronomy 24:1-4; Bible History Online, 2018).

Marriage – The state of being married or wedlock. A relationship between husband and wife in wedlock or Holy Matrimony. Meaning "to master" or "to take." Biblical Perspective: A divine institution designed to form a permanent union between man and woman that they might be helpful to one another (Genesis 2:18).

Paradoxical – Contradictory to the norm, and not consistent. Terms that describe paradoxically: inconsistent, absurd, ironic, contradictory, illogical, impossible, enigmatic, puzzling, irrational, unreasonable, unsound, opposing, clashing, conflicting, at odds, differing, incongruous, ambiguous, paradoxical inconsistent.

Union – The state of being one unit or united. Can be described as a "unity" to signify a oneness of sentiment, affection, or behavior such as, e.g., should exist among the people of God or "the unity of the faith."

Printed in the United States
By Bookmasters